## Books

# MacLarens of Boundary Mountain

Colin's Quest, Book One,
Brodie's Gamble, Book Two
Quinn's Honor, Book Three
Sam's Legacy, Book Four
Heather's Choice, Book Five
Nate's Destiny, Book Six
Blaine's Wager, Book Seven
Fletcher's Pride, Book Eight
Bay's Desire, Book Nine
Cam's Hope, Book Ten, Coming next in the series!

# *Romantic Suspense*

## Eternal Brethren, Military Romantic Suspense

Steadfast, Book One
Shattered, Book Two
Haunted, Book Three, Coming Next in the Series!
Untamed, Book Four, Coming Soon!

## Peregrine Bay, Romantic Suspense

Reclaiming Love, Book One
Our Kind of Love, Book Two
Edge of Love, Coming Next in the Series!

# *Contemporary Romance Series*

# MacLarens of Fire Mountain

Second Summer, Book One
Hard Landing, Book Two
One More Day, Book Three
All Your Nights, Book Four
Always Love You, Book Five
Hearts Don't Lie, Book Six
No Getting Over You, Book Seven
'Til the Sun Comes Up, Book Eight
Foolish Heart, Book Nine

## Burnt River

Thorn's Journey
Del's Choice
Boone's Surrender

**The best way to stay in touch is to subscribe to my newsletter.** Go to www.shirleendavies.com and subscribe in the box at the top of the right column that asks for your email. You'll be notified of new books before they are released, have chances to win great prizes, and receive other subscriber-only specials.

# Restless Wind

## Redemption Mountain Historical Western Romance Series

## SHIRLEEN DAVIES

**Book Thirteen in the**

**Redemption Mountain**

**Historical Western Romance Series**

Avalanche Ranch Press, LLC
PO Box 12618
Prescott, AZ 86304

Restless Wind is a work of fiction. Names, characters, places, and incidents are either products of the author's imagination or used fictitiously. Any resemblance to actual events, locales, or persons, living or dead, is wholly coincidental.

Book design and conversions by Joseph Murray at 3rdplanetpublishing.com

Cover design by Kim Killion, The Killion Group

ISBN: 978-1-947680-01-2

I care about quality, so if you find something in error, please contact me via email at shirleen@shirleendavies.com

# Description

A headstrong rancher determined to make it on his own.
A society bell intent on creating her own life.
Is there any chance they'll become each other's future?

**Restless Wind, Book Thirteen, Redemption Mountain Historical Western Romance Series**

**Dominic Lucero** is a man driven to succeed. Leaving his family's profitable ranch in Texas, he strikes out to build a new life. Becoming a U.S. Marshal for the Montana Territory and purchasing land near Splendor are two steps toward his ultimate goal. What he doesn't need is the distraction of a beautiful woman. Especially one from wealth with a fondness for a pampered life.

**Josephine Dubois** ran away from the comfortable, yet controlling life of her parents' New Orleans home. Seeking adventure and independence, she follows her dearest friend to Splendor. Falling in love with the town, she charges ahead with plans of her own. Plans that don't include the handsome transplant from Whiplash, Texas.

Unsettled by his attraction to Josie, Dom focuses on establishing his ranch. But unusual events, coupled with surprise attacks, stall his efforts.

When the danger shifts toward the woman he's come to care a great deal about, Dom can't shove aside his feelings any longer. No matter his unsettled heart, he won't allow an innocent to be caught up in actions targeted at him.

Can two such different people find common ground for a shared life? Or will stubborn pride and increasing danger force them apart, dashing their hopes for a future together?

Restless Wind, book thirteen in the Redemption Mountain historical western romance series, is a full-length novel with an HEA and no cliffhanger.

**Visit my website for a list of characters for each series.**
http://www.shirleendavies.com/character-list.html

# Restless Wind

# Prologue

*New Orleans, Louisiana*
*October 1869*

"What do you think you're doing, Miss Josie?"

Josephine Dubois gripped the folded chemise as she whirled around to face the short, buxom, older woman who'd been a second mother to her since birth. Teezy's bright smile against her coffee brown skin would fool most. Not Josie. She could see the exasperated gleam in the woman's eyes, hear the annoyance in her voice. Stiffening her spine, Josie jutted her chin out, a pose that hadn't worked in years.

Teezy glanced from the satchel on the bed to Josie. "I know that look. Don't be thinking you can lie to me, missy."

Refusing to be cowed, Josie met the woman's piercing black gaze. "Harriet and her parents invited me to stay with them for several days."

Lifting a brow, she crossed her arms under ample breasts. "At eleven at night?"

Josie almost stomped a foot in disgust, showing some of her infamous temper. "I'm packing to leave in the morning. Charles already knows to have the carriage ready for me."

Turning away, she placed the chemise into the satchel before folding a wool dress, setting it inside. Sensing Teezy step behind her, Josie turned, blocking the woman's view.

"It may be fall, missy, but it's as humid as an August night. You'd best be telling me where you're really going."

Josie blew out a frustrated breath, hoping Teezy would give up and leave. She didn't.

"I'm packing it for Harriet. She's always admired it, and I have so many dresses."

Beautiful, with multiple suitors, Harriet was the only person who knew of her plan to escape.

Teezy tilted her head back, laughing. "Her father has more money than yours, chérie. I doubt that young woman has ever taken a hand-me-down in her life."

Anger at the close scrutiny began rippling through Josie. She'd spent months devising her plan to leave New Orleans behind, joining her best friend in Splendor, Montana.

Over a year of begging her parents to let her visit Olivia had gotten her nowhere. Her father had refused to allow Josie to travel beyond the state lines without her mother or Teezy as a companion. Typical for a proper southern lady, her mother supported his decision.

At twenty-one, she'd never even gone into the city without one or both of her parents, sometimes

Teezy. Josie remembered how she'd felt when Olivia made the decision to find her real father, Nicholas Barnett. It had been a devastating parting, both young women crying when Olivia boarded the train for the long journey to Montana. As the train pulled away from the station, Josie had begun her plans to follow as soon as possible, wishing her parents were as understanding as Olivia's grandparents.

Mr. and Mrs. Moreau, the grandparents who'd raised Olivia after her mother, Charlotte, died not long after her birth, hadn't encouraged the trip, but didn't stop her. The money her great-grandmother provided after her death allowed her the funds to seek her father out.

When she was sixteen, Josie's own great-grandfather had left her a large amount of money when he passed. The funds became available for her use on her twenty-first birthday.

"You're welcome to travel with me in the morning, Teezy. I expect to be leaving the house a little before six."

Eying her skeptically, Teezy's lips twisted in a sardonic grin. "How long do you plan to stay with Harriet?"

"Several days." Josie held her breath, continuing to pack while Teezy pondered what to do. Her parents had given the older woman full authority while they were on an extended trip to Europe. They'd given her older brother, Rafael, the same. Thankfully, Rafe no longer lived at home, trusting Teezy to make decisions regarding his sister.

"You aren't planning to go anywhere else, are you, missy?"

"Of course not." Biting her lower lip, she closed and latched the satchel. "It will give you time to visit your daughter and grandchildren." Glancing up, she hid a smile at the wistful look on Teezy's face.

"It *would* be nice to see them." Her gaze narrowed on Josie, voice turning serious. "I'll expect you back on Tuesday."

Walking to her, Josie bent down, kissing her on the cheek. "Enjoy the time with your family and don't worry about me. I'll be fine."

A wave of guilt washed through her at the blatant lie. She loved the older woman who'd always been there for her, and hoped her parents wouldn't blame Teezy for Josie disappearing.

The same as her parents, she was overprotective, spoiling any attempt Josie made at freedom. This time, though, with her parents in Europe, Rafe living in town, and Teezy leaving to visit her daughter, she'd finally have the chance to escape their suffocating love.

Josie could barely contain her excitement. In twelve hours, she'd board the train, taking it as far away from her predictable, sheltered life as possible.

4

# Chapter One

*Splendor, Montana Territory*
*February 1870*

Olivia Barnett and Josie Dubois stepped into the cold winter evening, arms laden with packages from Petermann's General Store. Hurrying down the boardwalk, they were about to cross the street when a loud crack of thunder had them jumping and scrambling back toward cover. Seconds later, the sky burst open, rain beating down on the already drenched ground.

Josie adjusted the packages in her arms, a slow smile curving the corners of her mouth. "Even when it rains, it's so beautiful here."

"So different from New Orleans. It's beautiful in its own way, but—" Olivia startled at another flash of light, followed by a loud boom of thunder several seconds later.

"You two young ladies need to get in here." Betts Jones held the door open to McCall's, the restaurant she owned with her husband, motioning them inside. "It's cold, the rain's coming down in sheets, and the wind is picking up." She nodded toward a table by the window. "I'll bring you large cups of hot chocolate."

Olivia smiled. "Thank you, Mrs. Jones."

Setting their packages on nearby chairs, they sat down, staring outside. Thunder continued to rattle the windows as lightning flashed across the sky.

"So, tell me about your supper with Doctor McCord." Josie clasped her hands together, resting them on the edge of the table. "Did he take you to the Eagle's Nest?"

Feeling her cheeks heat, Olivia nodded, a shy smile appearing. "Yes."

Josie cocked her head to the side. "And?"

"Here you are." Betts set two steaming cups on the table. Hands on hips, she glanced outside, shaking her head. "The weather sure is cutting down on business. I do hope it clears up soon. Holler if you want more." She didn't look at the women on the last, her gaze fixed on the continuous flashes of lightning before abruptly returning to the kitchen.

Josie blew across the hot chocolate, her eyes bright with mischief. "All right. Now, tell me about your supper with the doctor."

Setting down her cup, Olivia flushed a second time. She and Josie couldn't be more different. Vivacious, inquisitive, and always ready for an adventure, Josie had been getting them in trouble since their days in boarding school. Shy, smart, and bookish, with a preference for small supper parties instead of the larger, boisterous gatherings Josie preferred, Olivia marveled at how close they'd become. She was the voice of reason, while Josie was the spark of life.

"He's a very nice man."

Josie waved her hand in the air. "I already know that. Tell me what you talked about."

She pursed her lips, brows furrowing. "We usually talk about what we're reading, places we'd like to see."

"Livvy," Josie prodded. "Did he ask your father to court you?"

Olivia's features sobered before she lowered her head to stare into the cup. "Clay didn't say anything. Father doesn't seem to mind him taking me to supper without formally courting me."

Josie sat back, crossing her arms, blowing out an exasperated breath. "If it were *my* father, I wouldn't be allowed to go anywhere with a man unless there'd been a formal show of interest. *And* he'd send Teezy with us."

Olivia couldn't contain her interest. "Have you ever been courted?"

Josie snorted out a brittle laugh. "Of course not. My father runs off every eligible suitor before they even get in the house." She smiled and leaned forward, talking in a conspiratorial voice. "There was this one young man I met at the market. My mother was with me when he introduced himself. His father and mine were founders of the Mistick Krewe of Comus. You remember, Liv. The businessmen who organize the Mardi Gras each year."

"Yes, I remember. Now that you're here, my grandparents and Mardi Gras are all I miss about home."

Josie nodded. "I'm certain I'll feel the same after a few more months. Anyway, because of the connection, the young man thought Father would be amicable for him to call on me."

Picking up her cup, Josie took a few sips, enjoying the look of anticipation on Olivia's face. Her mouth twisted into a grimace.

"Father wouldn't allow it."

Olivia didn't hide the laughter at the look of disgust on Josie's face.

"This is serious, Livvy, and the main reason I traveled across country to get away from him."

Olivia's eyes sparkled. "And I thought you came to see me."

"Of course I came to see you. You're my closest friend. The only person who understands me." Josie glanced outside at another flash of light and subsequent crack of thunder. Holding the cup in both hands, she took a slow sip, her gaze lifting. "And to get away from Father."

Olivia's green eyes softened. "He loves you. It's natural he'd want to protect you."

"You don't understand, Livvy. Your grandparents never tried to control your every move. Neither does your father. I'm not allowed to go anywhere without a chaperone. Mother or Teezy are my constant companions. If I'm invited to a party, one of them always accompanies me. It's stifling."

Finishing her hot chocolate, Olivia gave her a sympathetic look. "Well, you're here now, and Father will allow you the same freedom as me. I mean, we are in our twenties." She smiled.

"Barely. But you're right. It will be wonderful to not have to ask permission for everything." Josie's brows drew together. "At least until they discover where I am and order me home."

"How long do you think it will be before they discover you've left?"

Josie's features clouded. "They're due back from Europe in late March. I left a letter in their bedroom. The same as the ones mailed from St. Louis to Teezy and my brother, they don't reveal my destination. With luck, they won't discover my location for several months after their return. By then, I hope to be living in a house of my own instead of imposing on you and your family."

"You're welcome to stay as long as you like, Josie. Father and Suzanne love having you with us."

"And I love living with you. Who wouldn't? The home Nick built for Suzanne is beautiful."

A wistful expression moved across Olivia's face. "Father loves her so much, and she feels the same about him. I hope to have the same someday."

"With Clay?"

Olivia nodded. "I love him, Josie."

"From the way he looks at you, I'd say he feels the same."

"He does?"

Josie laughed. "You'd have to be blind not to know he's in love with you. Whenever you're together, he can't take his eyes off you. And if you haven't noticed, he's quite possessive."

Before Olivia could respond, the door opened, drawing their attention. Dominic Lucero, the newly appointed U.S. Marshal, walked inside.

"Good evening, ladies." Shrugging out of his duster, he hung it and his hat on hooks.

Josie's throat constricted, as did her chest, feeling a flush of heat. The same happened each time she saw Dom, which irritated her more than a little. She didn't understand her reaction to him. Yes, he was a striking man, with sharp features, ink black hair, and golden brown eyes. Tough, lean, and sinewy. She guessed he stood a little over six feet, his muscled shoulders filling the coat he always wore. Seeing him without it had her mouth going dry, something else which annoyed her. He wasn't remotely similar to the men her family considered suitable in New Orleans.

"Hello, Dom." Olivia smiled at the brother of her good friend, Sylvia Mackey. "I'd heard you were out of town." She glanced at Josie, wondering why her friend hadn't greeted him.

"Got back from Big Pine last night." He nodded at an empty chair at their table. "May I join you?"

"Please." Again, she glanced at Josie, who'd gone uncharacteristically quiet.

Taking a seat, he settled his gaze on Josie. "I hope you two will let me buy supper."

Olivia ignored an almost imperceptible shake of Josie's head. "That would be lovely. You can tell us all about your new job and the ranch." She didn't miss the way her friend's shoulders slumped. *Curious*, she thought, vowing to ask Josie about it after Dom left.

"Well now." Betts walked to their table. "Marshal Lucero. It's good to see you again."

"Good evening, Mrs. Jones."

She shook her head. "How many times have I asked you to call me Betts?"

Dom smiled. "Too many to count, Betts."

"That's better. Are you three going to have supper?"

"We are," Dom answered. "What do you have for us this evening?"

"Roast beef with boiled potatoes, meatloaf with mashed potatoes, and roast chicken. It also comes with potatoes."

Dom flashed a grin at Josie. "Miss Dubois?"

"The roast beef, please."

"I will have the same, please," Olivia said.

Dom didn't take his gaze off Josie. "I'll also have the roast, Betts. And coffee when you have a chance."

"I'll bring you ladies more hot chocolate." She didn't wait for a response before leaving for the kitchen.

"Have you seen Sylvia since you got back?" Olivia asked.

Dom looked at her, nodding. "I had breakfast with her and Mack this morning," he answered, mentioning Sylvia's husband. "I've never seen my sister so happy."

Olivia smiled. "They both are. I'm glad he finally came to his senses and asked her to marry him."

"It saved me from giving him a good beating."

"You were going to beat him?" Josie asked Dom, her eyes wide.

He grinned. "If I had to, yes. It doesn't mean I don't like Mack, but it's sometimes the best way to get a man moving in the right direction."

Josie glanced at Olivia, who seemed unaffected by Dom's words. "Wouldn't Sylvia have been outraged if you'd hurt him?"

His mouth edged up. "Not at the time, no."

Brows drawing together, Josie looked at Olivia, a question in her eyes.

"He's right. The way Mack acted was inexcusable. When he heard Sylvia might return to Texas, well..." She glanced at Dom, then back at Josie. "What Mack thought he wanted changed when he realized she might be gone for good."

"Oh," she whispered, not understanding at all.

"Three plates of roast beef and potatoes." Betts set them down, then returned with coffee and more hot chocolate. "I have apple pie for dessert." She grinned before leaving them to their meals.

Several minutes passed while they ate before Olivia spoke again. "How are the plans for your ranch coming along?"

Setting down his fork, Dom grinned. "I'm meeting with Bull Mason in the morning." He looked at Josie. "He's one of the foremen for Dax and Luke Pelletier, and is also an excellent designer."

"Bull helped Father and his partners, Gabe and Lena Evans, with the St. James Hotel. He also drew the plans for the new clinic," Olivia added. "I don't know how he has time to do both jobs and take care of his family. I believe you met them at Caleb and May's wedding."

"I met so many people, it's hard to remember." Josie did her best not to stare at Dom. She wanted to reach out, stroke a finger along his jaw, feel the stubble, brush a thumb over his lips. She stilled, confused at the direction her thoughts were headed. Confused *and* angry.

"I'm hoping to start building in March. You're both welcome to come out and see the property when the snow melts. In fact, I'd be honored to escort you."

"We'd love to see it. Wouldn't we, Josie?"

Fork pausing partway to her mouth, she nodded. "Um, yes. Perhaps Doctor McCord would like to join us."

Dom nodded. "I'll mention it to Clay as the time gets closer." His gaze wandered to Josie.

He'd been doing his best not to stare at the beautiful woman, the same as he'd tried to do since meeting her after she arrived on the stage. He wanted to reach out, remove the pins from her blonde hair, run his fingers through the silken tresses.

Dom wanted to do more. He couldn't recall the last time he had such an immediate and intense reaction to a woman. At one time, Dom had been attracted to Tabitha Beekman. Like his sister and May Covington, she'd come to Splendor as a mail order bride. He'd been tempted to ask to call on her, but never did. She'd ended up accepting an offer of marriage from a previous suitor, leaving Splendor the same day Josie arrived.

The moment he'd seen her talking with Olivia, all thoughts of Tabitha vanished. Now Dom couldn't get his mind off her. He didn't even try.

# Chapter Two

"What do you two young ladies have planned for today?" Nick Barnett, Olivia's father, poured another cup of coffee, resting against the back of his chair.

Josie shot a look at Olivia before returning her attention to Nick. An attractive man with the same black hair and green eyes as his daughter, he wore a patch over his left eye. It had rattled her when she'd first met him after departing the stage. After several weeks of living with him, his wife, Suzanne, and Olivia, she barely noticed it.

"We discussed having Mr. Brandt saddle our horses and—"

"No." The quick, firm tone of Nick's voice startled both young women. "You are *not* going riding without me or another man I approve of accompanying you."

"Nick?" Suzanne walked into the room from the kitchen, stopping next to her husband's chair. "Is everything all right?"

He reached out his hand, threading his fingers through hers. "Everything is fine, sweetheart. I was telling Olivia and Josie they're not to go riding without being accompanied by me or one of our male friends. Besides, the trails are covered with snow and will be icy in some parts."

Her hand tightened on his, an agonizing flash of a memory crossing Suzanne's face before she forced the pain away. "Nick is right. There are dangers you can't imagine. The storm from last night has passed, but another could come in without warning. They can be brutal and...deadly." Her voice broke on the last.

"Suzanne." Nick stood, his soft voice comforting as he settled an arm over her shoulders. "I believe they understand." He kissed her temple. "Are you ready to leave for the boardinghouse?"

Swallowing, she nodded, a wave of embarrassment coloring her cheeks. "Why don't you two join me for lunch today?"

"An excellent idea, sweetheart," Nick said. "May I join my three favorite women?"

"That would be wonderful, Father." Olivia pushed back her chair and stood, concerned over Suzanne's distress.

She'd heard the story of how her stepmother had lost her first husband and daughter in a freak winter storm. It had taken her years to get over the losses, choosing to work long hours to build the boardinghouse into a success.

"Suzanne and I will see you ladies at lunch. Enjoy your day." Nick sent them a pointed stare. "And stay out of trouble."

Josie finished her tea and stood, waiting until they'd left. "Is Suzanne all right?"

Olivia nodded. "She will be. I'd forgotten she lost her first husband and daughter in a winter storm. It had been a beautiful, clear day when they left." She looked at Josie, shaking her head. "They didn't return."

"Oh, no." Josie's hand flew to her chest. "I can't imagine losing your family in such an awful tragedy. Suzanne is an amazing woman to have lived through it and built a new life."

Olivia nodded. "I admire her a great deal. So does Father."

Clasping her hands in front of her, Josie moved across the room to the front window. "It's beautiful outside." She turned back to Olivia, an impish glint in her eyes. "So, what *are* we going to do today?"

Dom studied the plans Bull rolled out on a table at the Dixie, the saloon Nick owned with Lena Evans. Tossing back the whiskey he held in one hand, his gaze narrowed on the drawing, a slow smile curving the corners of his mouth.

"We can move the barn or bunkhouse, but I'd recommend leaving the house where it is." Bull pointed to the stream. "Even though it's below the location of the buildings, you don't want any of them too close to the water. Luke says it's known to flood in a hard rain."

Dom nodded. "He and Dax mentioned that to me when we looked at the land."

"I thought they would." Bull stared at the drawings. "Placing the house, barn, and bunkhouse as shown on the plans should resolve any issues with flooding. So far, we've had a mild winter. If it continues, we might be able to start laying out the buildings by late February." Bull glanced up at him. "Unless you want to wait."

"I'd rather start as soon as the ground thaws. The bunkhouse would be first, then the barn. Arrangements have been made for a herd of Texas longhorns to arrive in April. I've also signed a contract with a breeder in Kansas to purchase shorthorn and Hereford stock for delivery about the same time."

Sitting back in his chair, Bull stroked his stubbled jaw. "That's quite an investment for a new ranch. Are you planning to crossbreed?"

"I am. Dax and Luke are interested and plan to purchase a few of the longhorns from me to breed with their shorthorns."

Bull's eyes widened. "I hadn't heard about it."

Dom lifted one shoulder in a shrug. "I'm not surprised. We talked about it at Caleb's wedding, and there's been a lot going on the last few weeks. It's something my father has been wanting to try for several years at his ranch in Texas."

Leaning forward, Bull rested his arms on the table. "Is that where you're getting the longhorns?"

"Afraid so. In hindsight, I should've made a deal with one of the other ranchers I know." Dom thought about the numerous telegrams between himself and his family. Those from his father often contained veiled threats of disinheritance if Dom didn't return to Whiplash and accept his role on the Lucero ranch. "My father can be a hard man."

Bull's features clouded. "Most fathers are."

Dom had heard the stories of Bull and his father working together to design and construct many of the buildings along the Ohio River in Cincinnati. He'd also learned the Pelletier foreman had fought for the Union Army alongside the Squirrel Hunters and Black Brigade during the war. Afterward, he'd chosen to ride west instead of return home and continue to work with his father.

"Have you seen yours since coming west?" Dom asked.

Giving a slow shake of his head, Bull lowered his gaze to the plans. "No."

"I heard you were back in town." Beau Davis, one of Gabe Evans's deputies, strolled toward them, clasping Dom's outstretched hand before shaking the one Bull offered.

"Have a seat." Dom nodded to a chair. "We're going over the plans for my ranch. I'd welcome your opinions."

Chair scraping across the worn wood floor, Beau lowered himself onto it, already studying the drawings Bull had prepared. "Don't know if I'll be much help. Bull prepared the plans for my place and I'm real pleased with it." He shot a grin at Bull. "When do you plan to start building?"

Dom repeated what he'd told Bull, including the part about crossbreeding longhorns with shorthorns and Herefords. "The bunkhouse will be built first. I'll be looking for five ranch hands plus a foreman." He glanced at Bull. "You aren't interested in moving over, are you?"

"Not if I want to live," he chuckled. "The Pelletiers have been real good to me, and Lydia is close to Rachel and Ginny. She'd probably slit my throat if I mentioned leaving." His brows shot up. "Mal Jolly might be interested. He's good with the men and the cattle. Lately, he's been talking about moving on so he can work as a foreman."

"Do Dax and Luke know he's considering leaving?" Dom asked.

Bull shook his head. "I don't know. If you want, I'll mention the job to him."

"I'd appreciate it, but don't mention my name. I won't speak to Mal until after I've talked with Dax and Luke."

Bull nodded. "Sounds fair."

Beau rubbed the back of his neck. "You should talk with Noah Brandt, Dom. A good number of

21

cowboys who ride through town stop to have him check their horses."

"When it's closer to the time you want to hire, talk to the bartenders here and at the Wild Rose." Bull mentioned the other saloon owned by Nick, Lena, and Gabe. "Men looking for work usually stop there first."

"I'll do that." Dom studied the drawings again.

"Marshal?"

The three glanced at the man coming toward them. Bernie Griggs ran the telegraph and post office in Splendor, had been in town longer than most, and approached his job with unwavering dedication. He stopped next to their table, holding up a message.

"Got a telegram for you, Marshal."

A tight grin tilted the corners of Dom's mouth. He hadn't grown used to people referring to him by his profession.

"Thanks, Bernie. Can you stay a minute in case I want to reply?"

Nodding, his gaze skittered around the room. "Sure can." Below average in height with a slim build, he projected nervous energy.

Dom's gaze scanned the message, a scowl forming. Folding the paper, he tucked it into a pocket.

"Reply that I'll be there late afternoon tomorrow, Bernie. Can you put it on my account?"

Nodding several times, Bernie glanced around again. "Sure, Marshal. Well, I'd better be going." He scurried away, leaving the three to watch his hasty retreat.

"Never seen a man more jumpy," Beau chuckled.

"He's been that way as long as I've known him," Bull responded, a grin appearing on his face. It disappeared at Dom's disgruntled expression. "Bad news?"

Dom shook his head. "Not really. I'm needed back in Big Pine for a trial the day after tomorrow. I'd hoped to stay here at least another week."

As a U.S. Marshal, his job included protecting the judge from threats, such as the one the suspected murderer made against the man presiding over his trial.

His thoughts wandered to the woman he couldn't seem to get off his mind. Josie Dubois had lodged herself in his brain, and no matter how hard he tried, he couldn't find a way to remove her image.

As much as Dom tried to ignore the attraction, he found himself wanting to spend time with Josie, getting to know the intriguing woman. Instead, he'd be riding for hours to reach Big Pine, staying until the verdict had been read.

If found guilty, he'd be tasked with escorting the man to the territorial prison near Deer Lodge. Two to three days north and the same amount of time riding south to reach Splendor. Too long, but it was his job, and he enjoyed the work.

"There are still some things I need to do before riding out tomorrow morning." Dom stood, waiting while the others did the same. "Thanks, Bull. I'll ride out to Redemption's Edge when I get back. Beau, it's been good to see you. Maybe we can play a couple rounds of cards when I return." Tossing money onto the table, he walked outside, buttoning his coat to fend off the icy temperature.

Avoiding slow moving wagons and deep ruts filled with slush, he crossed the street in time to see Josie and Olivia coming out of Petermann's. When he saw them last evening at McCall's, they carried several packages. Today, they held far fewer.

They were laughing, something they seemed to do a great deal of most of the time. He'd never met a woman as animated as Josie. Even if she wasn't a raving beauty, her vigor and spirit would attract many men. It made him wonder how many had courted her and why such an obvious prize hadn't married.

Watching, Dom reminded himself Josie was staying in Splendor a brief amount of time before returning to her home in New Orleans. At least that was what he assumed. He'd never spent enough time with Josie to learn her plans. It appeared he wouldn't have a chance until returning after his latest obligation.

Dom stepped aside as they approached, so absorbed in their own conversation, neither noticed him. Coming alongside him, Josie glanced to her side, startling at the sight of Dom's amused expression.

"Oh." Her hand flew to her chest. "Mr. Lucero. I didn't see you standing there."

"It's Dom, remember?"

Josie's hand dropped, her tongue darting out to moisten her lips. "Dom then."

"Hello, Dom. Did your meeting with Bull go well?" Olivia asked, watching her friend's reaction to the handsome lawman.

It puzzled her. Outgoing with a broad smile for everyone she met, Josie could barely form a sentence when around Dom. Her actions were quite strange. Even though Josie's father kept her under his tight control, she never met a stranger, carrying on long conversations with new acquaintances.

For some reason, she struggled with every word spoken to Dom. It was as if Josie fell into a trance whenever he appeared, becoming skittish, ready to bolt.

"Our meeting went very well. If weather permits, we're hoping to start building later this month or early March. The bunkhouse and barn first, then the house."

"Wouldn't you normally build the house first?" Olivia asked.

"Sometimes. It depends on each rancher's expectations and needs. I've made arrangements for a herd to be delivered in April, and I'll need to have a place for the ranch hands to live. I'll bunk with them until the house is built."

"That's interesting, isn't it, Josie?" She glanced at her friend, noticing how her gaze focused on Dom, lips compressed. Olivia's brows furrowed. "Josie?"

Forcing her attention from Dom, she blinked. "I'm sorry. What did you say?"

Olivia looked at Dom, seeing the amusement in his eyes a moment before they both laughed.

"It's nothing important, Josie." Olivia glanced down the street, seeing Clay step between two buildings. "Oh, there's Doctor McCord." She shot Josie a quick glance. "Do you mind if I say hello to him?"

"Well, I..." Her voice stalled when Olivia hurried away. Biting her lower lip, she looked at Dom. "So, um..."

"How about we get a cup of coffee while Olivia and Clay talk?"

"I'm not sure..." Again, her words faded.

He leaned closer, his voice lowering. "It's only a cup of coffee, Josie. We can walk over to the boardinghouse."

She glanced over her shoulder, seeing Olivia slip her arm through Clay's, walking down the boardwalk in the opposite direction. "But Livvy won't know where we are."

"If she doesn't find us before you're ready to leave, I'll take you home." His eyes glittered. "I heard Suzanne made peach pie this morning."

Relaxing, a playful grin slid the corners of her mouth upward. "Peach?"

"That's what I heard."

Straightening her spine, she lifted her chin. "I don't share my pie, Dom."

His golden brown eyes darkened to a deep chocolate. "That's good, because I don't share anything, Josie."

# Chapter Three

Josie picked at her pie, still finding it difficult to meet Dom's intense brown eyes for more than a few seconds. Doing her best to appear disinterested in him, she responded to his questions, nodding when the topic moved to his job and new ranch.

Not wanting to appear rude, Josie asked a few questions of her own, hoping he didn't notice her profound interest in his responses. He was the most fascinating man she'd ever met. Much more captivating than the young men she'd known in New Orleans, who spoke of their social status and wealth, attempting to impress Josie and her family. Their self-serving words did the opposite, boring her to the point she found herself attending fewer social events each year.

Dom surprised her. He spoke of his family's ranch in Texas, relating amusing stories about his older brother, Cruz, and his sister, Sylvia. Josie had heard how his sister snuck away from their parents' home and became a mail order bride, ending up in Splendor with three other young women.

She hadn't heard about Sylvia's courtship with Mack. Dom went into enough detail to let her know the hurdles they'd overcome, leaving out the more painful moments, and the way he and Mack had almost come to blows over the deputy's treatment of his sister.

Other than being with Olivia, Josie couldn't recall when she'd had such a good time. And despite the desire not to let Dom notice her attraction to him, she found herself laughing, relaxing the longer they sat at the table.

"How long will you be in Splendor?"

Shrugging, she glanced outside before returning her gaze to him. "I'm not certain. Mother and Father are on an extended trip to Europe. They're due back in late March or early April." Josie pursed her lips, deciding how much to say. Her plans weren't a secret. They just weren't final. "I'd prefer to stay here, find a job, and buy a small house near town. Once they return and learn of my absence, they'll be furious. Especially my father." An involuntary shudder passed through her. "I've no doubt he'll hire a detective to locate me. Then either he or my older brother, Rafe, will come after me."

Dom set down his cup, brows furrowing. "Would he force you to return to New Orleans?"

A bitter chuckle escaped her lips. "Oh, yes. He might never allow me out of the house again." She forced away the anxiety at the thought of her father showing up and making a scene, embarrassing her, as often happened when he tried to bend her to his will. "He doesn't understand that I'm not his little girl any longer."

"My father was the same way with Sylvia. He had her future planned out, who she'd marry and when." His features softened. "I'm sure he and your mother will be frantic with worry when they return to find you gone. It's natural he'd try to find you, make sure you're safe." He wanted to reach across the table, settle his hand over hers. The opportunity was lost when she moved her hands to her lap.

"If he'd stop at locating me, everything would be fine. But he won't. He'll do all he can to force me to leave. I'm a grown woman, Dom, with money of my own, and dreams he'll never understand."

He nodded, crossing his arms as he leaned back. "I had to move here to get away from my father's plans for me."

Josie's eyes widened. "You did?"

"Not much different than Sylvia. I came to Splendor to convince her to come home. The problem was I felt the same as her. So much so, I began discussions with Dax and Luke Pelletier about buying land to start a cattle ranch. I returned to Texas long enough to turn in my badge, explain my decision to my parents and brother, then head back to Splendor."

A brow lifted. "Your badge?"

"I was a Texas Ranger for a short period of time. Not long after resigning and returning to Splendor, Neil Howie, the U.S. Marshal for the western Montana Territory, approached me about taking on his position when he retired. I'd completed the purchase of land from the Pelletiers and knew it would take time to get the ranch up and running."

"So you took the job Mr. Howie offered."

Nodding, one corner of his mouth tilted into a grin. "I don't know how long it will last. I'll need to resign once the ranch work gets too heavy to continue."

Studying his face, she realized her earlier reservations about being with Dom had disappeared the longer they spoke. She found him easy to be with, comfortable, as if they'd known each other longer than a few weeks.

Sitting up, a regretful expression crossed his face. "I should get you home before Olivia and Nick come looking for you."

Her eyes sparked. "Are you afraid of him?"

"I'd be a fool not to be. He may appear the southern gentleman, but I've seen him when he's angry. It's not a pretty sight. Nick knows how to protect himself and anyone else he cares about. You, Josie Dubois, would fall into that group." Standing, he moved behind her chair, pulling it out to help her up.

She looked at him, surprised at how relaxed she felt. "Thank you for the coffee and pie."

Dom waited until she slid her hand through the arm he offered, then smiled. "My pleasure."

Walking along the boardwalk toward Nick's house, she allowed herself to enjoy the comfort of having him close. Dom truly was a handsome man, one she wanted to learn more about.

"I'm leaving for Big Pine tomorrow. Probably won't return for at least a week. When I do get back, I hope you'll consider having supper with me."

Excitement coursed through Josie. If he'd asked her before today, before they'd spent time together at the boardinghouse, she'd have politely declined.

"I'd love to have supper with you, Dom."

Looking down, he studied her. "Do I need to ask permission from Nick?"

Sucking in a breath, her lips twisted. "It might be best. After all, he and Suzanne are allowing me to stay with them and refuse to accept any form of payment."

"Yeah, I was afraid of that."

Her head fell back on a deep laugh. "You *are* scared of him, aren't you?"

Stopping, he turned Josie to face him. "Clay has been sweet on Olivia since well before I came to Splendor. Nick has made no secret about his disapproval of the doc courting her. It makes no sense as Clay is educated, successful, and one of the best men I've ever known."

"Olivia is his daughter, Dom. He only recently learned of her existence."

"True, and I understand his hesitancy about making certain the right man spends time with Olivia." He looked down at her. "It won't stop me from asking Nick for permission to escort you to supper."

"And if he says no?"

Dom grinned. "He won't."

*Big Pine*

Dom stood with his feet shoulder width apart, hands clasped behind his back. Staring at the table where the accused murderer sat, he studied the man. Features contorted, fear evident in the way his gaze jerked at those seated behind him in the courtroom. The wild look in his eyes worried Dom.

The young gunslinger had been caught running from the scene of a bank robbery where two people had been shot. One a pregnant woman, the other a respected business owner. Both died hours later. The other robbers had gotten away.

The outraged town pushed for a quick trial, trusting the verdict would be a firm guilty. From what Dom had learned from the local sheriff, Parker Sterling, the gunman didn't stand a chance of being found innocent. The gallows had already been erected.

It didn't help his cause to have the woman's husband, a child in his arms, sitting in the front row, not hiding his anguished, yet stoic, features. Dom expected the trial to be one of the shortest he'd ever witnessed.

Unlike Splendor, and being the territorial capital, Big Pine had its own courthouse. The large courtroom had enough chairs for fifty observers, plus one table for the prosecution and one for the defense. Two rows of six chairs each had been placed along one wall on the right side of the courtroom for the jurors.

A platform had been built at the back, a table placed on top. This was where the judge would preside over the trial, determining the fate of the young man who'd begun to sweat, his face turning a blotchy red. Something in the gunman's eyes warned Dom, caused his back to stiffen, his body on alert.

The door to the judge's chambers creaked open, the courtroom going silent. A rotund man of average height emerged, a black robe draped over the rumpled suit Dom saw him wearing earlier.

"All rise," Dom announced when he realized the clerk who took notes hadn't arrived.

The judge nodded to him, taking his seat at the same time the harried clerk ran through the front door.

"Sorry, Your Honor. My cow—"

Holding up a hand, brows drawing together in a steely frown, the judge halted the clerk's explanation. Picking up the gavel, he struck the sound block.

"Court's in session," the clerk squeaked before sitting down, casting a furtive glance at Dom.

He didn't know what made him tear his gaze from the clerk to look toward the gunman. The instant he did, a flash of metal behind the outlaw caught his attention. Other than the six-shooter he carried, guns weren't allowed in the courthouse, yet Dom knew he'd seen the barrel of a revolver.

Hand carefully moving to the handle of his gun, his intent gaze studied the gunman, waiting for something he prayed wouldn't happen. His prayers weren't answered.

In what seemed a coordinated move, the prisoner jumped up, as did a man behind him and a third standing on the far side of the courtroom. All held guns pointed at the judge. And each one held a feral expression.

Cruel.

Cold.

Determined.

Dom took in the scene in less than a second, nostrils flaring in concentration. The fear on the outlaws' faces worked to his advantage, allowing a calm to wash over him.

The prisoner opened his mouth to speak, his gun trained on the judge. He didn't get the chance to voice whatever venom lodged in his throat.

Dom's bullet to the gunman's forehead had him crumpling to the table where he stood, eyes wide with shock. Half a second later, his partner gave a screeching cry, clutching at his chest, falling over the rail before him. The third hadn't switched his aim from the judge to Dom before feeling the cold metal of a gun barrel at his temple.

"Don't do it." Sheriff Parker Sterling stood beside the last of the three gunmen. "Drop your gun."

Instead of heeding the lawman's order, the man's jaw clenched, madness flashing in his eyes. Swinging his gun from the judge to Dom, he didn't have time to draw another breath before a bloom of red spread across his stained shirt. Parker barely had time to grab the revolver from the gunman's hand before the man fell against the wall, sliding to the floor.

Dom didn't spare a glance at the fallen outlaws before turning to the judge. "Are you all right, Your Honor?"

Eyes bulging, face flushed, he swiped a handkerchief over his face, nodding. Clearing his throat, he stuffed the cloth into his pocket. "Ye...yes." The judge's gaze flickered over his courtroom before returning to Dom. "That was an admirable display, Marshal."

Glancing over his shoulder, Dom shrugged, as if killing three men in the courtroom was commonplace. "As long as you and the others are all right."

Holstering his gun, Dom checked the two dead outlaws closest to him before joining Sterling. He nodded at the body slumped against the wall.

"Dead?"

"As they come," Sterling answered. "The other two?"

Dom cast a quick look at the undertaker and his men, who'd begun moving the other two bodies from the courtroom. "The same."

Rubbing the back of his neck, Sterling shook his head. "At least we don't have to go through a trial to determine if the prisoner is guilty. The way they went out says it all. You headed back to Splendor?"

"At sunup. I plan to get a bath, a decent meal, and a full night's sleep first. Any news you want me to pass along to Gabe?"

"Tell Sheriff Evans about what happened here today. There could be more than the three you killed." Sterling's brows lifted. "Mighty fine shooting, Lucero."

"Surprise and luck."

Choking out a rough laugh, the sheriff shook his head. "Surprise, yes. Those three didn't know what hit them until you'd laid them out. Luck? Nothing about those shots was luck. I didn't know you had such a fast gun."

Chuckling, Dom's eyes lit. "My brother and I used to practice all the time back home. Drove our parents crazy." At the thought, some of his amusement faded. His life would be easier if they tried to understand his need to explore, find his own life. "Over the years, Cruz and I both became pretty proficient."

"Well, you'd do well to watch your back. Word's going to get around about what you did today. If I'm not mistaken, you'll be finding some young guns hunting you down, testing their skills."

Dom blew out a breath, his features taut. "I've never faced off a man in a gunfight."

"Hope you never do. If you do, watch his eyes, the way his hand hovers over the handle of his gun. You can learn a lot about a man by the look he sends you, if his hands are steady or shaking. And don't assume he'll fight fair. Few of those types do."

Features somber, Dom swallowed the bile building in his throat. He wouldn't admit it to Sterling, but today was the first time he'd ever killed in the line of duty. The Luceros had run off rustlers, shooting a few before hauling them to jail. He'd witnessed his father kill a man who'd attempted to rob him and his family on a trip to town. As a Texas

Ranger, he'd been in a couple close calls, but never killed any of the men he'd hunted.

Today, he had no choice. Regardless, it gave him no pleasure.

Sterling clasped him on the shoulder. "Be prepared, son. You just set actions in motion you might never be able to change."

# Chapter Four

*Splendor*

"I'm so pleased with the way the quilt is coming together." Ruth Paige's praise at the beautiful stitch work made everyone else smile. "I know we still have a ways to go, but it's just so beautiful. The reverend is going to be so pleased."

"We have Josie to thank for the pattern." Olivia set a hand on her friend's arm. "I'd forgotten what an accomplished artist you are."

"It's a wonderful design, Josie. I'm so glad you shared it with us." May's hand traced over the top of the unfinished cross, continuing over one wing of the white dove."

For the last few weeks, Ruth, Olivia, Josie, Abby, May, and Sylvia had met at Nick and Suzanne's house to create the striking pattern. Allie Coulter, who owned the dress and millinery store, had donated several dozen pieces of fabric too small for her purposes.

Bright blues, greens, purples, and reds set off the golden yellow cross. Green vines would wrap around the base, putting an elegant finishing touch to Josie's design.

"I just don't know what we would've done if you hadn't provided the pattern, Josie." Sylvia flashed her a grateful smile. "We hadn't been able to agree on anything before you arrived in town."

Uncomfortable with the praise, Josie stood. "Would anyone like more tea?"

When everyone nodded, she lifted the teapot and returned to the kitchen. It didn't take long to boil the water and add the tea. Several minutes later, Josie lifted the teapot, grabbed the tea strainer from the counter, and started back to the dining room, then stopped.

An impish grin split her face, eyes sparkling. Remembering her mother's hot toddy recipe using tea instead of hot water, she opened a cupboard, taking out a small container of honey and tin of cinnamon. A second cupboard held whiskey, brandy, and rum. Pulling down the bottles, she set everything on a tray, then returned to the dining room.

Dom slid from the saddle, rolling his head and stretching to relieve his stiff shoulders. He'd ridden hard, doing his best to outrun a storm approaching from the north. Entering Splendor, he reined Blue, his roan stallion, to a stop in front of Noah Brandt's livery. He walked around his mount. As always, Dom appreciated the silvering effect of white hairs turning the animal's coat into a dark bluish hue. It was a rare combination, drawing his attention immediately when he'd spotted the colt on a neighbor's ranch outside of Whiplash.

"Afternoon, Dom. You just get back?" Noah wiped his hands on a rag, slipping it into a pocket before extending his hand.

Not hesitating to accept it, Dom nodded. "Came right here. Do you have time to take care of Blue for me? I need to get over to Nick's house."

Snickering, Noah didn't try to hide a grin as he took the horse's reins. "The ladies are there working on the quilt for the church. Are you sure you want to venture into that gaggle of women?"

Wincing, his mouth twisted. "Do you know if Josie and Olivia are there?"

"They're there, all right. Josie's the one who drew the design for the quilt. Abby says it's..." He scratched the stubble on his jaw, "*gorgeous.*"

"If Abby's with them, it can't be too much of a hen party. She's got the most level head of any woman I know."

Noah lifted a brow, shaking his head. "You've been warned."

Taking the trail to Nick's house, Dom bounded up the steps, hearing laughter coming from inside. Knocking, he waited. After a couple minutes, he knocked again. When no one answered, he gripped the knob and pushed the door open.

Walking in the direction of female voices peppered with giggles, he slowed his pace, body tensing at Josie's voice.

"Yes, he is quite handsome." She giggled, then hiccupped, causing him to smile.

"I think he is one of the most attractive single men in Splendor." He recognized May Covington's voice. "But don't any of you tell Caleb I said that."

Another round of snickers ensued before Dom's sister, Sylvia, spoke. "He's never lacked for female attention." A bark of laughter burst from her. "From the time he was thirteen, he complained of girls not leaving him alone."

Dom winced.

"I thought he held an interest in Tabitha Beekman." He recognized Abby's voice.

"Who is she?" Josie's surprised reply held a hint of jealousy.

*Good*, Dom thought, a smug expression crossing his face.

"One of the mail order brides," Olivia answered, a little louder than normal. "She left town the day you arrived. A previous suitor contacted her, asking for her hand in marriage." She giggled. "He sent a picture. If it had been me..." Olivia's voice transformed as another round of laughter had her face flushing. Several of the women added their own giggles. "I'm certain he's a very nice man, and Tabitha said he has a successful business. But..."

"Bu...but...what, Livia?" Ruth prodded, her voice slurred.

"What she's trying to say is Tabitha's betrothed is quite short and, well...rotund. His mustache drops well past the bottom of his chin, and his ears are," Sylvia lowered her voice, "rather large."

"Sylvia!" Ruth's admonishment was spoiled when she laughed.

Olivia looked at Josie, her voice thick with merriment. "Tabitha is a few inches taller than him, slender, with beautiful brown hair and caramel eyes. The truth is she's quite pretty. I do hope she's happy, but ..."

"Your brother would've been a much better match, Sylvia," Abby said. "It's a shame he didn't make his interest known sooner. Is there more tea, Josie?"

For no apparent reason, the women burst out laughing. Deciding he'd return another time to see Josie, he turned to leave before they spotted him.

"I don't know how I could've let you talk me into trying your family recipe for hot toddy, Josie."

Dom halted at Ruth's words. *Hot toddy?*

Understanding came to him in a gust of clarity, a smile tilting the corners of his mouth. Chuckling, he shook his head.

The quilting circle sat in the next room, indulging in hot tea with alcohol. And the reverend's wife had been hooked into it by Josie, the apparent ringleader. As he'd thought when first meeting her, the woman was trouble.

Turning around, he headed to the dining room, making certain his boots could be heard on the wood floor.

"Good afternoon, ladies." His gaze lit on the quilt draped over the dining table before nodding at each of them.

"Dom?" Sylvia set down her cup of tea before standing, a giggle bursting from her lips. "We weren't expecting you." She slapped a hand over her mouth to stifle a hiccup.

"I can see that."

Walking around the table, he held out his hand, drawing his sister into a hug. Gripping her shoulders, he studied her face, smelling the faint scent of alcohol. His eyes lit in amusement.

"Are you going to tell me what's got you flushed and your eyes glassy?"

Stepping out of his grasp, she stifled a hiccup with her hand before sitting back down. "My eyes are not glassy."

May stood, moving close enough to study Sylvia's eyes. "She looks fine to me." Narrowing her eyes, she shrugged. "Well, perhaps a little, um..." She chortled, quickly sitting back down.

Crossing his arms, he glanced around the room. "Uh-huh." Leaning down, he picked up his sister's cup, taking a sip. Wincing, he set it down, quirking a brow. "Tea, honey, and...whiskey?"

Biting her lower lip, Sylvia slumped in her chair, refusing to meet his gaze. "A tiny bit. Right, Josie?"

His focus turned to Josie. "This is *your* doing?"

Glancing at the tray holding a teapot, honey, and bottles of whiskey, rum, and brandy, she grimaced. Lifting her chin, Josie nodded.

"Yes, it's my doing, Mr. Lucero. As Sylvia said, we added a tiny bit of alcohol to our cups. Very little, really. Miniscule, in fact." She bit her lip so as not to laugh, but the amused look in her eyes gave her away.

He cocked his head. "And how many cups have you had?"

Clearing her throat, Josie glanced around the table at the other ladies, noting their flushed faces and glazed eyes. Frowning, she looked up at him and grimaced. "A few?"

Deciding to get to the bottom of the mystery, he turned to the reverend's wife. "Mrs. Paige?"

Straightening her back, she clasped her hands together, attempting to sober her features. "Well now, that is a very good question, Marshal Lucero. An excellent question, in fact." Drawing in a breath, she touched a finger to her temple, frowning. "Perhaps five or six cups."

Eyes flashing in disbelief, he shifted his hard stare to Josie. "How much alcohol did you add to each cup?"

A wicked smile slid the corners of her mouth upward. Holding up an oversized serving spoon, her lips twitched. "Three of these per cup." When his eyes widened, she clarified. "The alcohol *was* mixed with strong tea, honey, and cinnamon."

"Oh, that does make it *so* much better." Placing fisted hands on his waist, he stared at the ceiling. "Good Lord." Taking several deep breaths, he returned his attention to the women. "Josie, would you mind standing?"

She shook her head, wincing. "I don't—"

"Stand up, Josie." His hard voice broke through the haze in her brain.

"Fine," she spit back, skewering him with a haughty glare. Bracing her hands on the arms of the chair, she stood. Instantly, her head spun, forcing her to grip the back of the chair so as not to topple over.

"Sit back down, Josie." He turned his gaze to Sylvia. "Stand up, please."

Swallowing, she did the same with identical results, except she also slapped a hand over her stomach. "Oh. I do believe I may be sick, Dom."

"Oh, dear." May slapped both hands over her mouth, her face turning an odd shade of gray-green.

Mumbling curses under his breath, Dom dashed to the kitchen. Grabbing two buckets from under the sink, he hurried back, hearing uncontrolled retching through the closed door.

"Ah hell."

Shoving open the door, his eyes widened at the sight before him. All but Abby and Ruth were hunched over the table, chests heaving, throats constricting in an attempt to contain the contents of their stomachs.

Dropping the buckets, he tore the quilt from the table, tossing it aside. Retrieving the buckets, he handed one to Ruth, the other to Abby. He didn't have to explain. Without a word, Ruth rushed to Olivia, Abby to May, while Dom gripped Sylvia's arm, then Josie's. He hadn't yet reached the kitchen before the front door opened.

"What in the world..." Suzanne's startled voice trailed off.

Ruth glanced up from her task of holding the bucket before Olivia. "I'm so sorry, Suzanne."

Waving off the apology, she rushed to take hold of Sylvia's elbow, sending Dom a sharp look. "I'll take care of her. You help Josie."

Jaw clenching, he nodded, continuing into the kitchen. Within seconds, the two had Sylvia and Josie bending over the large sink. A full minute passed before the young ladies raised their heads, their features grim, coloring pale.

Grabbing towels, Suzanne handed one to Dom. "Do what you can for Josie." She dampened hers with cool water, blotting Sylvia's face. Placing a reassuring hand on her back, Suzanne stroked lightly. "Are you feeling better?"

An unintelligible groan trailed from Sylvia's lips.

"It may be best for you to lie down for a bit. Come along, dear." Suzanne put a reassuring arm around Sylvia's shoulders, guiding her to a door leading to the hall. "There are two beds in the room, Dom. Perhaps Josie would feel better if she took a brief nap."

"No," Josie ground out, holding the cool cloth to her face. "I must see to Olivia."

"Ruth and Abby will make sure she's all right." Dom cast a quick look at the door to the dining room, wrapping an arm around her waist. "I'll check on her and May once you're settled in the guest room, Josie."

"But—"

"No arguing. After what you've done, I'd think you'd want to spend some quiet time contemplating how you're going to explain your actions to Caleb, Noah, Clay, Mack, and Reverend Paige."

Tugging out of his hold, Josie glared up at him. "I've done nothing."

Lifting a brow, he crossed his arms, getting a bit of satisfaction at the uncertain glint in her eyes.

49

"Plying innocent women with whiskey, rum, and God knows what else isn't inappropriate?"

"Well, I..." Tearing her gaze from his, her lips twisted. "I suppose it wasn't my best idea."

"Indeed. It may have been your worst." Gripping her elbow, he continued down the hall, depositing her in the room where Suzanne tucked Sylvia into one of the two beds. "I'm going to check on May and Olivia."

Suzanne nodded. "I'll be out in a moment."

Casting Josie a look of utter disappointment, he shut the door behind him, missing the way her shoulders slumped at his dismissal. Letting out a breath, she sat on the edge of the bed, burying her face in both hands.

"Am I to assume all this is your doing, Josie?"

Dropping her hands, her face fell at the displeasure in Suzanne's features. Olivia's stepmother had done everything to make Josie feel welcome. A member of their family. In return, she'd convinced Olivia and the others to try a slight amount of alcohol in their tea, not expecting the ladies to enjoy it enough to drink several cups apiece.

Groaning, Josie nodded. "I'm so sorry. I didn't mean for the ladies to get sick." Misery flooded her voice.

Suzanne studied Josie at the same time her thoughts turned to Nick. Her husband wouldn't be happy once he learned what happened, but she doubted he'd show real anger. No matter her belief in how Nick might react, she wouldn't allow Josie to shirk the responsibility for her friends' misery.

"Try to take a nap, Josie. You'll want to be rested when Nick arrives and learns what you've done."

# Chapter Five

"It truly wasn't Josie's fault, Father." Olivia's stomach still roiled, her head pounding from the effects of the fortified tea, but she refused to miss supper. Doing so would show cowardice regarding her part in today's quilting party debacle. "She didn't force any of the ladies to accept spirits in their tea."

Nick studied his daughter's face before switching his attention to Josie, gratified at the mortification in the young women's features. They'd been at the table for close to a quarter of an hour, and as yet, Josie hadn't met his gaze. Neither had she met Suzanne's. Instead, she'd sent furtive, apologetic glances to Olivia.

Cutting a piece of meat, he slipped it into his mouth, chewing slowly. When finished, he washed it down with a large swallow of wine.

"Do you partake of spirited tea often?"

Josie's gaze shot up to meet his, giving a slight shake of her head. "No."

"Have you ever consumed it before today?"

Letting out an exaggerated sigh, she pursed her lips. "No. I've only helped our cook prepare it for my parents. She never allowed me to taste it or make my own. Today seemed the perfect opportunity."

Suzanne quirked a brow. "There are times you'll need to ignore the perfect opportunity."

Touching her heated face with a cool hand, she nodded. "I'm certain you are right. I just wished I'd thought of it today."

Nick stifled a grin. "Should I expect this will never happen again?"

Straightening her spine, Josie shook her head vigorously. "Never again."

Taking another sip of wine, Nick's features softened.

"Shall we discuss something else?" Suzanne asked.

"Oh, yes." Olivia flushed at her enthusiastic response. "I mean, anything except the quilting party."

Nick threw back his head and laughed. "If you ladies agree, we won't speak of your activities this afternoon again."

"The subject is quite closed." Suzanne shot a look at the young women and grinned. "What I *do* want to discuss is a shopping trip to Big Pine."

Josie's face brightened. "When?"

"We'd leave Monday and return Wednesday."

"That would be wonderful. Wouldn't it, Olivia?"

Excitement fused her face. "Oh, yes." She looked at Suzanne. "Is there something in particular you're seeking in Big Pine?"

Features stilling, she clasped her hands together on the edge of the table. Not meeting Nick's gaze, she shook her head. "A few trivial items. Lena is the one who suggested the trip. I believe she may have a few purchases in mind."

Nick's brows rose, but he said nothing. His expression, however, told Suzanne her husband didn't quite trust the reason for the sudden trip. Excursions to Big Pine were usually planned a couple weeks out, not a few days.

"Who's going with you?"

Suzanne's lips thinned. She'd been afraid he'd ask, and hadn't come up with a good answer as of yet. Women didn't ride alone to the territorial capital, not even when there were several of them.

Raising a brow, she did her best to appear calm. "Do you truly believe anyone would attack four women?"

His face hardened, incredulity in his voice. "You don't?"

Feeling her face heat, she nodded. "You're right, of course. I'll speak with Gabe. Perhaps he knows of someone going to Big Pine."

"I'll go."

"No!" Suzanne glanced at Olivia, then Josie, seeing surprise on their faces. "What I mean is, you're needed here. Especially with both Lena and I going." Biting her lower lip, she forced herself to take a slow, calming breath. She could not have Nick riding along. It would ruin everything she and Lena had planned.

"All right, but you will not be going alone. If needed, I'll pay someone to accompany you."

Standing, Suzanne stepped next to him, leaning down to place a kiss on his cheek. "Thank you, Nick. I promise it will all work out."

Nick stormed into the house the following day, stopping to calm his agitation. Olivia and Josie sat in the parlor, each focusing on the petit point in their hands.

"Olivia?"

She glanced up, setting the fabric on a table before walking to him. "Good afternoon, Father. I didn't expect you back so soon." Olivia hugged him, stepping away.

"I need to speak with you a minute."

"I'll leave you two alone." Standing, Josie began to walk past them, stopping at Nick's words.

"It seems I need to speak with you, too."

Shooting a quick glance at Olivia, she nodded. "All right."

"Please, sit back down." Nick waited until they'd settled into chairs, taking a seat across from them. Leaning back, he stretched out his long legs, clasping his hands in his lap. His gaze locked on Olivia. "Clay came to see me this morning." Nick didn't miss the slight catch in her breathing. "He asked my permission to court you."

One hand moved to her stomach, another to her chest. "What did you say?" She glanced at Josie, finding it hard to contain her excitement.

"Clay is a fine man, Olivia. Smart, loyal, and an excellent doctor." Straightening, he leaned forward, resting his arms on his thighs.

She felt her throat constricting, fear building at what her father may have said to him. "Yes, he is."

"He'll never be able to support you in the manner you've become accustomed."

Heart pounding, she stood, pacing toward him, clasping her hands so tight her knuckles turned white. "I don't care about that, Father. Not how much money he has, or if I have to live behind the clinic. If he ever proposes marriage," she bit her lip, glancing at Josie, then back at Nick, "I'll say yes."

The sound of Nick chuckling had her glaring at him.

"What is so funny?"

Shaking his head, he stood, taking the few steps to her. "Clay said the same."

Her brows knit together. "He did?"

Grinning, Nick took her hands in his. "He didn't believe his lack of wealth would bother you."

Body relaxing, she let out a ragged breath. "Clay is right. I don't understand why you don't like him."

Cocking his head, Nick's brows drew together. "I like Clay just fine. What I don't like is the way he seemed to sneak behind my back to be with you. I kept waiting for him to come forward with his intentions. I'd begun to think he never would."

"So, what did you say to him, Father?"

Shrugging, he dropped her hands, stepping away. "That I'd be speaking with you before giving him my consent."

"And now?" Olivia felt her chest squeeze when he didn't answer immediately.

Walking to a cabinet, he pulled out a bottle of whiskey, pouring a small measure into a glass. Letting the smooth, amber liquid slip down his throat, he turned back to his daughter.

"I'll let Clay know he has my approval to court you."

She clasped her hands to her chest, features full of joy. "Oh, Father—"

"I'm approving of a courtship, Olivia, not a wedding. You do understand, don't you?"

She hurried to him, throwing her arms around his neck. "Yes, I understand." Kissing his cheek, she stepped away. "Thank you."

His gaze wandered over her face, throat tightening at the joy he saw. "I only want what's best for you. It's all I've ever wanted, Olivia."

Turning, he looked at Josie. "Your turn."

Eyes wide, she sat forward on the sofa, uncharacteristically silent. By the time Nick returned to his chair, Josie thought she'd burst with curiosity.

"Dom Lucero has asked permission to escort you to supper Saturday. Although I'm not family, you are under my care and protection. I felt the need to speak with you, make certain it's what you want, Josie."

Catching her lower lip between her teeth, she stared at the floor. "After what happened, Dom still wants to be seen with me?"

Stroking his stubbled jaw, Nick grinned. "I believe he's willing to forget about it if you never exhibit such foolishness again."

Embarrassed, she offered a small smile. "No more tea spiked with spirits."

"I'm assuming you'd agree to supper with Dom?"

Her face lit with pleasure. "Yes, I would."

"Excellent." Standing, he walked to the door. "I must return to the Dixie." His eyes twinkled. "And speak with Clay and Dom."

Walking out, he stifled a self-satisfied grin, whistling as he rode the short distance to town.

*Houston, Texas*

Chandler Evans lay on the hard cot, hands threaded behind his head, staring at the water-stained ceiling of the Houston jail. He'd brought in a prisoner a couple hours before, surprised when the sheriff threw him in jail along with the outlaw. The slow-moving, slow-thinking man hadn't believed him to be a Texas Ranger, not even when Chan produced his badge. Now he waited for the lawman to obtain confirmation from Austin. At least he'd gotten a free meal and a couple hours of sleep out of it.

He rarely allowed himself time for reflection, preferring to focus on the future. The youngest of four sons, he'd garnered little attention in his youth, his parents expecting him to fall in line behind Weldon and Lawrence, the second and third oldest.

Instead, the brother he looked up to, wanted to emulate, was the oldest, Gabriel, and according to their parents, the embodiment of the black sheep. Never mind he'd been promoted to captain in the Union Army, fought valiantly against the Confederates, receiving numerous accolades.

Most confounding to Chan was that his parents ignored the fact Gabe had been the sole heir to their wealthy uncle's estate. An estate made up of pricey and successful hotels and restaurants in New York, businesses requiring a sharp mind and excellent management skills.

That he controlled those properties while holding the position of sheriff in Splendor, a frontier town in the Montana Territory, meant nothing to their parents. To them, as the oldest, he'd been groomed to enter New York society, marry for the financial benefit of both families, and accept his position within the city's elite.

From what Chan had learned through the gossip channel within the Ranger community, his brother had married for love. Miss Magdelena Campanel grew up in the back alleys of New Orleans, becoming a successful businesswoman in partnership with her childhood friend, Nicholas Barnett. All three now lived in Splendor, a town Chan meant to see in the near future.

"Guess you *are* a Ranger." The sheriff unlocked the cell, not a bit of remorse on his face as he held it open for Chan. "I suppose you'll want to take the prisoner with you to Austin." His voice held not a small amount of hope.

Walking to the front of the jail, Chan grabbed his gunbelt and coat from a hook. Turning to face the sorry excuse for a sheriff, he couldn't hide a smirk. "My orders were to apprehend and deliver the man to the jail in Houston. This is Houston, and I believe this is the only jail. Therefore, my obligation to you and the miscreant in the cell is over."

Red infused the sheriff's features. "You can't unload him on me."

"I can, and I have. My captain gave the order. If you don't like it, I'd suggest you let him know." Settling his hat lower on his forehead, Chan flashed a grin at the agitated sheriff. "I'll be on my way."

"Wait!"

Heading outside, he didn't stop at the man's shouted plea.

"Now see here, Evans." The sheriff rushed to catch up with him. "I don't have enough deputies to guard a prisoner until the judge arrives."

Looking up and down the street, Chan settled his sights on a bawdy saloon a few buildings away. "Tell that to your town leaders," he tossed over his shoulder, continuing down the boardwalk.

Shoving open the swinging doors, he headed straight for the bar, signaling for a whiskey. Moving into an open space, he lifted the glass, turning to rest his back against the bar.

Mid-afternoon and the saloon already held a good number of customers. Some played cards, others faro, a few stood around a roulette table, and several held scantily clad women in their laps. Overall, the mood was genial, patrons enjoying the games and other entertainment.

Experience told Chan the atmosphere would change a couple hours after sundown. Too much whiskey, lengthy losing streaks, and fights over the women would transition the saloon from convivial to dangerous. By then, he'd be enjoying a hot bath, big meal, and comfortable bed.

All three being requisites before the long trip he had in mind. His captain didn't know it yet, but Chandler Evans's tenure as a Texas Ranger was about to end.

# Chapter Six

*Splendor*

"Your table is ready, Mr. Lucero." Thomas led Dom and Josie to a table near the front window of the Eagle's Nest, the best restaurant in town.

As they approached, Josie's mouth slid into a grin. Clay and Olivia occupied two of the four chairs, and by the appearance of the table, they'd arrived not long before her and Dom.

"How wonderful." Josie looked up at Dom, not seeing the same degree of enthusiasm. "Don't you think so?"

"Wonderful." His whispered, lackluster response went unheard.

He shot a resigned look at Clay, noting the same disappointment on the doctor's face as he felt. Each had hoped to have a quiet evening with his lady, a rare evening alone to learn more about each other. It seemed Nick had a different experience in mind.

Standing, Clay kissed Josie's cheek before accepting Dom's outstretched hand. "Appears we will be sharing a table tonight. I hope you don't mind."

Pulling out a chair for Josie, he shook his head. "Not at all." An amused expression crossed Dom's face as he took a seat next to Olivia. "How are you feeling this evening?"

Remembering the quilting party, she knew he meant more than his words implied. Flushing, Olivia offered a strained smile. "I'm doing quite well, thank you."

Thomas handed a handwritten menu to each. "Would you care for wine this evening?"

"Yes, Thomas," Dom answered for the others.

After placing their orders, they sipped wine, relaxing into the evening. Instead of the intimate conversation Dom had envisioned, the four spoke of ordinary matters, subjects women discussed after church. Or, he grimaced, during a quilting party.

"Suzanne, Lena, Olivia, and I will be traveling to Big Pine on Monday." Josie threw the sentence out as if a trip such as this one happened every day.

Olivia warmed to the subject. "Suzanne mentioned Lena needed some items not available here. We won't be returning until Wednesday." She took a sip of wine, smiling. "I'm so looking forward to the trip."

Dom hadn't moved beyond the knowledge of four women traveling alone. "Who will be riding with you?"

Josie and Olivia exchanged glances, although neither answered.

He raised a brow. "Josie?"

Clearing her throat, she hesitated, not wanting to enter into the same discussion Suzanne had with Nick. "Well...we aren't sure."

"Not sure?" Dom pressed.

Setting down her glass, Olivia looked between the men. "Father plans to ask the sheriff if he can spare any of the deputies. If not, I'm certain he'll find someone."

Dom leaned back in his chair, crossing his arms. "I'll escort you."

Josie shook her head. "Oh, we couldn't ask you to take time when you are always traveling."

Picking up his wine glass, he shrugged. "I'm expected there on Tuesday anyway. Going a day earlier is no hardship."

"That would be so much better than Father coming, which he will if he can't find someone he trusts."

Clay's brows lifted. "You don't want Nick riding with you, Olivia?"

"It's not exactly that. He's wonderful and I love him dearly." She let out a breath, pursing her lips. "Father can be so, well...protective."

Clay chuckled, settling his hand on top of hers. "It's his job to protect you, Livia."

Staring down at their joined hands, she gave him a slow nod. "True. But does he have to be so good at it?"

Both Clay and Dom threw their heads back and laughed while Josie's eyes sparkled at the humor in Olivia's question.

Eyes wide, she glared at the three. "It's true."

Leaning closer, Clay cast her a considerate look. "I've no doubt he takes his responsibility to you seriously. After all, he didn't know of your existence until the last couple years. You must try to understand how he feels, Livia."

She played with the edges of the cloth napkin in her lap. "I know you're right, Clay."

"I wish my father were more like yours, Livvy." Josie toyed with the stem of her wine glass. "You have no idea what controlling is until you've lived under his iron resolve."

They quieted when a server arrived with their meals, pouring more wine before retreating. The silence remained, with only an occasional comment or observation as they ate. After the server cleared their plates, returning with dessert and coffee, the conversation resumed.

"What is the actual purpose of the trip, Josie?" Dom placed a spoonful of berry cobbler into his mouth, moving his leg to brush against hers. He smothered a smirk at her quick intake of breath, the way her lips parted, eyes darting to him. "There must be something quite important in Big Pine for the four of you to ride all that way instead of sending a telegram to order the items for delivery to Splendor."

At the feel of Dom's leg touching hers a second time, Josie forced down a bite of cobbler, doing her best to control the flares of heat spreading through her. She'd never felt anything so wonderful, yet concerning. How could a mere touch summon such a quick and strange reaction?

"Suzanne didn't share anything more with Josie and me. It's a little mysterious, which is why it's so exciting." Olivia smiled over the rim of her cup. "Don't you agree, Josie?"

"Oh, yes." She sent a glance at Dom, feeling an unexpected surge of disappointment when he shifted his leg away. Schooling her features, Josie looked back at Olivia. "By this time next week, the mystery behind our trip will be answered."

Scrubbing a hand down his face, Dom did his best to keep his gaze on the trail ahead and behind them rather than on the four women in the wagon. Suzanne and Lena sat on the front bench, while Olivia and Josie occupied the bench behind them, their conversation constant since leaving Splendor. Until today, he'd never appreciated how women could chat for hours. Through it all, he hadn't learned anything about the reason for the trip.

Nick hadn't offered any objection when Dom volunteered to accompany them to Big Pine. They spoke a few minutes before leaving town that morning about the possibility Dom may not be able to return with the women until Thursday.

The trials he'd been summoned to attend were scheduled for Tuesday, but delays sometimes happened. Or, as was the case the last time, the trial never took place. Instead, the town buried three men in the common cemetery with only a minister, Parker Sterling, and Dom in attendance.

About an hour outside of Big Pine, there'd been no sign of trouble. *We aren't there yet*, Dom reminded himself as they continued to plod along.

As they traversed the remaining miles, the women's voices grew louder, enough so he could now make out what they said. Reining closer to the wagon, he continued to scan the trail ahead while staying attuned to their ongoing conversation.

After a few minutes, he grew tired of hearing about the latest births and current fashions. Meaning to rein away, he stiffened in the saddle when Lena asked the question he'd been unable to voice.

"When will you be leaving for New Orleans, Josie?"

He studied her reaction, seeing her smile fade and shoulders slump, if only a small amount.

"My parents are due back in late March or early April. I assume Teezy sent word to them in Europe about my disappearance. If Father hasn't launched a search yet, he will upon their arrival home." Josie drew in a breath, staring into her lap. "I've no idea how long it will take for them to find me."

Lena turned on the front bench to look behind her at Josie. "Did you tell anyone about your destination?"

She shook her head. "No. But my brother, Rafe, has no doubt already gone through my belongings and found Olivia's letters. He knows of our friendship, so I assume it wouldn't take him long to conclude I'm in Splendor."

Dom reined closer, determined to hear what else was said while attempting to look disinterested.

"You *are* twenty-one, Josie. Of age to make your own decisions," Suzanne called over her shoulder, slapping the lines gently on the horses' backs.

Olivia patted her knee. "And you do have money from your great-grandfather's estate."

"I know you don't want to disappoint your parents, but don't you think it's time to follow your own dreams?" Lena asked, her face etched with compassion.

Dom's chest squeezed as he waited for her answer. He hadn't known Josie long, shared a couple dinners with her and Olivia, walked with them along the boardwalk, sat with her twice at

Sunday supper at Nick's, and taken her to supper Saturday evening. In that short amount of time, he'd become attached to the beautiful young woman. As foolish as it seemed, he'd begun thinking of a shared future.

"The only dream I had was to join Olivia. I never gave much thought to what I'd do beyond coming here."

"Are you situated so you don't have to work?" Lena asked.

"If I'm careful, yes. I do admire Nora and the work she does for Allie. My understanding is she also doesn't have to work but chooses to." She glanced at Olivia. "Perhaps you and I should open a shop."

Sitting on the bench behind Suzanne, she couldn't see the pleased expression on her stepmother's face.

"I know nothing about running a shop, Josie."

"You're smart, Livia. You'll be able to learn what to do in little time," Lena said. "Besides, you have Suzanne and me to help you. And your father is a brilliant businessman, as is Gabe."

Josie's face brightened. "You see, Livvy? We'll have all the help we need to get started."

A slow smile appeared as Olivia warmed to the concept of owning their own store. Then her brows drew together. "What type of shop should we open?"

Josie tapped her lips with a finger, her features growing serious. Dom's stomach twisted at the action, his body going taut. Mumbling a curse, he reined away, riding forward to clear his mind.

"I wonder what Dom saw," Lena said.

Leaning forward, Josie followed his path, sitting back on the bench when he turned to ride back toward them. He reined around, once again taking his spot next to the wagon.

"Did you see something, Dom?" Lena asked.

"No, ma'am. I wanted to gauge our location. Big Pine isn't far beyond the rise. We should reach it within half an hour."

Olivia nearly bounced on the bench seat. "We're almost there, Josie." Settling, she clasped her hands in her lap. "So, what business should we pursue?"

Smiling, she shot a quick look at Dom, wondering if he'd been following their conversation. "I think we should visit as many shops as possible in Big Pine, discuss our thoughts with Suzanne and Lena, then make a decision."

Suzanne glanced at Lena, her amused expression matching her friend's.

"We would love to talk about what is needed in Splendor. Supper tomorrow night would be the perfect time, after we've visited the shops." Suzanne's gaze moved to Lena, who nodded. "By the time we return home, the two of you will have the information you need to speak with Nick and Gabe."

Dom continued to listen as the women chatted about the shopping they planned and where to stay. Suzanne had spent little time in Big Pine, staying in the cheapest lodging available. Lena, with a more robust budget, always stayed at the Imperial Hotel.

Reaching the top of a low hill, Suzanne pulled the lines, stopping the wagon to enjoy the view. The territorial capital sprawled before them. Each of the women had traveled through the town, but this was the first time Olivia and Josie had seen it from this vantage point.

"It's really quite large." Josie rose enough for a better view. "There must be twice the number of people as in Splendor."

"A little more than twice." Dom adjusted the reins in his hand. "We should get moving, ladies."

Sitting down, Josie cast a quick look at him, enjoying the way he sat in the saddle. She'd been watching him ride all day, impressed at the way he and the horse moved as one. Both exhibited strength and a fluid grace not often seen in New Orleans. They were magnificent.

Josie hoped Dom would someday invite her to ride with him. She couldn't imagine a better way to spend a day.

# Chapter Seven

*Austin, Texas*

"I'm sorry to lose you, Evans. I'll save your badge for you, just in case you ever want to come back."

Chandler set his badge on the desk, feeling a touch of regret. Being a Texas Ranger carried a certain amount of prestige. He'd been offered free meals, the occasional beer or whiskey, and countless invitations from various women, mostly of the saloon variety.

It also meant dealing with all manner of criminals, putting his life on the line every day. Not much different from what he'd experience without a badge.

"Thank you, Captain. If things don't work out in Splendor, I may be back."

The man's brows arched. "Splendor, Montana Territory?"

A crease formed between Chandler's eyes. "Yes, sir. You know it?"

"Know of it. Pat Hanes, another Ranger, had a ranch there. When he died, he left it to two other Rangers, Dax and Luke Pelletier. I recently heard Caleb Covington was a deputy there. Another man I was sorry to lose." Standing, the man picked up the badge. "Suppose I'll have to get up there someday, figure out the attraction for myself."

Chuckling, Chandler grasped the outstretched hand. "It's been a pleasure, Captain."

"Same for me, Evans. Good luck."

Another brief rush of remorse hit him as he stepped outside, adjusting his hat on his head. Stepping off the boardwalk, he looked up and down the dusty street. At just over four thousand people, Austin had been the state capital for several decades, drawing dignitaries and men of wealth.

He'd miss it, but the time had come to continue his journey. Chandler would take the railroad to Salt Lake, then ride north, stopping when needed to avoid the winter snows. If all went as planned, he'd be sitting across the desk from his brother in less than four weeks.

*Big Pine*

"It's odd." Josie stopped outside the mercantile, the largest store in Big Pine.

"What's odd?" Olivia asked, her brows drawing together.

She glanced up the street, watching Dom enter the courthouse. All stayed at the Imperial Hotel, meeting for breakfast before he left for the first trial and the women started their shopping.

"Josie?"

Shifting, she stared at Olivia, forgetting what they'd been talking about.

"You said something about it being odd," Olivia prompted.

"Oh, yes. I was thinking how we grew up in a very large city. In comparison, Splendor seemed so tiny when I first arrived. Now, coming to Big Pine..." She glanced around again.

"It seems so large," Olivia laughed.

Grinning, Josie nodded. "Odd, isn't it?"

"Not so much. You've been in Splendor almost three months, become used to its size. Big Pine is more than twice as large, which is still miniscule compared to New Orleans."

"Are you two going to stand outside all morning or join Suzanne and me?" Lena held the door to the mercantile open, gesturing them inside.

Josie stopped next to the first table of goods, her gaze roaming over the cans of tomatoes, condensed milk, vegetables, and seafood. She'd seen similar fare back home, although where her mother shopped, the cans were organized, sections labeled.

"Suzanne and I have been looking at the clothing." Lena indicated for them to follow. When they reached the spot where Suzanne held a small top in the air, Josie's and Olivia's eyes widened.

Olivia moved next to her. "That's a gown for a, well…"

Suzanne smiled at her. "A baby. Yes, I know."

She stepped closer. "Are you thinking of buying it as a present?"

Setting it down, Suzanne picked up another, holding it out toward Lena. "How about this one?"

Lena lowered the baby gown she'd been holding, taking the cream colored one from Suzanne's outstretched hand. "This one is lovely. Will you buy it?"

Olivia shot a confused glance at Josie before whipping around to face Suzanne. "Buy it? Who's having a baby?"

"We are," the older women said in unison, then laughed.

"Lena and I are expecting. Isn't that wonderful?" Suzanne's expression could light up the darkest night.

Squealing, Olivia and Josie hugged each of the women, looking them up and down.

"It's fabulous news. But I didn't think either of you could have more children." Olivia swiped a tear from her cheek.

"Apparently, we were wrong." Suzanne pulled a handkerchief from her reticule, handing it to Olivia. "Doc McCord confirmed it, as did Doc Worthington. Both came back with the same answer. In fact, they believe Lena and I will have our babies within days of each other."

"Father must be ecstatic."

Suzanne flashed a wary look at Lena. "Actually, I haven't told Nick yet, and Lena hasn't told Gabe."

Lena set down the gown, picking up another. "We thought it would be best to buy a few things we need before telling them. Once they learn of our conditions, it's quite possible they won't allow us to leave Splendor."

Josie held up another gown, the corners of her mouth tipping into a broad grin. "They may not allow you to leave your houses. Now, tell us what you need and we'll help. This is such wonderful news."

Several minutes passed as the four sorted through the baby clothes, setting a few items aside. It didn't take long for Lena and Suzanne to find what they wanted.

"Allie is making each of us a few gowns and bonnets, but she's so busy making more dresses for Ruby's girls that we thought it best to purchase a couple items here." Lena held up another gown, then set it on the purchase pile. "Plus, it's hard for her to make what we need with Cash being one of Gabe's deputies. It will be easier once we tell them."

Josie leaned against the edge of a table while the others continued looking. "Nick and Gabe are going to be so surprised."

Lena's features stilled. "I hope so. Neither of us expected this. Jack is nine and used to being the center of our world." She let out a nervous breath.

"Lena, Gabe is going to be thrilled. And Jack will be a fabulous big brother." Josie turned toward Suzanne. "The same with Nick. He'd do anything for you."

"I am a little older." Suzanne felt the same knot of fear in her stomach she did when learning of the pregnancy. "It's been so long since I had my daughter..." Her voice trailed off, a melancholy look on her face.

She'd lost her husband and daughter in a freak winter storm years before, never quite recovering. Nick had been the one to give her hope, help her see she could love and be happy again.

Olivia wrapped an arm around Suzanne's waist. "Father is going to love this child as much as he loves you."

"And you," Suzanne added.

Josie watched the scene before her, feeling a pang of longing so unexpected, she had to step away. "I'm going to see if they have anything else for babies."

Moving around the store, she ended up close to the front, holding two small rag dolls and two wooden soldiers. Hearing the front door open, the bell above it ring, she turned, clutching the toys to her chest.

"Dom. We, uh...didn't expect to see you so soon."

An odd expression on his face, he walked to within inches of her, staring at the items in her hands. He looked up, cocking a brow. "Dolls and toy soldiers?"

Feeling her face heat, she shifted the items. "I thought they were cute, and, well..." Her voice faded when the other three joined them.

Dom's eyes focused on what the three held. "Baby clothes?"

Lena let out a ragged breath. "Oh, dear." She looked at Suzanne, who nodded. "We learned last week that we're both pregnant."

"Holy..." He scrubbed a hand down his face. "Do Gabe and Nick know?"

Suzanne shook her head. "No. And you won't tell them. We want it to be a surprise."

Dom chuckled. "I think it's a fair guess they're both going to be stunned."

"What do you think, Dom? Shall we open a variety shop selling merchandise Mr. Petermann does not carry in his general store, or an emporium offering men's and women's clothing? And accessories, of course." Keeping her arm linked with his, she smiled up at him.

They'd shared supper with Lena, Suzanne, and Olivia, talking of babies and the shops they'd visited. Neither topic interested Dom in the least.

After dessert, he'd invited her to take a stroll through Big Pine. At first, she'd hesitated, having never been allowed to be alone with a man in such a private way. When neither Suzanne nor Lena objected, she agreed, a thrill rolling through her at another first since arriving in Splendor. The excitement at being with Dom hadn't subsided since leaving the restaurant.

The bright smile and enthusiasm in her voice were as tangible as a fist to his gut. Glancing away, he severed the spell before becoming so captivated he'd be unable to speak.

"I'm not the best person to provide advice, Josie. Ask me about cattle, ranching, or tracking down outlaws, and I'll offer sound guidance. I know nothing of emporiums or shops." Glancing at her, he stifled a grin at the way her lower lip jutted out in a pout. When she licked her lips, it wasn't amusement he had to suppress.

"If we open an emporium, we could include Allie's designs, which are far superior to what we saw here. However, I would also like to bring fine perfumes, tobaccos, jewelry, and other accoutrements to Splendor. The townsfolk would no longer need to travel here to find such items."

As she spoke, Josie tightened her hold on Dom's arm, bringing her body closer to his. He could handle the occasional brush of an arm or leg, but this was turning into something more, and he doubted she'd want to discover what.

"Perhaps we could open in the new store Nick and Gabe want to build next to Allie's shop. Or the empty space between the newspaper office and the St. James. That location would be so convenient, don't you think?" Again, she glanced up at him, a question in her eyes.

Clearing his throat, Dom nodded. Knowing it unseemly, he guided her between two buildings, hearing her slight gasp when he turned her toward him. Cupping her face with his hands, he stared into her eyes, words escaping him.

"What..." Her voice trailed off when he brushed the pad of his thumb over her lower lip.

"I want to kiss you, Josie." Giving his head a quick shake, he revised his comment. "That is, I'm *going* to kiss you. Unless you object."

Eyes wide, she gave a slight nod, causing him to smile.

"Is that a no, or a yes? I don't want there to be any misunderstanding."

Staring at his mouth, she licked her lips. "Yes. Please."

Lowering his head, he hesitated an instant before brushing a kiss over her lush mouth, feeling an immediate rush of heat. The second brush confirmed his first reaction to having her in his arms. Miss Josephine Dubois was going to be trouble of the most perplexing and best kind.

The return trip to Splendor was more subdued. Suzanne and Lena spoke quietly about their plans to tell Nick and Gabe their news while Olivia and Josie discussed which idea to pursue. After studying the shops in Big Pine, they'd become even more determined to pursue a business opportunity of their own.

If they still lived in New Orleans, such a desire would've been quashed without discussion. In the frontier, women working in trade were common, sometimes required to put food on the table.

Choices for single women were limited anywhere in the country, but especially for those living in the western territory. Taking in laundry, mending clothes, cleaning rooms in boardinghouses or hotels, and teaching were the appropriate options. Offering their wares in saloons or brothels being the least acceptable.

Unfortunately, opportunities for the first were limited, thrusting many women into the second.

Owning a business of any kind wouldn't have been allowed under their strict upbringing in the upscale neighborhoods of New Orleans. In Splendor, they could explore their freedom in a way unavailable back east. The future seemed brighter, more interesting, and much more exciting.

After a while, the four fell silent, traversing the last miles in comfortable friendship while Dom rode alongside. Unlike some trips between the two towns, this one passed without the appearance of outlaws, highwaymen, or renegade Crow or Blackfoot.

The only real distraction came from Josie. Every few minutes, Dom caught her casting cautious glances his way. Glances he returned with a knowing grin. Her reaction to his touch the night before caught him unaware, along with the realization she hid a passionate nature he wanted to explore, yet couldn't.

Not only would he incur Nick's wrath, but also that of Gabe and several other men he respected. Men who saw themselves as Josie's protectors while she stayed in Splendor. If Dom wanted her, which he did, it would have to be achieved with serious intent.

Between his jobs as a U.S. Marshal and rancher, he had little time for a courtship. With her dreams of a shop, he wondered how receptive Josie would be to his interest. After last night, he concluded no matter her future plans, she might be quite amenable.

# Chapter Eight

Sharing a table at the Dixie, Nick and Gabe hunched over plans for their latest project while sipping beers. Today, their attention wasn't captured by the drawings Bull had prepared for another block of houses and shops. Instead, they puzzled over the actions of their wives, wondering at their odd manner since returning from their trip to Big Pine.

Over a week had passed since Suzanne and Lena arrived back in Splendor with a few items, none of which they'd shared with their husbands. Both had been unusually quiet, going about their work, preparing meals, and managing their homes.

Tonight, the four would be having supper at the Eagle's Nest, not an unusual occurrence, as the four were partners in the hotel and restaurant.

"Something isn't right." Gabe rubbed fingers over his brow as he studied the drawings.

Nick followed his friend's gaze. "What isn't right?"

"Lena." He took another long draw of beer, adjusting his tall frame in the hard, wood chair. "She's too quiet and spends more time at home than normal." Staring outside, Gabe's jaw tightened. "I'm afraid she may be ill and isn't telling me."

Surprised, Nick's features sobered. "Have you asked her?"

"Yes. Lena insists she's fine. More tired than normal, but not sick." Sucking in a deep breath, he exhaled, worry in his eyes. "She's lying, Nick. Lena never lies to me."

Rubbing his jaw, he thought of his years of friendship with Gabe's wife. They'd met as the offspring of New Orleans' whores, never knowing their fathers. Over time, he'd become her protector, then her business partner. She was family, a woman he loved as much as a cherished sister. Over all their years together, he'd never known Lena to lie.

"There are times she may not share all she knows, but I've never known her to lie. If Lena says she isn't ill, I'd accept it as true. If you'd like, I'll speak with her."

Shaking his head, Gabe picked up the drawings. "Thanks, Nick, but this is something Lena and I have to resolve. I need to get to the jail, then I'm going home."

Nick didn't stand at Gabe's departure, choosing to signal the bartender for another beer. He hadn't shared his same concerns about Suzanne. Similar to Lena, his wife had also been more tired than normal, returning home in the middle of the day instead of staying at the boardinghouse until supper. In all the time he'd known her, Nick couldn't remember a time she took a nap in the middle of the day or retired to bed before ten at night.

The same as Gabe, Nick had asked if she was sick. Suzanne denied it, leaving him wondering over the changes he'd noticed since her return from Big Pine.

Finishing his beer, he decided to follow Gabe's lead. Setting his empty glass on the bar, he spoke with the bartender before walking straight to the boardinghouse.

Reading the telegram from the sheriff of Moosejaw, a town east of Big Pine, Dom blew out a curse. Tossing the message on Gabe's desk, he walked to the stove to pour a cup of thick, black coffee. He ignored the urge to gag at the bitter taste. Walking to the back door, he tossed the remains outside before turning to see Cash Coulter, Dutch McFarlin, and Beau Davis walk inside.

Cash tossed his hat on a chair, heading toward the stove and coffee pot.

"Don't bother," Dom warned him before setting his cup on a shelf. "It's beyond horrible."

"Guess I'd better make more." Cash threw out what was left, looking up at Dom. "Have you seen Gabe?"

Crossing his arms, Dom leaned against the edge of the desk. "Came in a little bit ago. Said he was heading home and would be back later."

Dutch shot Cash a look, but didn't respond.

"What's this?" Cash picked up the telegram, holding it up.

"I'm needed in Moosejaw. Some reprobate shot a merchant during a robbery. The judge gave him ten years in the prison at Deer Lodge."

Beau picked up Cash's hat, setting it on a hook before sitting down. "So you're transporting him there? Could be rough. According to Enoch, weather's coming in and it's going to be bad. Worse than last year."

"Enoch, the town drunk?" Cash asked, setting the pot back on the stove.

Stretching his legs out in front of him, Beau nodded. "One and the same. He's a pretty interesting guy. If you can talk to him when he's sober."

"Which is almost never." Cash lowered himself onto a chair next to Beau. "When are you leaving, Dom?"

"In the morning. If Enoch's right, I want to get the prisoner to Deer Lodge and return to Splendor before the weather hits."

Reading the telegram, Dutch snorted. "You'll be lucky to get there and back in a week. It's a long way to Moosejaw."

"Then over the pass to Deer Lodge." Cash lifted his booted feet onto the desk, crossing them at the ankles.

Beau nodded. "Then through Blackfoot country to get back home. Glad it's you and not me." They turned at the sound of the door opening.

"Gabe here?" Caleb strolled inside, looking between the men.

Dom shook his head. "Headed home. Said he'll be back."

"Did he say when?" Caleb grabbed another chair, turning it around to straddle it.

"No. He seemed distracted. Came inside, saw me, and told me he'd be back after heading home. Nothing more. I swear, most of the time Gabe treats me as one of his deputies."

Chuckling, Cash flashed him a grin. "Might as well be. You drink most of the coffee and spend more time in here than any of the rest of us."

A moment later, the door flew open. Gabe looked around, stepping inside, his features drawn in shock.

"You all right, Gabe?"

He stared at Cash as if he didn't recognize him.

The men glanced at each other, raising brows and shrugging. Standing, Cash moved toward him, stopping a foot away.

"You look like you saw a ghost. Maybe you should sit down and tell us what happened."

Scrubbing both hands down his face, Gabe shook his head. "Lena..." He swallowed. Clearing his throat, he glanced around the room, seeing blank faces staring back at him. "Lena's..."

When he didn't finish, Cash clasped his shoulder, his voice raspy with concern. "Lena what?"

Rubbing the back of his neck, Gabe let out a strained chuckle. "Lena's pregnant."

Nick took slow strides toward the jail, his mind whirling. Suzanne's news shocked him beyond anything he'd ever experienced.

When he'd entered their house an hour ago, she, Olivia, and Josie were in the kitchen. Suzanne had both hands on her stomach, groaning, while the others took turns placing cool cloths on her face. The instant the young women had seen him, they'd patted Suzanne's shoulder, then left.

Fear clawing at him, he'd sat down, taking her hands in his. A few moments later, Nick fought lightheadedness. With a few simple words, his entire world, and future, changed. After carrying her upstairs, he stayed, rubbing her back until she fell asleep. Several minutes passed before he headed out, needing fresh air to clear his thoughts.

Without a specific destination in mind, Nick found himself standing outside the jail, hearing laughter coming from inside. Curious, needing to speak with his friend and business partner, he shoved open the door.

"Nick. Have you heard the news?" Caleb asked.

He looked at Gabe, seeing the same stunned look on his face that he felt. "What news?"

Looking up, Gabe gave him a lopsided grin. "Lena is pregnant."

Staring at him, Nick took the chair Beau offered, lowering himself onto it before glancing at the others. Before he could stop himself, a roar of laughter burst from his lips, surprising them all. Several moments passed, Nick's eyes watering as he continued to laugh. After a while, he dragged a hand down his face.

"I guess we both have a reason for celebration."

Gabe leaned forward, resting his arms on the desk. "What's that?"

A broad smile appeared, Nick allowing himself to feel the depth of his joy. "Suzanne is pregnant, too."

*Cheyenne, Wyoming*

Stretching both arms over his head to loosen sore muscles, Chandler glanced around the train platform, blinking at the bright afternoon sun. The trip from Texas had been uneventful. Much too boring for his taste.

The streets were quiet, almost eerily so, compared to many frontier towns. A salesman who'd shared a seat with Chandler on the train mentioned Cheyenne had grown since the opening of the railroad between it and Kansas City. The population now approached fifteen hundred residents. He expected considerably more activity.

The thought had just taken hold when shouts came from behind the train station. Running to the edge of the platform, he settled his hand on the handle of the six-shooter at his side, ready to take action. What he saw had him slowing his steps.

A crowd surrounded what appeared to be hastily erected gallows, their shouts traveling through the streets. Taking the stairs to the ground, Chandler moved toward the scene, curious about the bound man standing on the top platform.

As he grew closer, his stomach clenched. The prisoner couldn't have been older than sixteen. The young man's eyes were wild, filled with fear, searching the crowd for anyone who might help him.

He stopped next to an older couple. "What did he do?"

The man glanced at him, grunting. "Nothing we know of."

"He's a good boy. It's that rancher who's after him." The woman nodded toward a tall, rotund man near the front of the gallows. "The men standing around him with guns are his ranch hands. More like his hired guns," the woman bit out.

"Why would he want the boy dead?"

The man's voice lowered as more people congregated around them. "Word is he's in love with the rancher's daughter. Sheriff's got the gut ache, and his two deputies were called out this morning. No one's here to stop them."

"They're going to lynch that poor boy." The tears pooling in her eyes and distress on her face spoke to the injustice of the scene before them. "He doesn't have any family."

"Been working at the general store," the man added.

Chandler's hand settled back on the handle of his gun. "It's a lynching?"

The man nodded. "Best we can tell. No trial. Just the rancher's word the boy stole some cattle. The man's a crook. If anyone should be hung, it's him."

Chandler glanced around, not seeing what he sought. "Where's the jail?"

The older man pointed. "Behind you."

Taking a quick look at the gallows, he weighed his options for a brief moment before breaking into a run. Reaching the jail, he found the door open, the building empty. Hurrying to the desk, he opened one drawer after another until he found what he wanted.

Grabbing a badge, he pinned it on his chest before his fingers wrapped around a Springfield rifle resting against a wall. Checking it for ammunition, he took a couple deep breaths and headed back outside.

Walking with determination, his anger growing with each step, Chandler drew his six-shooter. Firing twice into the air, he holstered the gun before raising the rifle, aiming it at the rancher's chest.

"Hold it right there. There'll be no lynching until that boy's been found guilty by a legal trial."

As the crowd parted, he continued moving forward. What he'd first thought were angry shouts from the crowd turned to cheers of agreement.

"You've got no authority here." The rancher's loud voice didn't stop Chandler from his mission.

"Neither do you. Now, you and your men back away."

Snorting in disdain, the rancher took a step closer, flashing a feral smile. "You're outnumbered. You'll be dead before you get off a shot."

A cocky grin appeared on Chandler's face. "Are you willing to place a bet on that?"

The rancher's smile faded. Glancing between his men, he looked back. "Who are you?"

"Name's Chandler, and you'll be the one lying in dirt if you don't order your men to drop their guns and step away." Without taking his aim off the rancher, he shouted to the crowd. "Anyone here willing to help?"

Most moved away, shaking their heads, saying nothing. Thankfully, two men stepped forward, their guns drawn.

"We'll help you, Deputy."

Uncaring that his words would have no legal status, he nodded. "Consider yourselves deputized. Keep your guns focused on the rancher. No matter what happens, he goes down." He spoke loud enough so all could hear.

Taking several steps closer to the rancher, Chandler took a slow breath, readying himself to squeeze the Springfield's trigger. "Drop your guns or your boss is dead."

Worried eyes shot to the rancher, the ranch hands waiting for his command. A moment passed before the man nodded for them to comply with Chandler's order.

Not lowering the rifle, he glanced at the two new deputies. "Get their guns, then help the boy down and take him to the jail."

"Yes, sir."

The crowd dispersed, giving Chandler a clear view of the rancher. He didn't allow his guard to weaken, prepared if the man should do anything reckless.

When the deputies moved past him, their arms full of weapons, another man escorting the boy toward the jail, he slowly lowered the rifle.

The rancher raised his arm, pointing a finger. "You're a dead man, Chandler."

Ignoring the threat, he took a step closer, his right hand ready to draw, if necessary. "You may be right, but that boy will still be alive."

# Chapter Nine

"How long will you be gone?" Josie leaned toward Dom, her arm threaded through his as they strolled along the boardwalk.

He'd stopped by Nick's house to speak with Josie and stayed for supper. Afterward, he'd invited her to join him on a walk, explaining his orders to transport a prisoner to Deer Lodge from Moosejaw would take him away for several days.

Glancing down at her, his breath hitched at her beauty in the moonlight. "A week, at least. If the weather worsens, it could be much longer."

"I'll miss you." She felt her face heat. The words came out before Josie could stop them, a flaw she'd suffered from her entire life. Her parents always accused her of speaking without thought, ill-considered notions bursting from her mouth, whether appropriate or not.

Stopping, Dom turned her toward him. Staring down, he felt a rush of desire at the way her clear, chocolate brown eyes, so vulnerable and trusting, held his. Until now, he hadn't noticed the specks of gold. Specks which flashed in the bright, star-filled night.

Leaning down, he kissed her cheek before tucking her arm more firmly through his and continuing on. "Tell me more about the store you and Olivia want to open."

Dom's question surprised her as they'd talked briefly of it during supper. "I'm not certain there is much more than what we talked about earlier. Although we did decide to use the empty shop next to the St. James."

Glancing down, he realized he wanted to learn everything there was to know about her. "I want to know what your dream is, Josie. Nick believes it would be best to open an emporium offering men's clothing and designs from Allie's shop. You didn't seem too excited. Is that what you want?"

They passed the Dixie, heading down the boardwalk toward the St. James Hotel. For a while, he thought she wouldn't answer. Then she looked up, giving a quick shake of her head.

"No. I'm certain an emporium would do well. It's just..." Her voice trailed off as she searched for the right words.

Stopping, he lifted her chin so their eyes met. "It doesn't give you the same sense of excitement as other choices."

The corners of her mouth edged up. "Yes."

"I thought so." Dropping his hand, Dom kept walking.

"Nick doesn't believe a shop selling accoutrements would thrive in Splendor. He says the town isn't yet big enough to sustain it. When

Olivia pressed him, he did admit the town is growing by almost twenty-five percent each year. That means we'll be as large as Big Pine in a few years, and they have two similar stores. From what we saw, they're doing well."

Her voice became more animated as she spoke. "Olivia and I believe beautiful scarves, perfume, Meerschaum pipes, and high-quality tobacco would sell, but Nick says there isn't enough money in the area. That doesn't make sense to me. Look at the St. James." She nodded toward the hotel ahead of them. "It and the restaurant are always busy, and the rates are much higher than the boardinghouse."

They stopped outside the St. James, Dom taking her hands in his. "Perhaps there is a compromise."

Her eyes flashed with excitement. "Do you think so?"

"I think it's possible. Come on." Gripping her hand, he led her up the steps to the lobby. "Are you still open, Thomas?"

The young man grinned. "We are, Marshal Lucero."

"We'll want coffee and dessert. And a quiet table."

Thomas nodded. "Of course."

"But we just had cake at supper," Josie protested on a soft laugh, following Thomas to their table.

After seating her, Dom leaned close. "You forget. I've seen how much you can eat."

"Dom," she gasped, slapping his hand. "A gentleman wouldn't mention a lady's appetite."

Sitting down, he flashed a wolfish grin. "Whoever said I was a gentleman? Certainly not me."

Brow quirking upward, she gave a soft, unladylike snort. "Sylvia has warned me about you, Marshal Lucero."

He didn't respond, waiting until Thomas set coffee and slices of golden spice cake topped with sweet icing before them. "May I get you anything else?"

"This is fine. Thank you." Dom watched Josie pick up her fork and take a bite.

"Oh. This is wonderful. You must try it."

He scooped up a portion of cake. Lifting it to his mouth, he stilled. "I thought you had no appetite." Chuckling at the narrowing of her eyes, he slipped the dessert into his mouth. "You are right. This is excellent."

"Of course I'm right."

Amused at her impish comment, Dom ate while taking quick, sly glances at her. He found her delightful, confusing, and thoroughly entertaining.

Swallowing the last bite with coffee, Dom set down his cup. "Would you like to hear my ideas for your shop?"

Eyes sparkling in interest, she set down her fork, leaning toward him. "Very much."

Lips slightly parted, she stared at him in rapt attention, as if his words would provide the answers she so desperately sought. Dom's throat clenched, the pressure in his chest building at the trusting gleam in her eyes. He couldn't recall a time when anyone had looked at him with such unconcealed confidence. The thought had him shifting in his seat.

Glittering golden specks in eyes the color of warming chocolate stared at him, waiting. Shoving aside his discomfort, Dom began.

"I think it's a wonderful idea. Olivia will love it, and Nick should have no objections."

Standing, Dom didn't respond as he pulled out Josie's chair. When she stood, he placed a hand on the small of her back, guiding her outside. Gripping her hand, he slipped it through his arm, taking the steps to the boardwalk.

"Nick is an excellent businessman. He'll look at your ideas from a financial perspective, probably speak with Gabe, then make a decision. You're lucky to have both men so interested in helping you and Olivia start your store. Many would turn away."

"I know." Her voice came out on a resigned groan. "My father would be one of them. He believes a woman's job is to support her husband, bear children, and run the household. Working outside the home would be unthinkable." A spirited chuckle burst forth. "In truth, he'd consider it blasphemy."

Dom stared down at her a moment before throwing back his head on a deep, throaty laugh. "Let's hope he never visits to find you ringing up a purchase."

Sobering at his comment, her mouth twisted into a grim line. "Let's hope he never discovers where I am."

Dom patted her hand. He'd been stunned to hear of how she'd vanished from her home, taking trains and stagecoaches to reach Splendor while her parents traveled in Europe. It bothered him how she showed so little regard for how her lady's maid or her brother would take her disappearance.

Dom figured they'd have been frantic at the way she'd lit out on her own. The same as he and his family had been desperate with worry when Sylvia ran away from their home in Whiplash, Texas. Her running resulted in marriage and Dom ending up in Splendor. The outcome could've been much worse.

"Do you expect your brother will try to find you?"

She shot him a questioning glance. "As you and your family wanted to find your sister?"

Dom felt not the slightest amount of regret at hiring Allan Pinkerton's agency to track Sylvia down. "Yes."

Taking a moment to respond, Josie stared into the darkened windows of the stores they passed. "I'd expect nothing less. He'd want to find and steal me back home before our parents return from Europe. It wouldn't surprise me if Rafe found the letter I left for our parents and destroyed it, hoping they'd never learn of my disappearance."

"What will you do if Rafe shows up, expecting you to leave with him?"

Licking her lips, she met his questioning gaze with a wide grin. "I'd do the same as your sister."

Brows bunching, he tilted his head toward her.

"She told me all about how you came to take her home, but she spurned your every effort."

Barking out a laugh, he shook his head. "Did she tell you how I'd also wanted to leave Whiplash?"

"Well...no."

"It's true. If our oldest brother, Cruz, had been sent, I can assure you Sylvia wouldn't have married Mack. She'd be living back at the ranch, readying herself for an arranged union."

Shaking her head, she snorted in disbelief. "I doubt that. She'd have run away again."

"Perhaps, but Father would've made it much more difficult the second time. He can be quite formidable when needed."

Passing the jail, she looked up at him. "Has he been *quite formidable* regarding your purchase of land from the Pelletiers?"

Dom didn't answer at first, glancing into the jail. The light from one oil lamp illuminated Hex Boudreaux and his brother, Zeke, sitting inside, playing cards. The deputies often volunteered for night shifts, leaving their days open for whatever they chose. Dom liked them, although he knew little about the two men from New Orleans. He shifted to look at Josie as they continued toward the livery.

"Did you know Hex and Zeke Boudreaux in New Orleans?"

She shook her head. "No. I didn't meet them until arriving in Splendor." The corners of her mouth edged up. "They are quite handsome, don't you think?"

Her question caught him off guard, causing an unwanted stab of irritation to grip him. Stopping abruptly, he glared down at her. "Handsome?"

Her eyes glinted in amusement. "Why, yes. I don't believe I've met such fine looking men in a long time."

Dom's features tightened, jaw working at her comment. Without thought, he tugged her between two buildings, eliciting a surprised shriek. Glancing around, satisfied no one watched, he lowered his head to capture her mouth. She didn't resist, slipping her hands up his arms to wrap around his neck.

On her deep moan, and before he could be dissuaded, Dom deepened the kiss. A small voice told him he might be pushing her, moving too fast. He couldn't miss her tentative movements, the way she followed his lead. Josie had little experience, which only heightened his desire.

Tightening his arms around her, he continued exploring her mouth, his hands moving over her back to settle on her waist. He couldn't recall a time he desired a woman as much as Josie. Realizing how much more he wanted, Dom gentled the kiss, allowing space to grow between them. If they didn't stop, he'd continue, doing things they might later regret.

From the way Josie clutched his shoulders, he knew she wouldn't object, and would allow him to do whatever he wanted. She deserved better than a quick taking in the darkness between two buildings, and Dom wanted so much more from the lovely New Orleans lady. Breaking the kiss, he rested his forehead against hers, feeling her hot breath against his jaw.

"We must stop, sweetheart." Glancing down, seeing her glassy eyes and swollen lips, he almost gave in to the urge to kiss her again. Instead, he took a step away, his hands resting on her shoulders.

Searching his face, her brows drew together. "Is there something wrong?"

A low chuckle broke from his throat. "Ah, Josie." He stroked his knuckles down her face. "There's nothing wrong, which is why we must stop. If we don't..." Dom continued to study her face, letting out a ragged breath. "Do you have any idea what I'm talking about?"

He continued to watch her, giving Josie time to understand his meaning. Dom saw the instant she did.

"Oh..." Her face flushed, heated as the meaning of his words became clear. "Surely we couldn't..." She glanced around the empty space, trying to convey her thoughts without speaking it.

Clutching her chin, he turned her face to him. "Believe me, sweetheart, we certainly could."

Eyes going wide, she pressed her face into his shoulder on a muffled groan.

On a thread of regret, Dom stepped back, creating enough distance to look at her. "I should get you home before Nick comes looking."

Not looking up into his eyes, she nodded. "I suppose you're right."

Chuckling, he took her arm, slipping it once again through his. Silence enveloped them during their walk to Nick's. As they approached the front steps, Dom stopped.

"Will you let me call on you when I return?"

Going on tiptoes, she braced her hands on his shoulders, placing a lingering kiss on his lips. Lowering herself, she shot him an elfin grin.

"You had better, Marshal Lucero. If you don't, I'll be forced to find you." Turning, she ran up the steps, disappearing into the house before he had a chance to reply.

Staring at the closed door, Dom considered what seemed to be happening between them. There was so much to like about the precocious young lady. Independent, with definite ideas on many subjects, she didn't allow anyone to squash her dreams.

Unlike some of the women he'd known, her unpretentious intelligence impressed him, keeping him focused on her every word. And she made him laugh with her surprising comments and actions. He couldn't recall a woman who'd captivated him to such a degree.

Turning, he pondered what he wanted, his plans for the future, wondering if Josie would hold any place in them. Dom had no plans to marry. At least not until he'd built his ranch into a success, which could take years. And not while he worked as a U.S. Marshal, a job which could take his life with the slightest miscalculation.

His plans for the future had been why he'd never approached Tabitha Beekman. There'd been a definite attraction between them, one others noticed and often commented about. Still, he'd never seriously considered courting the beautiful young woman. Unbeknownst to others, relief had flooded him when learning she'd accepted a proposal of marriage from a previous beau, leaving

Splendor within a few short days of receiving the telegram.

Josie presented an entirely different dilemma. His feelings for her were already stronger than intended, his desire to be with her dragging him from thoughts of the ranch he dreamed about. The idea of any woman having this effect on him was preposterous. And unwanted.

Without thought, he walked toward the jail, his mind muddled with what needed to be done. Tomorrow, he'd leave for Moosejaw. The following days would be spent taking the prisoner to Deer Lodge before returning to Splendor.

As much as the thought disturbed him, the trip would give him time to decide how to let Josie know they had little chance of a future. She had her dreams, and he had his. Both would take all their time, leaving little for building a relationship. Perhaps in a few years...

His steps faltered on the thought. It wouldn't be right to give her false hope for something which might never occur. Ignoring the sharp pain to his chest, the burning ball of regret in his gut, Dom forced himself to make the difficult choice.

Taking the final steps to the jail, he shoved open the door. Grabbing a chair, he swung it around to straddle it. "Deal me in."

# Chapter Ten

Josie sat on the window seat in the Barnetts' parlor, watching Olivia and Clay walk down the path toward town. Her heart tripped when Clay threaded their fingers together, remembering how she felt at Dom's touch.

It had been over a week since he'd left. Nine days without word. At least that was what Gabe had told her. Josie didn't doubt him. She just didn't like knowing something could happen to Dom and she might never know. No matter the reassurances from Olivia, Suzanne, and others, Josie couldn't keep her mind off him, wondering when he'd return.

After he left, Josie and Olivia had spoken with Nick about Dom's idea. It surprised both how much he liked what they proposed. So much so that he'd asked Gabe for his thoughts. By the same evening, the four had drafted plans for the new business, identified the location, and listed what Olivia and Josie had to do before opening.

The two men had also agreed to fund the business, as long as the women followed the detailed notes they'd agreed upon.

"I doubt it will be long before Clay asks Nick for Olivia's hand."

Josie turned at Suzanne's voice, seeing her walk into the parlor, a book in her hand.

She felt a surge of melancholy at Suzanne's comments, but didn't disagree. "It's obvious how much he cares for her."

"I hope Clay loves her," Suzanne chuckled. "Otherwise, his discussion with Nick will be quite short. My husband doesn't believe there is any other reason to marry."

"Not even for financial benefit?" Josie had a hard time grasping the idea, her father telling her for years how she'd be expected to marry to join two wealthy families. "According to my father, money, power, and social status are the only reasons to marry."

Suzanne quieted a moment, considering Josie's words. "I do understand how some would want that for the future of their families. But how miserable would it be if the marriage didn't also include love."

"I know you're right. It's one of the reasons I left." Shifting on the window seat, she faced Suzanne. "Mother and Father care about each other, but I doubt they'd call it love. The truth is Father keeps a mistress and Mother has been known to take lovers. It's all very discreet, but Rafe and I have always known of their activities. I've often wondered if that was why our mother was so miserable when Father would leave the house at night."

"If Nick ever took a lover…" Suzanne's voice faded off on a deep, uneven breath.

"It's a good thing you'll never have to worry about that, sweetheart." Nick strolled into the room, bending to kiss her reddened check. "Sorry to eavesdrop, but it couldn't be helped." Sitting beside her, he took her hand in his, kissing her knuckles. "You're more than enough woman for me." He turned his attention to Josie. "Do you have time to discuss your shop?"

Straightening, she stared at him with an eager expression. "Of course."

"Gabe and I believe another trip to Big Pine is required so you can select the goods you want to offer and discover who offers them to merchants."

Her face lit up. "So soon? I thought you didn't believe we'd need to make the trip for another couple weeks."

"We're taking advantage of the good weather. We don't know how long it will last, so it would be best if we left tomorrow."

"We?" Josie asked.

"Caleb and I will be riding alongside, while Sylvia and May accompany you and Olivia in the wagon."

Clasping her hands together, Josie stood. "It will be wonderful to have Sylvia and May with us. We'll be able to get their opinion on a number of items. I'd better return to my room and start making notes so we don't forget anything." Hurrying to the doorway, she stopped, turning back. "Thank you so much, Nick."

His brows rose. "For what?"

Her face split into a broad smile. "For everything."

*Big Pine*

Dom's head pounded, his back aching as he rode into town after delivering the prisoner to Deer Lodge. He'd no more than entered the prison grounds before one of the administrators handed him a telegram from the judge in Big Pine. The orders were to return right away.

Staying one night to rest his horse and eat a couple decent meals, he saddled Blue, prepared for the long ride back. It had taken three long days and nights to return. At least the weather had been in his favor.

After a hot bath, a meal at the hotel restaurant, and good night's sleep, he woke to a man pounding on the door of his room. Sitting up, he rubbed his eyes.

"Hold on." Standing, he didn't take time to glance at what he wore before opening the door.

Sheriff Parker Sterling stood in the hall, his gaze moving over Dom's disheveled appearance. "You look like hell, Lucero."

"Did you come here to insult me?"

"I wouldn't waste my time." he smirked. "The judge wants you at the courthouse in thirty minutes."

Scrubbing a hand down his face, Dom shook his head. "I thought the trial wasn't scheduled until tomorrow."

Sterling walked past him into the room. Grabbing pants off the floor, he tossed them to Dom. "Seems our judge is seeing a woman in town. She has *plans* for them tomorrow, so..." He shrugged. "Do you need details?"

Groaning, Dom shook his head. "No."

Stabbing his legs into the pants, he slipped on his shirt and slid into his boots before running fingers through his mussed hair. Glancing around the room, he strapped on his gunbelt before settling his hat on his head.

"Let's go."

Walking beside Sterling to the courthouse, his mind moved to Josie. Once the trial ended and he completed any additional duties the judge ordered, he'd be returning to Splendor, no longer able to put off their conversation. Although, over the last week, he'd mellowed a great deal on what he wanted to say.

Instead of discussing their tenuous relationship, he'd explain his plans for the ranch, adding how long it could take to find success. If she appeared to accept his reasoning, he'd take the next step and ask if she'd be willing to grant him a long courtship. One of indeterminable length.

Hands going moist at what he proposed, he slid them down his pants. Dom didn't understand why her agreement meant so much to him, but it did. The days away had given him another perspective on his feelings for Josie. No matter how many times he tried to talk himself out of it, Dom wanted her. Not for a few weeks or months. He wanted Josie in his life forever. A life which included laughter, love, and as many children as she'd give him.

Josie couldn't sleep the night before they left for Big Pine, unable to stop the excitement coursing through her. Each new thought led her to pick up the well-worn journal, adding another item for consideration. By morning, she'd gotten perhaps two hours of sleep.

The ride passed more quickly this trip. Hours before suppertime, they arrived in the bustling town, going straight to the hotel Nick always used. Not as nice as the St. James, it was still many degrees above what most frontier towns offered.

Instead of resting in their rooms, the four women decided to walk around town, making a list of the stores where they wanted to spend more time.

"Look at the one across the street." Sylvia nodded to a haberdashery. "Are you planning to carry men's hats?"

Olivia looked at Josie before they both shrugged.

"You should at least consider it." May moved to the edge of the boardwalk, getting a better look at the haberdashery. "My father owns many hats. He buys one in almost every town he visits."

"All right. I'll add the store to our list for tomorrow." Josie jotted down the name, slipping the journal back into her reticule.

Continuing along the boardwalk, they poked their heads into one store after another, adding a few to the journal, ignoring others. Within an hour, the list had grown well beyond what Josie and Olivia expected.

Sylvia stopped, looking up and down the boardwalk. "Do you think we have time for tea before meeting Nick and Caleb at the hotel?"

"We have more than enough time," Josie answered. "Where would you like to go?"

Tapping a finger against her lips, Sylvia shook her head. "I'm not sure. Shall we see what's up this way?"

Olivia swept her hand in a circle. "Lead on."

Dom removed his hat, threading fingers through his hair. The trial had lasted much longer than expected, the defendant being found not guilty. Instead of having to guard the judge from friends of the prisoner, he found himself guarding the defendant from the crowd of disgruntled spectators.

By the time he finished his duties, the day had slipped away. Dom craved a whiskey and a few games of cards before a meal at the hotel. If the judge needed him for nothing more, he'd be on the trail at first light tomorrow.

Stepping into the late afternoon sun, he strolled down the boardwalk, a destination already in mind. Glancing down the street, he failed to notice the person stepping out of a store and right into his path. Colliding, he heard a female grunt of surprise, the sounds of packages falling to the ground.

A cluster of pink fabric spread out across the wood planks, her purchases lying in a wide circle. Shoving his hat back, he bent down, holding out a hand.

"Ma'am, are you all right?"

A sharp crack of laughter broke forth, surprising him. "Yes, I'm fine." Shoving her own hat aside, she brushed hair from her face, not meeting his worried gaze.

"Let me help you up."

Glancing up, she saw his hand, gripping it with her own. Standing, she took her first good look at the man who'd graciously helped her up. Breath catching, she stared at his face, unable to believe her eyes.

"Dominic?"

Stilling, he took his first good look at the woman before him. It took a moment before his eyes widened, recognition coming in a rush. "Mattie?"

"Yes!" She threw her arms around his neck, hugging Dom to her before realizing the spectacle they made. Stepping away, a flush of embarrassment heated her face. "I'm sorry."

Dom grinned down at her. "I'm not." Giving himself a moment to adjust to seeing the woman he'd once thought he loved, he studied her face. "What are you doing in Big Pine?"

"My parents own the mercantile on the next street over. They moved here while I was away at school back east. I've been here a couple years."

Watching the play of emotions on her face, Dom experienced a brief flash of the past. They met when her parents had moved to Whiplash. Her father owned the mercantile, while her mother opened a millinery. She'd been fifteen, him seventeen, and he'd fancied himself in love.

Smitten, Dom had mentioned it to his older brother, Cruz, who'd been unable to stop himself from telling their father. After a time, news of their attraction reached Mattie's parents. They'd promptly shipped her back east to live with relatives and attend school. The memory seemed a lifetime ago. For Dom, it was.

He'd moved on, had many women since then, understood more about what he wanted. More precisely, he knew who he wanted, and it wasn't Mattie.

"Do you have time to talk? Perhaps we could have coffee or tea somewhere."

Dom was tired, ready for whiskey, not coffee, but the expectant look in her eyes had him agreeing. "Let me gather your packages and I'll follow you."

Talking in rapid sentences as they walked, Mattie led him to a restaurant not far from his hotel. Inside, they found a table in the back corner, far enough out of the way where her packages wouldn't be in the way. Setting them down, he pulled out her chair, taking a seat next to her.

It didn't take long to become lost in conversation, reminiscing about their time in Whiplash. Drinking coffee, eating slices of cake, neither noticed the door opening, the four young women entering.

"Are you married?" Dom asked, sipping his coffee.

"No, but I do have a beau. He's an attorney. Mother believes he'll offer for me soon. What about you?"

Shaking his head, he set his cup down. "Not married." He didn't explain more, not ready to share his uncertain future with Josie.

Reaching out, Mattie touched the badge pinned to his shirt. "You're a marshal? I always thought you'd continue in ranching."

Lost in their own conversation, they spoke in low voices, unaware of the drama unfolding a few tables away.

Josie sat down, exhausted from the long trip and their tour of town. Ordering tea, she relaxed, her gaze wandering around the room, stopping in disbelief. Her chest squeezed at the sight of a man she knew well sitting at a back table with a lovely young woman, his hand resting over hers. Letting out a pained groan, she swayed in her seat.

Sylvia leaned close, her voice soft. "Josie, what's wrong?"

She looked down to see Sylvia's hand on her arm. Swallowing, she forced herself to return her gaze to the couple.

Following Josie's stare, Sylvia gasped. "It's Dom."

"And he's with a woman," Josie whispered, her heart pounding a painful beat.

"What are you two looking at?" May swiveled to glance behind her. "That man looks like Dom."

"It is Dom," Olivia said, her face hardening. "Who is he with?"

Looking more closely, Sylvia groaned in disbelief. "If I'm not mistaken, he's with Matilda Lawson." Sympathy filled her voice when she turned back to Josie. "They met back home when they were young. Dom, well...he fancied himself in love with her."

"In love?"

"Josie, it's not what you think. They were seventeen and fifteen." Sylvia explained what happened when Mattie's parents learned of their feelings for each other. "I wonder why she's in Big Pine."

"Perhaps she's here to meet Dom." May turned back to the table, grimacing at the disapproving stares. "Or they might've just run into each other. It is a big town."

Staring down at her hands clutched in her lap, Josie tried to calm her scattered thoughts. Glancing up, a hard ball of ice formed in her stomach when Dom leaned over, kissing the woman's cheek. A tight spasm of pain rushed through her. Unable to watch more, she stood, knocking over the chair in her haste to leave.

Rushing out the door, she didn't see Dom turn away from Mattie in time to see her running out.

Mumbling a curse, he murmured a quick apology before following her. Stepping outside, he caught a glimpse of her rounding a corner.

Dashing after her, he called her name as he closed the distance. When she didn't slow, Dom shouted again.

"Josie, wait!" Reaching her, he gripped her arm, halting her retreat.

Not looking up, she tried to pull from his grasp. "Let me go."

"No." As he'd hoped, his response got her attention.

Lips thinning, her eyes sparked in anger. "No?"

Shaking his head, he drew her closer. "I'm not letting you go until you let me explain."

Lifting her chin, she tried again to pull away. "Sylvia already told me who the woman is. You should've told me you had an interest in someone else. And you shouldn't have led me to believe you cared for me. Now, let me go."

Instead of loosening his grip, Dom grasped her other arm, drawing her to within inches of his face. "The only woman I'm interested in is standing in front of me." He leaned down, but she twisted her head away at his attempt to kiss her.

"Stop it, Dom, and let me go."

Letting out a breath, he guided her to a bench. "Sit down and let me explain about Mattie."

The name sat like a burning coal in the bottom of her stomach. "I don't want to hear about her."

Gently pushing her down, he sat next to her, not loosening his hold. "Well, you're going to."

# Chapter Eleven

Over the next few minutes, Dom spoke of his history with Mattie in Whiplash, her being sent away, then stepping into his path today. All the while, he kept his gaze fastened on Josie's face, seeing her flinch at times, relaxing as he continued the story.

"Her parents own a mercantile in Big Pine and she's being courted by an attorney. Mattie is an old friend, Josie. Nothing more."

After a moment, she met his gaze. The relief he saw speared his chest. Dom wondered how he'd ever considered walking away from her.

"This is the first time you've seen her since she left Whiplash?"

"Yes. We were talking about the ranch when I heard a chair tip over and saw you."

Catching her lower lip between her teeth, she stared at a spot somewhere behind him. Feeling his hand stroke up and down her arm, Josie squared her shoulders, forcing a calm she didn't feel.

"Are you certain you have no feelings for her, Dom? I would understand if you did. She really is quite lovely, and—"

Whatever else she meant to say was lost when his mouth covered hers. Unconcerned of any passersby, he wrapped his arms around her, tightening his hold on her soft moan. The sound of a man clearing his throat had Dom pulling away, glancing over his shoulder.

"Sterling," he ground out. "Don't you have criminals to catch?"

"Sorry, Lucero, but the judge needs to speak with you before you leave for Splendor."

Standing, Dom held out his hand for Josie. "Josie, this is Sheriff Parker Sterling. Sheriff, this is Miss Josephine Dubois. She's from Splendor."

He tipped his hat at a blushing Josie. "Ma'am."

Stepping away to create a respectable distance between her and Dom, she nodded, not quite meeting his amused gaze. "Sheriff."

Tucking a few errant strands of hair behind her ear, she righted her hat. "I should find Olivia and the others."

Reaching out, Dom slipped his fingers through hers. "We'll find them together before I meet with the judge. I'm certain my sister is ready to give me a good tongue lashing."

"I'd best be going, Lucero. Don't keep the judge waiting." Touching a finger to the brim of his hat, Sterling headed toward the main street.

Pressing a kiss to her forehead, he tugged Josie back to the restaurant. "Why are you and the other ladies in Big Pine?"

Explaining as they retraced their steps, she glanced through the front window. "It seems *your* Mattie has joined Sylvia, May, and Olivia."

Gripping her shoulders, Dom turned her toward him. "Mattie isn't mine." He didn't say more as he studied her face. "Let's go inside and I'll introduce you."

Stepping over the threshold, Josie felt a wave of humiliation at her spiteful comment. Dom had made it clear Mattie held no place in his life. At the same time, he hadn't asked Nick's consent to court her. He'd only admitted having an interest in her.

Confused at his true intentions, she lifted her chin, determined not to let her misgivings show.

Removing his hat, Dom's gaze moved between the ladies. "It appears you've all met Mattie." Ignoring the look of consternation on Sylvia's face, he placed a hand on the small of Josie's back. "Mattie, this is Miss Josephine Dubois. Josie, this is Miss Matilda Lawson."

The two exchanged polite greetings before Dom grabbed two chairs, offering one to Josie.

"Dom told me he wasn't married, but he didn't mention a special lady." Mattie offered a small smile, glancing between the two.

Shifting away from Dom, Josie pinned her with a forced smile. "Probably because Dom and I are just friends. He tells me you live in Big Pine now."

Dom listened as the conversation continued, his jaw clenching at Josie's statement. The truth of her words irritated him. He'd escorted her to supper with Clay and Olivia, taken her on a few long walks, had coffee and dessert with her at the Eagle's Nest. Each time, he'd carefully avoided any mention of an actual courtship, knowing he had no intention of marrying.

Accepting his role in her thinking, his reaction to her comment about them being just friends shouldn't have had such a fierce impact. They'd shared kisses and passionate embraces, none of which were accompanied by an acknowledgment of how she'd begun burrowing into his life. Nor had they resulted in him pursuing a formal courtship. He had no intention of changing the status of their friendship, which left him in a foul mood.

Standing, he made a slight bow, avoiding Josie's confused expression. "Ladies, I have a meeting. Where are you staying, Sylvia?"

"At the Imperial Hotel."

"I'm staying there as well. Unless you have other plans, I'll join you at supper."

Giving a quick nod, Sylvia didn't look at Josie before answering. "We're all dining together, along with Nick and Caleb."

"Count me in as well." Without looking at Josie, he walked out, his mind whirling with thoughts of the woman he'd begun to care a great deal about.

125

"You should keep a chair next to you open for Dom, Josie."

After the way he'd left her at the restaurant, she'd chosen to sit between Olivia and May at supper. Sylvia's suggestion didn't sway her as she lowered herself onto the chair. Adjusting her skirt, she folded her hands in her lap with a resigned sigh.

"I'm sure he'd rather sit next to Nick and Caleb. After all, they're having drinks at the saloon next door."

Stepping next to her, Sylvia placed a hand on her shoulder. "Don't let his actions today worry you so much. It's obvious my brother cares about you."

"Not enough to want a formal courtship as Clay has with Olivia." A flash of guilt had her looking at her closest friend. "It's not that I'm not thrilled for you, Livvy. It's just I allowed myself to believe Dom might want more than a casual friendship. Today made me realize the fallacy of my thinking."

May saw the severe disappointment on Josie's face, recalling how she'd once felt the same about Caleb. "Some men take longer than others to realize what is right in front of them. My husband certainly was one. I believe Dom is as well. You shouldn't put too much stock in his actions."

Nodding at the waiter who silently asked if she cared for coffee, she waited until he made a tour of the table and left.

Picking up the tiny bowl of sugar, she added a small amount to her cup and stirred. "It truly doesn't matter. Livvy and I have much to do if we're going to open our business in a month."

Olivia choked on a sip of coffee. "A month? I thought we'd agreed with Father and Gabe it would be eight weeks."

Waving a hand in the air, Josie lifted her cup. "Eight weeks then. Regardless, we have a great deal to do before we open the store. Seeing Dom would only make the task more difficult."

"But I'll be seeing Clay."

Features softening, Josie smiled. "Of course you will. And you should see him as much as his time allows. In the meantime, I'll tend to tasks which may be completed by either one of us."

"Sorry we're late, ladies." Nick walked to Olivia, placing a kiss on his daughter's forehead before sitting beside her.

Caleb followed him into the dining room, taking a seat next to May. Dom strolled in a moment later, spotting the only empty chair on the other side of Nick. Ignoring Josie's obvious refusal to acknowledge him, he greeted the women before ordering wine for the table.

"Did you accomplish what you wanted?" Nick asked Olivia.

"More than I'd thought possible. We have a list of the stores we want to visit again tomorrow. With four of us, we should be able to discover what we need to begin ordering for our shop."

"What you need are the names of the drummers, Olivia." Dom's casual remark had the women gaping at him. "They're men who work for the big wholesale houses in large cities. You tell them what you want, they provide a price. If it's agreeable, you enter into a contract to purchase." He focused his explanation on Olivia, pointedly ignoring Josie. "There's a possibility you'll need to work with more than one, but one will get you started."

With each word, Josie's world tilted a little more, her heart crumbling from innumerable small cracks. The reality she'd earlier suspected came crashing down. His lack of attention, the way he noticed everyone except her, left no doubt of her importance to him.

Shared meals, several stolen kisses, and a few passionate embraces meant little to him. Certainly not what they'd meant to her. Josie had allowed his attention to sweep her away, make her believe he cared about her as much as she cared for him. The truth had her throat tightening, unshed tears burning behind her eyes.

Josie now understood the depth of her innocence. His numerous encounters with women made her feel insignificant, naïve in a way she'd allowed herself to ignore until now.

She had one more day in Big Pine before returning to Splendor. Once there, her time would be spent preparing the store for its opening. There'd be no time for anyone. Especially not Dom and his insincere considerations.

"Is that agreeable to you, Josie?"

Hearing her name shook her from the morose mental ramblings. It was hard to accept, but thoughts of her and Dom were nothing except childish musings.

"I'm sorry, Livvy. What did you say?"

"We'll split up tomorrow. You and Sylvia will visit half the shops while May and I visit the others. That way, we'll be able to spend more time in each one."

A taut smile formed on her lips as sadness crashed over her. Tonight might be the last time she ever sat with Dom for a meal, and there was nothing she could do but accept it and go on.

"I think you've come up with a grand idea."

"Actually, it was Dom's idea."

Refusing to concede his part, she looked at Sylvia. "Where should we start tomorrow?"

Dom had planned to get a solid night's sleep before riding back to Splendor after breakfast. Instead, he'd lain awake for hours, thinking about

Josie and the way he'd treated her, until the sun peeked over the eastern mountains.

During last night's supper, he'd noticed the numerous times she'd snuck a peek at him, refusing to look at him directly. It bothered him a great deal. Even more so because he had to take the blame for how she acted.

From the moment she'd spotted him with Mattie, her behavior toward him changed. At first, she'd been confused and hurt. Once he had a chance to explain his brief history with the young woman, Josie had been mollified. Then something changed, and Dom felt certain he knew why.

Josie had concluded what he hadn't yet been able to voice. Suddenly, the need to be alone with her, explain his intentions, became urgent.

Dom couldn't let her spend hours in the wagon believing he held no interest in her. Putting off his return wouldn't make a difference. Staying in Big Pine to speak with Josie would.

Dressing, he headed downstairs to the hotel dining room, shoving aside the lump in his throat when he saw Josie and the others sitting at a table. He quickly occupied the empty chair beside her.

"Good morning, Josie."

She spared him an almost imperceptible glance. "Marshal Lucero."

"What may I get you for breakfast?" The server stood over him.

"Eggs, bacon, flapjacks, and coffee."

"I'll make certain your food comes out with the others, sir."

"Thank you."

Dom didn't take his gaze off Josie, even though she didn't spare him a glance, which amused more than frustrated him. "When do the four of you start on your rounds?"

Olivia's excited voice answered for the group. "Right after breakfast."

"We believe it will take us until almost supper to visit all the stores on the list," Sylvia added.

May nodded. "It will take a while to discover the names of the drummers."

Conversation stilled while plates of food were set down before them.

"I'm so glad you mentioned drummers, Dom. Josie and I were perplexed about how the shops obtained their goods." Olivia took a sip of tea. "Father and Gabe order alcohol directly from wholesale merchants, and they brew their own beer. Isn't that right?" She looked at Nick.

Nodding, he lifted another forkful of eggs. "It is. While in New Orleans, I developed connections with the larger wholesale companies. When we opened the Dixie, I was able to arrange direct orders, allowing us to avoid using drummers."

His comment caught Josie's attention. "Why don't you want to use drummers?"

Setting down his fork, Nick lifted his cup of coffee. "They add a percentage to the wholesale price. We make more money buying directly from wholesalers."

Josie leaned forward, warming to the topic. "Why can't Olivia and I do that?"

"Unfortunately, the products you want to offer often require you to deal with drummers. You won't make as much, but you'll be able to get the goods you want." Nick resumed eating, using a biscuit to sop up the last of his eggs.

Waiting until everyone finished, Dom leaned close to Josie, lowering his voice. "We need to talk."

Although his hoarse voice startled her, she hissed back. "I'll be busy all day. Besides, I thought you were riding to Splendor today." She still hadn't looked at him.

"I'll ride back with the rest of you tomorrow. Would you have time to talk before or after supper?"

"We'll meet you outside, Josie."

"I'm ready." She set her napkin on the table, standing when Dom pulled out her chair.

Walking to the door together, he gripped her arm when they stepped outside. "A few minutes is all I want, Josie."

She knew the proper reaction was to agree to see him for a few minutes, giving him enough time to explain why he no longer desired her company. As the knot in her stomach tightened, she couldn't find it in herself to hear his apologies or excuses. It may not be fair to Dom, but it would be much less distressful for Josie if she made an excuse and moved on.

"I'll be quite busy today, Dom." Clasping her hands in front of her, she let out a slow breath. "Perhaps when we return to Splendor, I'll have time to talk with you."

Crossing his arms, he lifted a brow. "Perhaps?"

He saw a flash of distress before she deftly concealed it. "I don't mean to be difficult."

"Don't you?"

Taking hold of his arm, she led him away from the others. "I'm going to be very busy with the store, and you have little time between your job as a marshal and starting your ranch. You've been wonderful, Dom, and I enjoy being with you more than you know."

"But?" His features tightened.

Her throat worked as she swallowed. "I'll be honest, as I know no other way to say this."

His brows rose, but he stayed quiet.

"We both know if you had any interest in courting me, you would've said something by now." She rushed on when he opened his mouth to speak. "I understand, Dom. Truly, I do. You've no desire to have me in your life as more than friends." Her brave façade began to weaken on the word. "I hope we may continue our acquaintance...as friends."

"Friends..." He gritted out the word as if it were a curse.

"Maybe someday, when you've achieved what you want—"

"Josie. Are you ready?"

She glanced over her shoulder at Olivia. "One minute, Livvy."

Josie hoped he'd stop her, tell her she was wrong and he did want something more than friendship. Instead, he stared at her as if she were a puzzle he couldn't solve.

"Well, I need to go. I do hope you'll join us for supper this evening. I'd love for you to hear what we accomplish today."

When he didn't respond, she leaned up, placing a chaste kiss on his cheek before turning away.

# Chapter Twelve

Dom stared after her. Within a couple minutes, Josie and Sylvia made their way across the street while Olivia and May disappeared into a store near the hotel. She hadn't looked back since leaving him standing on the boardwalk.

Other than during a few arguments with his father, Dom had never been dismissed in such an efficient manner. It bothered him how easy it had been for Josie to wrap up their last few weeks in a proper package, dismissing their time together as if it meant nothing.

To Dom, it meant a great deal. He suspected if Josie hadn't been so defensive, she'd admit he mattered to her. What he couldn't do was argue with her reasons for continuing as nothing more than friends. He'd used the same arguments when struggling with whether or not to request a formal courtship. Dom hated having his own thoughts thrown back at him without a chance to explain.

"Are you staying or heading back today?"

So lost in his own thoughts, he'd failed to hear Nick come up beside him.

Until that moment, he hadn't made a decision. "As soon as I get Blue saddled, I'll be on my way. Unless you and Caleb want me to ride along with you."

"No need. We'll be leaving tomorrow." Nick's attention wandered across the street to where Josie and Sylvia stood outside a store. "Are you certain you don't want to wait?"

Following Nick's gaze, Dom's jaw tensed. "I must meet with Bull about my ranch. It would serve no purpose to wait any longer."

"If you're certain." Nick held out his hand, Dom grasping it as Caleb joined them.

"You aren't staying?"

"I have business back in Splendor. I'll trust you and Nick to see the women home safely." His mocking grin flashed between the two men.

"We will," Nick assured him. "Have a safe trip, Dom."

Touching a finger to the brim of his hat, he headed to the livery, ready to put as much distance as possible between himself and the woman who mystified him more than any other.

*New Orleans*

Rafael Dubois held the message in his lap, disbelief mingling with anger, his throat closing in time to stop a roar of anguish. No tears of loss pooled in his eyes.

Denial coursed through him, his mind muddled with useless memories.

"Mr. Rafe?" Teezy's broken voice sounded miles away, as if caught in the whirlwind of a tornado.

He didn't look at her, his mind in disarray, scrambling to make sense of the useless tragedy. "Yes, Teezy?"

"Can I get you anything?" She choked on a sob, unable to contain her own anguish.

"Whiskey, please. And leave the decanter."

The rustling of her skirts caught his attention for an instant before his thoughts turned back to the notice from Oceanic Steam Company. In the fall, his parents had boarded the Ocean Queen for Europe and were due back to the port of New York in late March. Less than a week from today. From there, they'd make their way home by train.

Rafe had already begun plans for a soirée in their honor, the invitation list approaching two hundred, not including his father's mistress. If the senior Dubois did as expected, he'd sneak the woman into the spacious home, sequestering her in a guest room for him to visit in the wee hours of the morning.

None of that mattered now. The list would be shredded, as would Teezy's ideas for decorations and food. Tossing the message aside, he stood, running both hands through his thick, dark hair.

Taking a couple steps, he stared back at the missive, feeling his stomach roil.

*Oceanic Steam Company: We regret to inform you of the deaths of Mr. Charles Dubois and Mrs. Charles (Eugenia) Dubois, who perished while passengers on the Ocean Queen. Their remains have not been recovered and are presumed lost. Our offices will be in touch with more information as it becomes available.*

"Here you are, Mr. Rafe." Teezy handed him a glass already filled with whiskey before swiping a tear from her cheek.

"Why don't you join me, Teezy?"

"I've already had my share." She glanced at the table, wincing. "What are we going to do?"

Tossing back the whiskey, he set the glass down. "Nothing yet. I need to send a few telegrams and meet with the family attorney. Until I get answers, we'll keep what we know between us."

Her lips drew into a thin line. "Not even the other servants?"

"No one, Teezy. With luck, I'll have answers by tomorrow."

Biting her lip, she glanced away.

"What is it?" Rafe asked.

"What about Miss Josephine?"

Scrubbing a hand down his face, he gave a slow shake of his head, letting out a weary sigh. "I don't know. There's been no word from Pinkerton. That's one of the telegrams I'll be sending."

If possible, Teezy's face sobered even more, her body beginning to vibrate in agitation. "Have you thought of looking through Miss Josephine's personal items?"

He moved to stand next to her. "What are you thinking?"

"Well, she kept a journal, but I believe she took it with her." Pursing her lips, she locked her eyes with his. "But she also keeps every letter. There's a chance..." Her voice faded when Rafe rushed to the stairs, taking the steps two at a time to the second floor.

Reaching Josie's bedroom, he shoved the door open, going straight to her bureau. Hesitating for only a moment, he pulled out the top drawer, rifling through the contents. Finding nothing, he moved to the next, then the third. Digging under the clothes, he touched what felt like papers. Tossing out the clothing, his eyes lit on a stack of envelopes, held together with a bright red ribbon.

Grabbing them, he sat on the bed. Staring at the red ribbon, he felt a pang of indecision at reading correspondence meant only for her. The guilt lasted a few seconds before he loosened the ribbon, took out the first letter, and began to read.

He recognized the author right away. Olivia Moreau Barnett. Rafe stared at the last name, the one she'd taken after locating her father in some frontier town out west. He liked Josie's closest friend, a quiet, beautiful young lady with an easy laugh and sweet manner. At one point, Rafe had thought of courting her, but before he could make a decision, she'd left to seek out a father she'd never met.

Reading quickly, his gaze settled on the name of a town. Splendor, in the Montana Territory. Setting it down, he picked up another letter. Again, the town was mentioned, this time with the name of a saloon, Dixie, and her father's name. Nick Barnett.

Rafe hurried through the rest, noting they were all from Olivia. Stacking them together again, he secured the pile with the red ribbon, slipping them into his pocket.

Moving back to the bureau, he replaced the items he'd dislodged, placing a hand on a sleeping gown his sister loved. It made him wonder why she hadn't taken it with her. Glancing around the room, he saw so many keepsakes she might've packed if there'd been time, and room in her satchel.

Walking to the door, he patted the package in his pocket, a remorseful smile curling his lips.

He had a great deal to do in a short amount of time. Afterward, when he'd done what was necessary to keep his parents' estate going, making sure Teezy had the appropriate authorization to make household decisions, he'd leave.

It could take weeks to arrive in Splendor. Much less time to find his sister. When he did, Rafe would return her to New Orleans to take her place as the mistress of their family home.

Chandler Evans, arms folded across his chest, hat pushed low on his forehead, hoped the repetitive sounds of the train rolling over the tracks would lull him to sleep. He'd stayed a few days longer in Cheyenne than anticipated.

The sheriff's gut ache didn't heal as expected. Chandler stayed until he improved, as did the two new deputies. The original ones, to the surprise of no one except the sheriff, had been on the rancher's payroll, their disappearance during the attempted lynching planned. Neither had returned to Cheyenne.

With the sheriff on the mend and the two men deciding to keep their positions as the newest lawmen, Chandler had taken the first train west.

The blast of the train whistle had him sitting up, shoving his hat back. Shifting to get a better view out the window, his eyes widened at the sight of the town ahead.

Salt Lake City spread out across the valley ahead. He'd heard the population was close to ten thousand. Chandler hadn't believed it, but his eyes didn't lie. Whether ten thousand or eight, it sprawled in all directions, big enough for him to purchase a solid mount, have a hot bath, and get a good night's sleep.

Slowing as it drew near the station, the train stopped alongside the platform, giving him a good look at this part of town. Stepping into the afternoon sun, he tossed his satchel over a shoulder, gripping his coat in a hand.

Making his way along the walkway, he spotted the car filled with personal items. Retrieving his saddle and tack, he headed down the street, taking in the stores, restaurants, and hotels. Selecting one appearing not too expensive, he registered, paid for a room, then deposited his gear inside.

Delaying a meal, he continued along the boardwalk, going straight to the livery he'd spotted near the train station. A smile tilted the corners of his mouth as he got closer.

He counted at least twenty horses in the corral in back, doubting all could be boarded animals. Seeing the smithy inside, he walked as close as possible to the forge before the heat had him stopping.

"I'm looking to buy a horse. Any of those out back for sale?"

Setting down a hammer, the man straightened, wiping grimy hands down his leather apron. "Got a few. Follow me and I'll point them out."

As they got closer, Chandler saw some of the animals were in reasonable condition, others sickly or recovering from an injury. Resting a boot on the lowest rung of the corral, he settled his arms on the top rail.

"See the buckskin in the back? He's the best mount I've got, also the most expensive. Gelding about five years old with a good temperament."

"What are you asking?" Chandler didn't flinch at the amount the smithy gave. "I'd like a closer look."

After making a thorough inspection of the buckskin, he and the smithy haggled on a price, reaching an agreement several minutes later. Adding the cost of boarding the horse another night, Chandler handed him the agreed upon amount before returning to the hotel.

Emerging an hour later, he stopped in the dining room for a hearty supper, then left to find a suitable saloon for the evening he envisioned. After a few minutes of searching, he turned in a circle, scratching his jaw. He'd walked several blocks and hadn't found a saloon.

"You looking for something?" A man dressed much like him in jeans, a chambray shirt, boots, and hat came closer, stopping next to him.

"You wouldn't know where a man can get a drink, would you?"

Chuckling, the man nodded. "The people around here don't hold with drinking or gambling, or much of anything else."

"No saloons?"

Mouth tipping into a grin, the man turned and pointed. "If you walk about four blocks that way, you'll end up in the part of town where you can get a drink, play cards, or get entertainment in other ways. I'm headed that way myself."

They walked in silence for a couple minutes before Chandler spoke up. "Do you live around here?"

"I have a ranch about half of a mile out of town." Opening his coat, he turned to Chandler, showing his badge. "I'm also a deputy."

"Since we're headed to a saloon, I'm guessing you aren't a Mormon."

"I'm not, but my wife was. She was forced to leave the church to marry me." He winced on the last. "It was a difficult decision. Her family and friends shunned her. After three years, she has a new family and a passel of friends. We're expecting our first child in a few months. You married?"

Chandler snorted out a laugh. "No, and I've no intention of tying myself down to one woman."

"I said the same before meeting my wife. If you ever meet the right woman, you'll understand what I'm saying."

Reaching the nearest saloon, the two walked inside, taking seats at the same table. All through the game of cards, Chandler thought of what the man said. The comment didn't leave his mind as he strolled upstairs with a pretty, young woman. Nor did his words disappear as he lay in his own bed at the hotel later that night.

Until tonight, he'd never considered any type of permanent relationship with a woman. After living in a house where the lack of love between his mother and father couldn't have been more obvious, he had a bitter taste in his mouth when it came to marriage.

Still, the story of how a young woman would give up her entire life, leaving behind her family and friends for the love of one man, moved him in an unexpected way. He fell asleep, still pondering what the man said.

By morning, he'd forgotten all about the conversation the night before. Riding out of town on his sturdy buckskin, Chandler's thoughts settled on the journey ahead, and the reception he'd receive when he arrived in Splendor.

# Chapter Thirteen

*Splendor*

"I do like how the store is coming along, Livvy." Josie stepped away from the new cabinet, grinning in appreciation. "We may need another counter over there." She pointed to a spot in the center of the room. "What do you think?"

Olivia finished unpacking the last oil lamp, setting it on one of the new counters. "I think this is coming along quite well."

"No. About ordering an additional counter in the center."

Crossing her arms, Olivia walked to where Josie indicated, making a slow circle. It was a large space, much bigger than either woman had expected when they'd first spoken with Nick about their idea.

Since returning from Big Pine over two weeks ago, Josie and Olivia had spent endless hours preparing the store. Starting soon after sunup each morning and falling into bed close to midnight had become common. For Olivia, the hours had been an exciting adventure, but for Josie, instead of the joy she'd hoped to feel, the time had become a way to forget about Dom.

She hadn't seen him since leaving him on the boardwalk in Big Pine. Suzanne mentioned seeing him several times at the boardinghouse where he rented a room, had even spoken to him a few times. Josie had no idea if he'd asked about her and refused to pose the question to Suzanne.

"Yes. I believe a counter in the center would be useful and allow for more merchandise. Should I speak with Father about ordering one?"

"That would be wonderful, Livvy."

"I'll do it now. Shall I get food from the boardinghouse while I'm out?"

Josie hadn't thought of eating until her stomach growled at the mention of food. "I'd appreciate it."

Settling her bonnet over her head, Olivia tied it before reaching for her reticule and leaving. Josie busied herself pulling the empty packing crates to the back. It took three trips before she'd cleared the space in front. Brushing her hands down her already dusty skirt, she surveyed the back room, deciding they needed more shelves for extra merchandise. The sound of the bell over the front door alerted her to Olivia's return.

Stomach growling again at the thought of food, she didn't think to call out a greeting before returning to the front. Glancing up, her steps faltered. A man of above average height with broad shoulders and a trim middle stood inside, his clothes covered in what she assumed to be trail dust. His dark beard and mustache hid a face she thought might be quite handsome once the grime had been washed away. Bright blue eyes assessed her, then moved around the room. She'd never seen anyone quite like him.

"May I help you?" Josie didn't move from her spot close to the back. Something about him had her thinking of the door to the street in back, trying to remember if she'd locked it. She hoped not.

"Perhaps. Are you Miss Dubois?" He took a step forward, stopping when she noticeably stiffened.

"I am. And you are?"

Instead of answering, he made a show of studying the dark-stained cabinets and shelves positioned along the walls. "I heard you and Miss Barnett are opening a store."

"An emporium."

"An impressive venture for two young women."

Brows scrunching, she clasped her hands in front of her. "We're fortunate to have financial backing from two distinguished businessmen."

"So you plan to stay in Splendor?"

Stomach coiling with unease at the odd question, she forced a calm she didn't feel. Before she could form a response, the door opened, the bell ringing. Olivia staggered inside, her arms laden with bags of food.

"Suzanne packed too much food for the two of us." She closed the door with a thrust of her foot. "I told her..." Her voice faded, noticing the man standing a few feet away. "Oh. I didn't see you."

Walking past him, she set the wrapped food on one of the counters. Turning back toward him, she grinned. "I don't believe we've met."

"No, ma'am, we haven't." Sending what appeared to be an apologetic glance at Josie, he studied her for another moment. "I'll let you ladies get back to your business." Tipping his hat, he left, shutting the door with a quiet click.

"Wait!" Josie ran to the door, throwing it open. Frantically glancing around, a burst of air left her lungs. Sensing Olivia beside her, she shook her head. "He's gone."

"Who is he?"

Unaccountable fear lodged in her throat. "I don't know."

Olivia followed her to where the food awaited. "He's quite an odd man."

"I'm afraid he's much more than odd."

Dom massaged the back of his neck, letting out a groan as he continued along the trail to Splendor. It had been a long, difficult week. The prisoner he'd been escorting escaped on the way to Deer Lodge. It had taken twelve hours to find him sprawled on the ground, his horse long gone.

Tying the man to a tree, he'd wasted another five hours searching for the animal before finding it grazing in a pasture a mile away. He should've been glad. Five hours didn't compare to having to bind the man behind him on Blue. It was that or make the convicted man walk the rest of the way. Thankfully, he didn't have to resort to either.

By the time he led Blue into a stall at Noah's livery, his wage would be sitting in his account at the bank. More than enough to pay Suzanne for another month at the boardinghouse, and settle his accounts at the general store and livery.

Reaching the outskirts of town, his thoughts moved to Josie, wondering how much progress she and Olivia had made on their store. As happened every time his mind turned to her, he felt empty. A deep, unquenchable longing for a woman who had no place in his life. She'd made her feelings clear.

*Friends.*

Even two weeks later, the word stuck in his throat. Her decision to sever whatever had been building between them should've relieved Dom. He had a ranch to build and a job requiring a good deal of time. Before she'd admitted her lack of interest, he struggled with how he'd ever have the time to court Josie. The problem had been taken from him with a few quiet words.

Reining up at the gate to the stables, he slid to the ground and unhooked the latch, flashing a tired grin when Noah came out to greet him.

"You must've had trouble. I expected you back days ago." Taking the reins from Dom's hand, he walked the horse to an empty stall.

A self-deprecating chuckle broke from his lips as he unsaddled Blue. "The prisoner got away from me. Took me almost a day to find him and his horse." Setting the saddle on a rack, he shook his head. "I made a mistake I'd expect from a greenhorn."

"We all make mistakes. Whatever happened, I doubt you'll do it again. At least it didn't end with a bullet in your head."

Dom snorted his agreement. "I'll be back tomorrow to pay what I owe you, Noah."

"I know you're good for it. Have you stopped by to see Josie?"

The question had him whipping his head toward Noah. "No."

His brows drew together in a frown. "Thought you two were getting close."

"Friends," he ground out without further explanation before tossing his saddlebags over his shoulder and stalking to the boardinghouse.

Stomping his mud-encrusted boots on the boardwalk, he removed his coat before doing his best to brush dirt from his pants, deciding something to eat was more important than securing his personal items in his room upstairs.

Seeing little activity in the dining room, he picked an empty table with a view to the street and stretched out his legs. Long days in the saddle had cramped his muscles. He hoped the washroom wasn't being used when he finished eating. Dom couldn't think of anything he wanted more than a soak in a warm bath. Then his gaze landed on the emporium down the street and he knew there was something he wanted more.

"Did you just get back?" Suzanne walked toward him with an empty cup in one hand, a coffee pot in the other. Filling the cup, she set it in front of him. "There's meatloaf and potatoes left."

"Thanks, Suzanne."

"I'll save you a piece of pie, too."

Grinning, he returned his gaze to the building down the street. It didn't take much to imagine Josie inside, fussing with whatever had arrived since he'd left town. Everything he knew about what would soon be the emporium came from hearing what others said about it. Refusing to ask about her, he settled for what he could get, which didn't amount to much. His depressing thoughts were interrupted when Suzanne arrived with his food.

"Thanks." In the next instant, he'd slid a large piece of meatloaf into his mouth.

"Let me know if you want more. There's plenty." She nodded toward the kitchen. "I'll bring out the pie and more coffee." Before turning to leave, she gave him a stern look. "When are you going to talk with Josie?"

The question had him choking on a second forkful of meatloaf. Grabbing the cup, he swallowed a large gulp of coffee before answering.

"I've been busy with plans for the ranch and my job."

Pulling out a chair, she sat down, crossing her arms. "That's an excuse. You've had plenty of time to see how she's doing."

Setting down his fork, Dom leaned back in his chair, his features taut. "Josie doesn't want to see me."

"Is that what she told you?"

Blowing out a breath, he gave a quick shake of his head. "She made it clear a courtship with me isn't what she wants. I'm honoring her decision by leaving her alone."

Lowering her hands into her lap, she gave him a sympathetic look. "You know she cares a great deal about you, Dom."

Feeling awkward, he rubbed the back of his neck. "I'll think about finding her tomorrow."

"She'll be in the store with Olivia. The same as each day since you left." Standing, Suzanne placed a hand on his shoulder. "I'm certain you won't regret it."

Closing his eyes for an instant in pure frustration, he picked up his fork. Stabbing a pile of carrots, he stuffed them into his mouth. Chewing, he thought of his ranch, vowing to ride out to

Redemption's Edge tomorrow. He had to talk with Bull about the building schedule for his place.

The bunkhouse should be almost finished by now, and the barn started. The house would be next. He needed his own home, and it couldn't be ready soon enough.

"You're certain neither of you recognized the man?" As was his habit, Nick sipped a brandy after supper before returning to the Dixie for the evening.

"I'm certain I've never seen him before."

Olivia nodded at the certainty in Josie's voice. "He didn't look at all familiar, Father."

Nick looked at Suzanne, who shook her head. "There isn't anyone with his description staying at the boardinghouse. Perhaps he's staying at the hotel."

"I'll speak with Lena about it. Then stop by the jail to see if Gabe knows him." Finishing his brandy, he set the glass on a nearby table, rubbing his chin. "Bernie Griggs at the telegraph office knows a great deal about what goes on in town." He looked between Olivia and Josie, a promise in his eyes. "We will find him."

"Thank you, Nick. I'll say goodnight to everyone." Standing, Josie headed for the stairs, exhausted and ready to retire.

They'd gotten a lot done at the store, but it had been another long day. Olivia had spoken with Nick about their request for a center counter. He'd agreed with little discussion, offering to send an order the following morning. Now he'd be trying to track down the man who'd shown up at the store.

The stranger's appearance bothered Josie more than she wanted anyone to know. So much so that she'd removed the gun from its hiding place, deciding to keep it with her. It had been the last item she'd stuffed into her satchel before leaving New Orleans.

It had been months since she'd practiced with the weapon her brother gave her after their parents left for Europe. With Rafe living in town, he wanted Josie to have some protection, giving her lessons and making certain she felt comfortable holding, loading, and discharging it.

Josie had brought little ammunition with her. Tomorrow, she'd stop by the general store and purchase more. Even if the man never appeared again or Nick discovered his identity, she'd feel better knowing a form of protection was nearby.

The idea turned her thoughts to Dom. She'd seen him ride in today, hoping he might come see their progress with the store. Spreading out her paperwork at the front window, she'd kept watch outside, her stomach a painful knot of anxiety as she waited.

Dom never came. Instead, she saw him cross the street, disappearing into the boardinghouse.

If only she could take back what she'd said to him in Big Pine. Though convinced what she told him was true, Josie should've taken more time to think about her words, waited until they'd returned to Splendor.

It hadn't taken long to feel regret. She'd been upset about Mattie. It was a ridiculous reaction driven by insecurity and her lack of experience with men. He'd made it clear the woman was a friend from the past and nothing more.

Changing into her nightdress, Josie slipped into bed, tucking the covers under her chin. She stared at the ceiling, trying to get her mind off Dom and what couldn't be changed.

# Chapter Fourteen

"We've ordered the merchandise, arranged the cabinets and counters, hung mirrors, set lamps around, decided on prices, and ordered signs." Josie made a slow circle of the store, a sense of pride curving her lips. "There isn't much more we can do until everything arrives."

Another week had passed since Dom rode back into town, yet she hadn't seen him again after the first day. Josie had almost convinced herself their time together had been nothing but a dream.

Since returning from Big Pine, she'd had invitations from more than one man to escort her to supper. She'd turned each down, using the store as her excuse.

Olivia boosted herself up and onto a counter, leaning back to survey the room. "There are times I still can't believe we're going to be the owners of a store. We never would've been allowed to do this in New Orleans."

Boosting herself up next to her, Josie laughed. "We wouldn't have been allowed to do much of anything except wait around for the right suitor."

"I'm so glad you came," Olivia said on a long sigh. "I can't imagine being in Splendor without you."

They fell silent for a few minutes before Olivia spoke again. "It's almost April, Josie. Do you think your parents have returned from Europe?"

"Probably." She glanced away, not wanting to ruin their good moods by thinking of her family. "I've been considering the invitations to supper."

The change in subject had Olivia's eyes going wide. "And?"

"I believe it's time for me to, well, get to know more people. I've decided to accept one or two of them."

"Truly? What a wonderful idea, Josie." Shifting toward her, Olivia's eyes sparked with enthusiasm. "Which one will you accept?"

"I believe the one from Hex Boudreaux."

Olivia's face brightened. "He's a wonderful choice. Handsome, with a good job. Gabe trusts him, so that says a great deal about him. And he's from New Orleans." Her brows furrowed a moment. "You aren't doing this to hurt Dom, are you?"

She responded with a wave of her hand. "He feels nothing except possibly friendship for me, Livvy. We never truly courted." Josie thought of their heated kisses, the way she'd felt in his arms, and shivered. Their brief moments together had been wonderful and sweet. She missed them. Missed him.

"You did spend a good deal of time together. More than would be expected from a man who has no interest in you."

Josie shook her head. "I haven't seen him since we returned to Splendor almost a month ago. He hasn't stopped by the house or the shop. Accepting a supper invitation from another man won't bother Dom at all." Her mouth drew into a thin line. "I'm not doing this to hurt him, Livvy. I'm doing it for me."

Nodding slowly, Olivia slid to the floor. "I do believe it's time you did something besides worry about our store. Supper with Deputy Boudreaux will be a wonderful change for you, Josie."

*Yes, it will be,* she thought, slipping to the floor next to Olivia. "There is one problem. How to get Hex to approach me again."

*Big Pine*

"Another." Hex lifted his empty glass toward the bartender before using the mirror behind the bar to scan the saloon.

Several tables were filled with men drinking and playing cards. A few scantily clad women moved between the tables, making certain the customers were content while offering other personal services.

"Are you sure you want to head to Denver?" Zeke Boudreaux shoved his empty glass forward for the bartender to fill. "You haven't seen her for years."

Hex glared at his brother. "And I won't see Alice now." The bitter words were followed by a large swallow of whiskey.

Flinching, Zeke stared into his glass. "Sorry." Bringing the glass to his lips, he tipped it back. Swiping an arm over his mouth, he shifted to face him. "But it's curious. Why would her mother go to all the trouble of finding you to tell you about Alice's death? It's been close to five years since you last saw her. And that was in New Orleans."

Resting his arms on the edge of the bar, Hex sucked in a slow, ragged breath. "I had asked Alice to marry me."

Zeke's brows shot up in surprise. "What?"

"She turned me down. Told me she had no intention of marrying. Ever."

"You must've loved her."

Holding up his glass again, he gave a terse nod. "I thought she loved me. Especially after..." Hex let the last go unsaid.

Zeke swore as the meaning became clear. "You fell in love and took her to bed, thinking she'd marry you."

"Yeah."

"You never said anything about her until you got the telegram," Zeke bit out, angry his brother hadn't mentioned a woman who'd meant a great deal to him.

Hex turned to glare at him, his face hard as granite. "What would I have said?" Jaw tightening, he gripped the glass so hard it was in danger of breaking. "What would you have said if you were in my place?"

Zeke's throat worked as he remembered the days before he and Hex had decided to leave New Orleans. Their mother died not long after his birth, leaving their father bereft. Although he'd done his best to raise two boys while keeping their plantation profitable, he'd never been the same.

When the war began, the boys stayed as long as possible to help their father, finally joining the Confederates. Their father died not long after they returned from the war. Still, they'd done their best to revive the family plantation. Lack of funds and men to work the fields brought them to the hardest decision of their lives.

They'd been fortunate to find a buyer from Pennsylvania. A few weeks later, they packed up their necessities and left for Texas. Sometime during those weeks, Hex had fallen in love, yet Zeke never knew about it. Until today.

Clasping a hand on Hex's shoulder, he didn't respond to his brother's question. "I should ride with you to Denver."

"No."

"I can send a telegram to Gabe, let him know."

"You aren't going with me, Zeke." His voice was tight, uncompromising. "This is a trip I have to make alone."

*Splendor*

"I'm looking for the sheriff."

Caleb and Dutch stared at the stranger, taking in the set of his shoulders, the way his gunbelt sat low on his hips. He had the look of a hired gun.

"He's not here. Is there something we can help you with?" Caleb stood, keeping his gaze locked on the stranger.

"If you don't mind, I'll wait." Grabbing a chair, he rotated it, resting his arms on the back as he straddled it. "I'm guessing you boys work for the sheriff."

Dutch studied him, giving a curt nod. "You'd be right." He held out his hand. "I'm Dutch McFarlin. That's Caleb Covington."

Grasping the hand, he nodded at both before shaking Caleb's outstretched hand. "Chandler. Most people call me Chan."

Rubbing his jaw, Caleb's gaze locked on his. "Chan. There's a gunslinger down south by that name."

He shrugged. "That so?"

Caleb began to answer when the door burst open, Gabe stepping inside. Removing his hat, he looked at the deputies, not noticing the man sitting behind him. "There are more reports of rustling. This time at the Miller ranch."

Caleb snorted, remembering their experiences with the eldest Miller and his sons last year. Several years before, the ranch had been divided in three parts, each man taking possession of one.

"Did you talk to Morgan or Curt?" Dutch asked.

"Not sure I'd trust either one," Caleb said.

Crossing his arms, Gabe scowled at both. "Curt's foreman was in the general store. You two need to head out and learn what you can. It's doubtful you'll find much, but the Millers aren't men we want to rile."

Standing, Dutch adjusted his gunbelt. That was when Gabe's gaze landed on the other man. Stepping closer, he settled his hands on his hips, looking down at him.

"Something I can do for you?"

Slowly, Chandler raised his face, staring into eyes so much like his own. Instead of the reception he'd envisioned, strong hands grabbed his shirt, hauling him up before kicking away the chair.

"Dammit, Chan. Where the hell have you been?"

"I think it's a wonderful idea, Livvy. No one would see us, and we wouldn't be gone long." Josie shifted on her bed, hoping her argument would sway her friend, who sat on a nearby chair, sifting through a dime novel. "Clay is in Big Pine getting supplies, so you know he won't be coming by to see you."

Setting down the thin book, Olivia shook her head. "If Father, Suzanne, or anyone finds out, it will get back to Clay."

"No one will find out if you don't say anything." Josie's teasing tone concealed the hope Olivia would agree to the plan. "It will be fun."

Lifting a brow, her voice held doubt. "Have you ever been to a dance show?"

"No. Have you?"

"Certainly not." Olivia's indignant smile faded. "What makes you believe it will be fun?"

Sliding off the bed, Josie walked to the window of her bedroom, drawing back the curtains to peer outside. "The men all seem to enjoy it."

Barking out an unladylike laugh, Olivia stood to join her at the window. "Of course they do, Josie. Women wearing who knows what, dancing to music you'd never hear in the drawing rooms back home. What man wouldn't enjoy it? Have you noticed none of the ladies in town have been there?"

"That isn't true, Livvy." Dropping the curtain, Josie walked back to her bed and sat down.

Rushing to sit beside her, Olivia crossed her legs. "Who has been there?"

Glancing at the door, confirming it was closed, Josie grinned. "I heard Suzanne and Lena talking about the time they, Abby, and Rachel visited the Palace."

Olivia's eyes widened. "What?"

"They arranged it with Ruby Walsh."

Brows raised, Olivia couldn't stop the gasp of surprise.

"She agreed to help them get inside and watch a show." Josie lowered her voice. "Without any of their husbands knowing. Unfortunately, Lena and Suzanne never talked about what they saw. But they both enjoyed it." She flashed an infectious smile. "We can go tonight while Suzanne is still at the boardinghouse and Nick is at the Dixie. We'll be back before either gets home."

Olivia bit her bottom lip, brows scrunched together.

Walking to her wardrobe, Josie drew the door open. "We won't wear our best clothes." She pulled out a plain gray dress, holding it up. "You have a similar one. We can wear the plainest bonnets we own."

Still not sure, Olivia stared at the dress. "I don't know, Josie. We don't even know how to get inside."

"There's a side door," she smirked.

"How would you know such a thing?"

Setting the dress on the bed, Josie sat on the edge. "That's how Ruby got the women in without anyone spotting them."

A groan broke through Olivia's lips. "You aren't going to give up on this until we go, are you?"

Josie shook her head, doing what she could to hide a grin of satisfaction. "You know I won't."

Sliding off the bed, Olivia moved to the door. "Why do I feel this is not going to end well?"

# Chapter Fifteen

"This is amazing," Josie whispered over her shoulder as she slipped inside, holding the side door open for Olivia.

They made their way along the back wall, stopping every few seconds to confirm no one had seen them. A nearby table, lost in the shadows in the back of the cavernous room, caught their attention.

"There." Josie moved to it, quietly dragging out a chair so her back was to the wall. Olivia did the same, eyes wide at the spectacle on the front stage.

A piano stood to one side, the musician tapping out a raucous tune. A fiddle leaned against a wall, but no player stood nearby. No more than fifteen men took up spaces at several tables, drinking and playing cards while shifting their gazes to the stage every few minutes.

"When does the dancing start?" Olivia asked, pulling back into the shadows when the bartender looked their way.

"I don't know. Soon, I hope."

Olivia spotted one of the serving girls talking to a group of men. "What will we do if someone sees us?"

Mouth twisting, brows scrunching together, Josie shrugged. "Order a drink?"

"Tea?"

Before she could stop it, a laugh burst from Josie's lips. Slapping both hands over her mouth, she shook her head.

Straightening in her chair, Olivia made a decision. "We'll order brandy, the same as Father drinks after supper."

Dropping her hands to her lap, Josie pursed her lips. "Anything but rum." She shivered, remembering how she felt the day after the tea party where she'd had several cups of rum toddy.

"Good evening, ladies."

A woman of average height with wavy red hair and bright emerald green eyes watched them, her mouth curved into a knowing grin. They didn't have to ask to know she was Ruby Walsh, the owner of the Grand Palace.

"Is this your first time?"

Neither had ever seen her in work clothes. A silk dress, matching the color of her eyes, flowed to the floor. The neckline dropped off her shoulders, bodice low enough for an unobstructed view of the swell of her breasts. Forcing her gaze from Ruby's striking appearance, Josie cleared her throat.

"Yes."

Pulling out a chair, Ruby sat down, resting her arms on the table. "Do Nick and Suzanne know you're here?"

Josie's eyes flashed while Olivia's widened, both shaking their heads.

Leaning forward, Ruby rested her chin in the palm of one of her hands, studying the young women. "Have either of you ever seen a dance performance before?"

"Oh, yes." Olivia brightened. "In New Orleans. My grandparents took me to the theater to see *Hamlet* and *The Merchant of Venice*. Is that the type of performance we'll see tonight?"

A throaty chuckle arose from Ruby's throat. "Not exactly."

Warming to the subject, Josie's eyes flashed in curiosity. "Please tell us what you'll be presenting."

Ruby's features softened. "Why don't I order you a sherry and we can talk more about the entertainment at the Palace?"

"May we have brandy instead?" Josie asked.

"You can have whatever you want, sweetheart." Signaling to the bartender, Ruby leaned back in her chair, an indulgent grin tipping the corners of her mouth. "Once you've had some refreshments, we'll talk about my girls and what you can expect."

Zeke, Dutch, and Dom sat around Gabe's well-worn desk, indulging in a friendly round of cards. It was all the sheriff would allow within the confines of the jail. If they wanted to bet, they could do it on their own time at the Dixie or Wild Rose.

"Your run of luck has to break at some point, Dutch." Zeke tossed his cards on the desk in a disgusted groan, followed an instant later by Dom.

"Wish this would happen when I'm at the Dixie." A wry grin curved Dutch's mouth. "Doesn't do me much good against you amateurs." Stretching his arms above his head, he stood, grabbing his cup before walking to the stove.

A soft knock had the three looking at each other. Shrugging, Zeke stood, stalking to the door and opening it.

"Ah, Sir Baker. Come on in."

Ruby's friend and assistant at the Palace, Bruno Baker, stepped inside, glancing between the three men. Clearing his throat, he raised his chin in a gesture all three had seen many times. Slight of build with a deep British accent, he always dressed as an East Coast dandy.

"Miss Ruby asked me to come here." Clearing his throat again, he continued. "There are two young women in the Palace. She thought it would be wise to let someone know."

Dom stood, meaning to leave, then stilled at Baker's next comment.

"One of them is Miss Olivia Barnett. The other is Miss Josephine Dubois."

Muttering a curse, Dom didn't wait to hear more before rushing out the door, ignoring Zeke's shout in his haste to reach the Palace. The theater and dance hall stood behind the jail, next to the clinic. It took a mere two minutes to get there.

"Dom, wait up." Zeke joined him. "We can't go charging inside."

Bruno stepped next to them. "We should go through the side door. The ladies are at a table near the back." Walking around the building, he opened the door, gesturing them inside.

The instant Dom crossed the threshold, he spotted Josie, Olivia, and Ruby. A glass of dark liquid sat in front of each. He wondered if those were their first drinks of the night. Lost in their own conversation, the women didn't notice the men approach until Dom stood right behind Josie, his hands coming down on her shoulders.

Jumping, she glanced behind her. Lips parting, she stared at him. "Dom."

His name came out in quiet welcome, not the annoyed greeting he anticipated. "Good evening, Josie, ladies. Do you mind if Zeke and I join you?"

"Why don't I leave you four to talk?" Ruby rose, gesturing for Bruno to follow.

Olivia shot a worried look at her friend. Instead of being ungracious, she nodded at the empty chairs. "Please."

Dom took a chair next to Josie, his chest tightening at being this close to her after weeks of avoiding each other. As his hungry eyes wandered over her, he found himself trying to remember why he'd stayed away. Josie said she wanted to be friends. Looking at her now, searching her face, he saw regret, hoping it was about them.

Shifting to look at the stage, he rested his arm over the back of her chair, then looked back at her. "So, you want to see a show." It wasn't a question.

Squirming in her chair, Josie gripped the glass of brandy with both hands. "We were curious."

"Are you still?"

Jutting her chin out in indignation, she glared at him. "Yes. The ladies haven't come out on the stage yet, but Ruby told us a little about what to expect."

Cocking a brow, he chuckled. "And you still want to watch a show?"

Letting out an irritated breath, she picked up the glass, taking a small sip. "Ye...yes."

Leaning toward her, he whispered next to her ear. "Are you certain?"

She shot a look at Olivia, seeing her in deep conversation with Zeke, wondering what they were talking about. If possible, she'd ignore Dom and join their discussion. It was a futile wish.

Giving a quick shake of her head, she groaned. "Not really. It isn't what Olivia and I expected."

Expression sobering, he relaxed next to her, his voice soft. "What did you expect, Josie?"

Shrugging, her face flushed. "*Hamlet*?"

The vulnerability jabbed at his conscience. Working to suppress a bark of laughter, he reached over, taking her hand in his. "It's a logical thought, Josie. This *is* a variety theater and dance hall."

Feeling his warm hand encompass hers, she felt a flash of desire so strong she had to stifle a sigh of longing. Squeezing his hand, she forced a small smile. "Even if it's not what we expected, I'm glad we came. The Palace is really quite beautiful."

Dom couldn't stop the brief chuckle. He'd never thought of Ruby's place as beautiful. Sweeping his gaze around the large room, he began rubbing the palm of her hand with his thumb.

"I suppose it is."

"Have you been here many times?" Her face flushed at a question she hadn't meant to say out loud.

Scooting his chair a few inches closer, he bent his head. "Are you asking if I came to see a show or for other reasons?" He tightened his hold when she tried to pull her hand from his.

Stiffening, she tried to move away. "Olivia and I need to get home before Nick and Suzanne return."

Face somber, he refused to loosen his hold on her hand. "I came here twice with Gabe and Nick to see the shows Ruby's girls put on. They wanted to see what drew customers to the Palace. Nothing more, Josie. The only woman I spoke with was Ruby."

She hoped her face didn't show the burning sensation moving up her cheeks. "Oh."

Standing, he helped her up. "Come on. I'll walk you and Olivia home. Once we're there, if you have time, I'd like to talk."

His words tugged at her heart. "All right."

Shoving aside the desire to bend down and kiss her, he straightened. "Good. Zeke, we should escort the women out of here. I'm sure they don't want anyone in town to know they're here." Without mentioning names, they all knew he meant Nick and Suzanne.

Standing, Zeke held his hand out to Olivia. "Are you ready to leave?"

Taking his hand, she stood. "Yes."

Giving a brief wave of thanks to Ruby, Dom tossed money onto the table, settling his hand on the small of Josie's back. It didn't take more than a few minutes to walk to the end of the short block, avoiding the main street where Nick or Suzanne might spot them.

Dom felt a slight wave of guilt at doing what he could to hide their movements. Skirting along the edges of the buildings, they reached the short trail to the Barnett house. Stopping, Zeke tipped the brim of his hat.

"Enjoy the rest of your evening, ladies. See you tomorrow, Dom."

Olivia sent him a grateful smile. "Thank you, Zeke."

"Anytime, Miss Olivia." Flashing one of his brash grins, he turned back to town.

"He's a very nice man," Olivia said as they headed toward the house. "If I didn't care so much for Clay..." Glancing at Josie, she stifled a giggle, but not a small smile.

Walking up the front steps, Dom opened the door, stepping aside for Olivia to enter. "Josie and I are going to talk for a few minutes."

"What an excellent plan. If Father or Suzanne come home, they'll believe we've been here the entire evening." Her eyes sparked with understanding before the door closed behind her.

"Is this all right?" Dom nodded toward the chairs on the porch.

Letting out a shaky breath, she nodded, taking a seat. Shoving aside her anxiety about what he planned to say, she prayed the reason Dom hadn't been to see her wasn't because he'd met someone else.

Lowering himself next to her, he reached over, settling a hand over hers before threading their fingers together. Several long moments passed, neither speaking. The sounds of the night surrounded them.

The creek rippled behind the house, frogs croaked from their spots along the water's edge, birds nested within the rushes. The sounds should've been soothing. Instead, they increased Josie's trepidation.

"I've missed you, Josie."

She let out an audible sigh of relief. "I've missed you, too."

Giving a slow nod, he smoothed his thumb over the back of her hand. "I made a mess of things when we first started spending time together. I'm hoping you'll allow me to rectify my wrongs."

Confusion clouded her eyes. "Rectify?"

Turning her hand over, he began stroking his thumb over her palm, causing her heart rate to rise. "You told me in Big Pine you only wanted to be friends. Was it the truth?"

Throat constricting, body reacting to his slow ministrations, her haunted eyes bored into him. "No."

Letting out a long, slow breath, his mouth tilted into a grin. "Good. I want to do it right this time."

"Do what, Dom?" She breathed the question out, trying to concentrate on his words, not her body heating at his continued touch.

"I know Nick isn't your father, Josie, but I plan to ask his permission to court you."

Lips parting, her heart squeezed, the beginning of hope stirring inside. "I'd like that."

Relief washed over him. Leaning toward her, he hovered his mouth inches from her lips when the sound of footsteps on the porch steps stopped his progress. Sitting up, he turned to see Nick and Suzanne standing a few feet away.

"Am I to assume you want to ask me a question, Dom?" Nick asked.

Standing, he clasped his hands behind his back. "Yes, sir."

Hearing the serious tone of Dom's voice, seeing the worried expression on Josie's face, Nick's lips twitched. "And that would be?"

"I'm asking your permission to court Josie."

Stepping forward, Nick's face broke into a smile. "It's about time."

# Chapter Sixteen

Chandler strolled around the office in Gabe's home, picking up a framed family photograph, staring at the image of their mother. He'd never received their father's telegram, telling him of her death. Nor had he known of Nora, their half-sister, a result of their father's long-term affair.

"He can be a real sonofabitch, but I do believe he loved Nora's mother."

Still holding the photograph, Chandler turned to see Gabe standing in the doorway. "Is Father capable of love? If so, I've never seen it."

Walking toward him, Gabe shook his head. "He's changed since Mother's death."

Snorting, Chandler set the photograph back on the shelf. "His mistress is dead, as is his wife. He has four sons he's spent little time around, and from what you've told me, a daughter he supported with money but little love. It would have to be a drastic change for him to turn all of that around. Sorry, Gabe, but it's hard for me to imagine."

Lowering himself into an overstuffed chair, Gabe stretched out his long legs, regarding his youngest brother. "He and a friend from New York are in San Francisco."

Chandler raised a brow. "Friend?"

"Baron Ernst Wolfgang Klaussner." His lips twitched at the surprised look on his brother's face. "He and Father met in New York. Klaussner bought land not far from Splendor and is building a house. A mansion, really. They'll be heading back here after they're finished in San Francisco."

"Father is coming back here?" Massaging his neck, Chandler poured two glasses of whiskey, handing one to Gabe before taking a chair across from him.

"He showed up here early last summer to explain about Mother and take Nora back to New York with him. You'll meet her and her husband, Wyatt Jackson, at supper tomorrow. Instead of Nora leaving, Father stayed here. Eventually, he'll need to return to New York, but he's been talking about building a house near town."

Choking on a sip of whiskey, he shook his head. "Father plans to live here?"

"That's what he says. If you stay, Chan, you and Father will have to come to some type of truce."

"It's not as if we fought, Gabe. As the youngest, he rarely noticed me at all." Rolling his glass between his forefinger and thumb, he stared at the amber liquid. "Weldon and Lawrence weren't any better," he said, mentioning the two brothers between him and Gabe. "The decision to leave for a different life wasn't difficult."

"What about Mother? She always doted on you."

That drew a bitter laugh. "Her attention was for show. She saw me for maybe five minutes each day, leaving the nanny to serve in her place. Social obligations and Father's commitments were her first and only priorities."

Leaning forward, Gabe rested his arms on his knees. "What have you been doing, Chan?"

Tossing the last of the whiskey down his throat, he thought back on the last few months. "My last job was as a Texas Ranger. Before that, a gun for hire, gambler, and a bodyguard for a prominent rancher. Except for the Rangers, all were good money. I don't have to work at all for at least a year."

"Mother left all of us a trust."

Chandler's brows rose. "I didn't know."

Standing, Gabe grabbed a piece of paper from his desk, handing it to his brother. "We'll get a telegram off tomorrow so you'll have immediate access." Crossing his arms, he leaned against the edge of his desk, watching various emotions pass over Chandler's face.

Still staring at the slip of paper providing information on the trust, his mother's death became real. "Did Father take another mistress after, well....after Nora's mother and ours died?"

"I didn't ask. Nora's mother died years ago. It's doubtful he took up with someone else while Mother was still alive." Shrugging, he blew out a weary breath. "I could be wrong. I often was when it concerned Father. Are you planning to stay in Splendor?"

Folding the paper, Chandler slipped it into a pocket. "I don't know."

"You'll stay here while you decide."

"I've got a room at the St. James."

"I'll take care of it. There's plenty of room here at the house. Besides, it'll give you time to get to know my wife, Lena, and our son, Jack." A grin appeared on his face. "We're expecting another baby in a few months."

Shoving up, Chandler set his glass next to the decanter. "Congratulations. You've done well for yourself, Gabe." His voice held no hint of jealousy. "If you're sure there's enough room."

"For as long as you want, Chan."

*East of Big Pine*

Rafe Dubois stared out the window of the stagecoach, body aching, eyes gritty, and throat dry from the unending swirls of dirt. He'd taken a train route ending in Cheyenne, Wyoming, before boarding the stage for the rest of the trip to Splendor.

The report from the Pinkerton agent had come days after the memorial service for his parents. After providing Teezy with copious instructions during his absence, Rafe met with his banker and accountant, then packed for the long trip.

The agent's report included a note on Josie's condition. *Happy, content, opening a business with the daughter of a prominent Splendor citizen.* Rafe knew the agent meant Olivia Moreau Barnett, his sister's best friend. The reason she'd traveled to the remote frontier town in the first place.

*Happy and content.*

The words rolled around in Rafe's head, making him wonder if he'd made a mistake coming after her. Learning Josie's location, he could've sent a telegram to explain the death of their parents, the same as he'd been notified. The news had been a blow, one he didn't want her to go through alone. Olivia would be there, but it wouldn't be the same as having her older brother nearby. They'd always been close. He supposed that was the reason her leaving had been such a shock.

Hearing the driver call out their next stop, Big Pine, he leaned out the open window. He lasted seconds before drawing back inside, choking on the thick dust.

A few minutes later, he and the other passengers, wide-eyed and curious, stood on the boardwalk of the territorial capital. The town was larger than Rafe expected. From his vantage point, he could see several saloons, hotels, restaurants, a saddlery, millinery, and haberdashery. There were many more, which he wished he had a little time to explore.

They'd been given thirty minutes to grab some food before the stage would leave for Splendor. Or he could wait several days for another stage. Or…

Rafe stepped inside the stagecoach office, spotting the clerk behind a counter. "How far to Splendor by horse?"

Looking up, the slim man with thinning hair shoved his spectacles up his nose. "Depends on the horse and how fast you ride." A grin didn't accompany the droll tone.

Rafe stepped closer. "Prime horse with an excellent rider."

Rubbing his jaw, he studied Rafe. "Well, about six hours. 'Course, that's if you don't come across any Indians or bandits. You got a gun and plenty of ammunition?"

"A gun and a rifle, but I'll need more bullets."

"You just might live through the trip. Or you can continue on the stage. It'll get you there in about five hours."

Rafe glanced outside once more before turning back to the clerk. "I want my bags to go on to Splendor. They can be left at the St. James Hotel."

"If that's what you want." The clerk's head lowered to whatever he'd been reading. "Let the driver know, then grab whatever you need from the stage."

Explaining what he intended to the driver, he removed a small satchel and rifle from inside the coach before handing the man a coin. Kissing it, the driver slipped it into his pocket.

"Your belongings will be at the St. James, mister. Hope you get there in one piece."

Rifle in one hand, satchel in the other, Rafe headed down the boardwalk. Crossing the threshold of the Imperial Hotel, he spent a few minutes registering before plying the man behind the counter with questions. By the time he tossed his satchel onto the bed of his upstairs room, he had the information needed to purchase a horse, saddle, and other tack.

Fifteen minutes later, he sat in a hot bath, an unlit cigar between his lips, the thought of a hot meal and good night's sleep within reach.

"These are wonderful." Josie unwrapped the perfumed soaps, lining them up on a counter next to scented powders and pomades.

"Look at these." Olivia held up packages of stockings and corsets. "These are supposed to be the best available." Setting them aside, she opened the third box, squealing at the contents.

"What's in there?" Walking over, Josie looked over her shoulder.

"Hairpins, face cream, and those little bottles of red liquid you insisted on buying."

"They're rouge, Livvy." Josie reached inside the crate, pulling out another wrapped package. Peeking inside, she smiled. "It's those beautiful tea infusers and the Clobbered tea jar. I'm so glad you talked me into these." Digging further, she unwrapped jars filled with expensive candies not available at Petermann's.

The fourth and last box contained at least five dozen books. Olivia joined her, both unwrapping, calling out the titles. *Pride and Prejudice*, *Uncle Tom's Cabin*, *Moby Dick*, *Three Musketeers*, *Wuthering Heights*, and many more.

Josie held up *The Last of the Mohicans*. "I'm certain Nora and Wyatt will buy at least a couple of these books. They love reading."

"As do Nick and Suzanne," Olivia said, unwrapping *Rip Van Winkle*.

Both stilled at the sound of the bell over the front door. Ever since the stranger had frightened them a few weeks before, they'd been cautious.

"Dom." Jumping up, Josie hurried toward him, wanting to throw her arms around his neck. Instead, she stopped inches away. "I thought you were working on your ranch today."

Looking around, the great idea he'd had earlier didn't seem so spectacular now. "I was going to invite you to ride along with me, but I see you're busy."

"She's not that busy," Olivia called.

Her lips clenched, eyes narrowing. He could see the struggle on her face. "I can't leave you to do it alone."

"Of course you can. We aren't opening the shop for at least another week, Josie. Probably longer. Go with Dom. It'll do you good to get away for a while."

She turned back to him, a tentative smile on her face. "I need a horse."

"All taken care of, Josie."

Catching her bottom lip between her teeth, she nodded. "All right. Let me get my hat and coat." Hurrying to the back, she returned less than a minute later, his stomach clenching at the excited smile on her face.

"Ready?"

"I should say something to Suzanne or Nick."

"I've spoken with both. Anything else?"

"No. I'll see you later, Livvy."

"Enjoy yourself. You, too, Dom."

Chuckling, he escorted Josie to the horses out front. "Noah saddled the mare you like." Helping her up, he handed her the reins before mounting Blue.

"Food?" she asked as they started down the main street.

Leaning back, he patted his saddlebags. "Suzanne packed some when I let her know my intentions."

It didn't take them long to get to one of several forks in the trail north. Taking one toward the east, they rode next to each other. Not long after, the trail opened up. A hundred yards ahead were buildings in various stages of completion.

"The barn is almost completed. So is the bunkhouse beyond it. The house is to the right and is going to take a few more weeks." He pointed to each as he spoke, then reined up, staring ahead.

"Is that smoke, Dom?" Josie's urgent voice preceded her kicking the mare forward.

"Stay here." Rolling a heel into Blue's side, he urged the stallion toward the thin ribbon of smoke curling up from the far side of the house. He didn't glance behind him, assuming Josie would obey his command.

If he had, Dom would've seen she didn't take orders any better than he did.

# Chapter Seventeen

Jumping off Blue before reining to a stop, Dom ran toward the source of the fire. What appeared to be a small blaze began to bloom, spreading rapidly over still damp ground toward the bunkhouse. He didn't want to consider how fast it would travel if it happened during the dry months of summer.

Taking a quick glance around, he saw none of the workers who should be there. Wasting no more time, he started back toward the front, coming to an abrupt stop. Josie stumbled forward, gripping a bucket of water.

"There's only one bucket, Dom."

Grabbing it from her hands, he headed back to the fire, pouring the contents on the worst spot.

"Give it to me." She held out her hand, gripping the handle before running back to the trough outside the barn.

Frustrated, watching the fire continue to spread, he rushed back to Blue. Grabbing his canteen and the one off Josie's horse, he ran around the house, emptying the contents. By then, she'd returned with another full bucket. He exchanged the canteens for the bucket, dumping the water over the blaze.

"Fill those as best you can." Running beside her to the only trough on the property, he glanced around again. Irritation thundered through Dom.

His father and older brother were on their way to Splendor with a small herd of Texas longhorns, the cornerstone of their new breeding program. If not extinguished before reaching the bunkhouse, the fire could set them back weeks.

Handing him the full canteens, Josie hurried into the barn, coming out with two shovels. "We can douse the fire with dirt." Handing him one, she took the canteens and ran to the house. Emptying the contents, she tossed them aside, then dug into the semi-hard ground.

A moment later, Dom joined her, shoveling and tossing the dirt onto the fire. They worked without stopping, following the path of the blaze toward the bunkhouse, until the flames died down. Tightening his grip on the handle, he stomped his boots over the last remaining spots while Josie continued to scatter dirt. A few minutes later, both stopped, their breaths coming in rapid gasps.

"We did it."

Dom would've chuckled at her comment if he hadn't been so concerned with learning how the fire started and where the men had gone. Walking to her, he placed an arm over her shoulders, pulling her close, placing a kiss on her forehead.

"Thank you. I wouldn't have been able to stop it without your help."

Leaning into him, she stared at the still smoldering embers.

Dropping his shovel to the ground, he wrapped both arms around her. Resting his chin on the top of her head, he closed his eyes.

After a few minutes, he pulled away, bending to kiss her lips. The brief contact ended at the sound of horses riding toward them.

Bull and several others from Redemption's Edge reined to a stop around them. Sliding to the ground, he walked toward the charred ground, lifting a brow at Dom.

"Where are the men?"

"I'd hoped you could tell me."

Taking another look around, Bull stalked to the bunkhouse. Throwing open the door, he muttered a low curse, then motioned for Dom and the others to hurry over. Not waiting for them, he stepped inside, bending down to loosen the gag in one man's mouth.

"What the hell happened?" Bull bit the question out, moving to the man's bound wrists and ankles. By then, Dom and the others, including Josie, were inside, helping untie the other two men.

Rubbing his wrists, the first man shoved himself up. "A Crow raiding party rode in before we had a chance to grab our rifles. They tied us up, stole all our provisions, and started the fire." Scratching the back of his head, he looked around the bunkhouse. "I don't know why they didn't kill us."

"Too risky," Bull said. "Not only would we go after them, but so would Gabe and his deputies, along with Colonel McArthur at Fort Connall." He turned to one of the men from Redemption's Edge. "Ride back and get enough supplies for a few days. Let them know what happened here. The rest of us will get to work finishing the barn and bunkhouse." Bull stalked to the door where Dom stood, waiting.

Hiring Bull to draw the plans and hire the workers had been a good decision. One of two foremen at the Pelletier ranch, he'd grown up helping his father construct buildings along the Ohio River waterfront. He also had a deep knowledge of the local Blackfoot and Crow tribes, knew the other ranchers in the area, and had a good relationship with the businessmen and women in town.

Dom stared beyond the burnt earth to the woods beyond, making a slow circle to survey the rest of the property. "I need to hire more men to help complete the house and guard against future attacks. I'll put out the word as soon as I return to town."

"Dax and Luke can spare me and the four men here today, but I don't know for how long."

"You'll be needed to start spring roundup soon."

Bull nodded. "I suspect it'll be about the same time the longhorns arrive."

"Then we'll need to get the house finished before then."

Scratching his jaw, Bull motioned for Dom to follow him away from the others. "I spoke to Mal Jolly about a possible foreman job at a neighboring ranch. He's interested, but you'll need to speak with Dax and Luke."

The ride back to town took little time, but didn't include the excitement of the ride out. Dom's thoughts were on the raid, Mal Jolly, and the need for more men. There were always a few looking for work, whether to provide them funds to leave or to build a life near Splendor. Most were hard workers, willing to do whatever their new boss asked.

"Nick and Gabe seem to always know about men looking for work," Josie said. "Silas Jenks at the lumber mill and Noah Brandt also seem to know much about what's going on."

Reaching over, Dom grasped her hand as they neared the edge of town. "Have supper with me tonight."

She didn't hesitate. "All right."

"We'll go to McCall's. It will be more private and quieter than either the boardinghouse or Eagle's Nest." Squeezing her hand, he pulled his away. "I'll call on you at six. That will give us more time alone."

A burst of laughter left her lips. "We've been together most of the day."

A wolfish grin lifted the corners of his mouth. "Not alone."

Stomach fluttering, she shot him a flushed look. "We won't be alone at McCall's."

"We will be during our slow walk to and from the restaurant. There'll be nothing requiring us to hurry tonight."

Dismounting at the livery, Dom took the reins of both horses, walking them to the stable in back. Following behind, Josie caught up with him, turning to see Noah join them.

"How's the ranch coming along?" Nodding at Josie, he removed the saddle and tack from the mare.

"A band of Crow raided sometime this morning." Dom slid the blanket and saddle off Blue, placing them on a nearby rack.

Noah's hands stilled. "Are the men all right?"

"There were three men working when the raid occurred. The Crow bound them, stole food and other supplies, and set a fire near the house. If Josie and I hadn't arrived when we did, it might've spread to both the house and bunkhouse. Bull and some men from the Pelletier ranch arrived right after we got the fire put out."

"We need more buckets." Josie flushed, realizing what she'd said. "Well, *you* need to buy more."

Chuckling, he glanced at Noah, whose lips twitched. "And a couple more troughs. There's plenty of water from the well, and the creek runs behind the house." Dom's somber face met Noah's. "I need at least four more men."

"You could talk with Lena. She and Gabe believe one of the mines is playing out."

Dom nodded, eyes flickering in understanding "They could be losing men."

"You might also send a telegram to Sheriff Sterling. He'll spread the word around Big Pine."

"Thanks, Noah. I'll get a message right off."

"And you and Josie will join Abby and me for supper on Friday. Assuming you aren't called out of town."

Dom shot a questioning look at Josie, who nodded.

"We'd be glad to join you, Noah." And with those few words, Dom recognized how important Josie had become.

"I believe these are the last of the items we ordered." Josie held up a selection of silk brocade men's vests, plus another group of embroidered silk waistcoats. Beautifully detailed leather belts, men's accessories, and ivory handled brushes with matching mirrors were also included.

Olivia opened another crate. "It's the women's wear we ordered." The top half contained intricate knit stockings, corsets made of fine satin in reds, blues, and greens with fine lace trim, and ribbons not available at Petermann's. Moving to the last crate, she levered off the top and began to dig inside. "This one contains the candles and candlesticks." She checked further. "There's also the Spode china, Minton vases, and majolica vases, pitchers, and platters."

Standing, Josie wiped her hands down one of the aprons Suzanne provided. "It's going to take days to price and place everything. I'll get the journal."

Everything they'd selected had been listed in the thick journal, including descriptions, cost, and estimated retail price. Entries also identified specific wholesale vendors and the name of the drummer, if one had been used to gain access to the product.

As a precaution, Nick had persuaded them to keep the journal in the safe they'd brought back with them from Big Pine. Using the key and combination, Josie opened the safe, pulling out the journal. Closing but not locking the door, she glanced at the desk against one wall.

On top sat a vase with a single flower. Dom had given her both when he called on her the night before. After they returned from McCall's, she'd set it on the night table in her room. In an impulsive move, she'd grabbed it before walking to the shop with Olivia.

A smile crossed her face each time she saw it. No one had ever given her flowers. It was a sweet surprise she refused to take for granted. Picking it up, she took the vase and journal to the front, not seeing the man who'd entered while she'd been gone.

Setting the vase down, she turned toward Olivia, mouth dropping open in surprise. Her chest constricted, legs heavy as she walked forward.

"Rafe," she breathed out before running to him. Jumping into his open arms, she wrapped hers around his neck. "How did you find me?"

Setting her down, he rested his hands on her shoulders. "It wasn't easy. Teezy suggested I check for letters." He held up a hand when she opened her mouth to protest. "There's a very good reason it became imperative to find you, Josie. Once I explain, I'm certain you'll forgive me for rummaging through your belongings."

The three glanced at the front door at the sound of the bell. Stepping inside, Dom's gaze moved over them, landing on a man he didn't know whose hands gripped Josie.

"Dom." Moving out of Rafe's grasp, she walked to him. "Are you riding out to the ranch?"

Keeping his attention on the stranger, he nodded. "I'll be gone most of the day, but wanted to see if you're available for supper."

Seeing his narrowed gaze focusing behind her, Josie turned. "Dom, this is my brother, Rafael Dubois. Rafe, this is Dominic Lucero. He's a U.S. Marshal."

Closing the distance between them, Rafe held out his hand. "Good to meet you, Marshal."

"Dom," he said, clasping the offered hand. "What brings you to Splendor?" He didn't ask how he'd found Josie.

Rafe's face paled before he let out a breath. Shifting, he looked at Josie, shoving aside the flash of pain. "It's a private family matter."

"Family matter?" Josie asked, a knot of dread forming in her stomach.

"Perhaps we should go somewhere private."

Shaking her head, she reached out, grasping Dom's hand. "Livvy is my closest friend, and Dom, well...he's..." She sent him a pleading glance.

"I'm courting your sister, Rafe."

Eyes widening for an instant, he stilled his features. Josie and he would discuss her interest in the lawman later. The news he had couldn't wait any longer.

"All right. Dom, would you mind locking the front door?"

Nodding, he locked it before returning to Josie's side, threading his fingers through hers.

Rafe's haunted eyes latched onto Josie. "You may want to sit down."

Worry creasing her features, she shook her head. "You're scaring me. Please, just tell me."

"If you're sure." At her nod, Rafe sent a warning look at Dom, alerting him to the extreme seriousness of what he had to share. "It's Mother and Father."

Sucking in a breath, she moved closer to Dom.

"The ship bringing them home from Europe..." Swallowing, he ignored the tightening in his chest. "Their ship encountered an unexpected storm. Some people made it to lifeboats and were rescued."

"Mother and Father?" Her voice broke on the question.

He shook his head. "I'm sorry, sweetheart. They didn't make it."

Dom slipped his arms under her, sensing her knees buckling. An instant later, she fainted. "Get some water, Olivia."

Rafe stepped to them, arms outstretched. "I'll take her."

Dom shook his head, moving across the room to an empty counter. Laying her on top, he stroked hair from her face, leaning close. "Josie?"

"She never faints." Rafe stood next to him, face etched in concern.

"It happens when learning your parents are dead."

Scrubbing a hand down his face, Rafe turned, settling a hip against the counter. "I didn't find out her location until after the services."

"Dom?" Josie's soft, confused voice caught their attention.

"I'm here, sweetheart."

Rafe's brows rose, but he said nothing.

"Here, Dom." Olivia handed him a cup filled with water.

Sliding a hand under her head, he held the cup for her. "Drink a little water."

Taking a small sip, Josie placed a hand on her chest to quell the intense ache. "Mother and Father are dead?"

"Yes," Rafe answered.

Shaking off Dom's offer of more water, she braced her arms on the counter, trying to sit up.

"Let me help you." Slipping an arm under her back, he helped her when she swung her legs over the edge.

"How long?" she asked Rafe.

"Several weeks, Josie. I didn't know how to reach you. That's when I searched your room and found your letters from Olivia. Instead of a telegram, I contacted Pinkerton in Chicago."

Dom nodded as the pieces came together. "The man who came into the shop. He must've been an agent."

Taking a slow breath, she slid to the floor. "I suppose you've already taken care of the services."

"A few weeks ago. I learned you were here a couple days later and made travel plans." Moving to stand in front of her, Rafe took her hands in his. "As soon as you pack your belongings, I'll take you home."

# Chapter Eighteen

Straightening, Josie pulled her hands from Rafe's, glaring at her brother. "Home?"

"Of course. With Mother and Father gone, you have responsibilities that can't be put off any longer."

Seeing Josie's features harden, face flush, Olivia stepped closer, placing a hand on Rafe's arm. "Perhaps it would be best if you discuss this later. She's had a shock and needs some time." She sent a pleading glance at Dom.

"Why don't I take you home, Josie? You can lie down for a bit."

"Home?" Rafe growled.

"She lives with my father, stepmother, and me," Olivia said. "The house is just beyond the edge of town. I'm certain they'll invite you to stay with us, Rafe."

The tension between the four increased as the silence continued. After a few long minutes, Dom wrapped an arm around Josie's shoulders, pressing her to his side.

"Why don't you three go to Nick's and talk? I'll let him and Suzanne know what's happening, then join you." He felt Josie turn her face into his shoulder, heard a muffled sob. Stroking her hair, his attention focused on Rafe, allowing Josie to release her sorrow. "You need to hear what these ladies have planned, what they've accomplished." Dom glanced around the shop. "It's impressive."

Rafe took the hint. They needed to concentrate on one issue at a time, the most important being the deaths of their parents. Stepping to them, he held out his arms.

"Come on, Josie. We'll go to the house, make you some tea, and I'll answer your questions about what happened to Mother and Father."

Lifting her head, eyes red, face wet with tears, she moved into her brother's arms.

"I just need to lock the back door." Olivia hurried away, returning a moment later with their coats and reticules. "It isn't far, Rafe. Do you have a horse?"

He nodded to the outside. "The chestnut gelding."

"The livery is on the way. You can leave him with Noah Brandt."

Dom opened the door. "I'll take him over while you get Josie home." When she pulled from Rafe's arms and started toward Dom, he shook his head. "I won't be long." His mouth twisted into a sardonic grin, eyes glinting. "Maybe you and Olivia can make one of your infamous toddies for me."

Dom found Nick, Gabe, and Chandler standing at the bar of the Dixie. Greeting each, he leaned an elbow on top, turning to look at Nick.

"Josie's brother arrived from New Orleans an hour ago. He's been trying to find her for months. Their parents died when their ship encountered a bad storm. Some passengers made it. Mr. and Mrs. Dubois didn't."

Noticing the pallor of Dom's face, Nick signaled the bartender for a whiskey. "Here." Sliding the glass to him, Nick ran a hand through his hair. "Where is she?"

"I asked her brother, Rafe, and Olivia to take her home." Tossing back the drink, he swallowed, feeling the burn of the dark liquid. Setting the glass down, he pushed away from the bar. "I'm heading over there now." Giving the men a curt nod, he walked toward the door, then shifted back around. "Rafe plans to take her back to New Orleans when he leaves."

Dom made it a few feet along the boardwalk before Nick joined him. "Did he tell her that?"

Giving a disgusted snort, Dom nodded. "Sure did. After hearing about her parents, she wasn't too receptive to him ordering her to pack up."

Chuckling, Nick waved to a couple across the street. "Wish I'd have been there. Have you told Suzanne about all this?"

"Not yet. Thought I'd stop on my way to your house."

"I'll do it. You go ahead. Josie's pretty strong, but she may need you there if her brother pushes too hard. If I know my wife, we won't be far behind you."

Dom figured the same. Suzanne was as protective of Olivia and Josie as if they were her own. In her mind, they were. The same as several other young women in town.

"Thanks, Nick. I'll see you at the house."

Increasing his pace, Dom thought of all the work waiting for him at the ranch. He'd sent three men to speak with Bull this morning, hoping at least a couple would stay on. Even with his experience growing up on the family ranch, he'd learned how different raising cattle was in Montana compared to Texas. Harsh winters, the change in grazing land, and distance to market made ranching a challenge most men weren't prepared to confront.

Dom admired the Pelletiers and what they'd accomplished. They also seemed to find and hire the best men. He needed someone like Bull or Dirk Masters, the other foreman at Redemption's Edge. Maybe Mal Jolly would be that man. In the meantime, he'd take whatever help Dax and Luke offered.

Bounding up the steps to the front door, he didn't bother knocking before stepping inside. The instant he did, the sound of loud voices, primarily Josie's, drew him to the kitchen.

"I'm not going to talk with you about leaving, Rafe. Olivia and I plan to open our shop in a week. I've made friends."

"Including the marshal," Rafe grumbled.

Fisting both hands on her waist, Josie glared at him. "And what is wrong with Dom?" She held up a hand. "If I may guess, is it because he isn't of our social standing, doesn't come from wealth?"

Dom stood outside the kitchen door, wincing at the not quite accurate assessment of his family. Reminding himself neither he nor Sylvia had shared much about their family's circumstances, he made a show of clearing his throat before striding into the kitchen.

"Hope I'm not interrupting." Moving to Josie, seeing her face flushed, eyes sparking, he slipped an arm around her waist. "Did you make the hot toddy I requested?"

Olivia choked out a laugh, ready to move beyond the tension. "I'll make a pot of tea."

Tugging Josie closer, he leaned down. "How are you doing?"

"Fine," she gritted out, still glaring at Rafe, who held up his hands in surrender.

"Where is she?" Suzanne entered the kitchen, taking a swift look around before opening her arms to Josie. "I am so sorry."

Nick was a few feet behind her, holding out his hand to the man he assumed to be the brother. "Nick Barnett."

"Rafe Dubois."

"Sorry to hear about your parents."

Lips thinning, he nodded. "Thank you. It wasn't something I expected for many years."

Studying the young man, Nick could still see the pain on his face weeks after the loss. "You'll be staying with us while you're in Splendor."

"I don't want to intrude."

"It's no intrusion at all. And I'm certain Josie would prefer having you close."

After the anger of a few minutes before, Rafe wasn't as sure. "Thanks, Nick. I'll need to get my bag. It was delivered by coach to the St. James."

"I'll take care of that for you. Let me speak with Josie, then I'll show you upstairs." Moving to the women, he hugged Josie. "I'm sorry, sweetheart. Whatever we can do..." He let the rest trail off, knowing she'd understand his meaning.

Pulling away, Josie offered a small smile. "Thank you, Nick." Seeing Dom leaning against a counter, she moved to him, comforted when he threaded his fingers through hers.

"Can I talk you into taking a walk?"

A grateful expression crossed her face. "Sounds wonderful."

Leading her to the back door, Dom turned to the others. "We're taking a walk. We won't be gone long." Ignoring the disquieted expression on Rafe's face, he ushered her outside. "Along the creek?"

She tightened her grip on his hand, nodding.

They walked in silence for several minutes, Dom giving her the solitude she seemed to need. Reaching the creek, he took the narrow trail along the edge. Before long, they came upon a fallen tree, old and long ago stripped of any foliage.

"Do you want to sit down?"

Nodding, she lowered herself onto the log, staring into the rippling water. Sitting beside her, Dom placed an arm around her shoulders, pressing a kiss against her hair.

The comfortable silence stretched on, neither moving. Dom didn't know how much time passed, Josie lost in her thoughts, him wishing he could do more.

Leaning down, he lifted her chin with a finger, brushing a kiss across her lips. It was meant to be comforting, getting her mind off the grief for a few minutes. When her hands snaked up his arms to wrap around his neck, thoughts of comfort turned to passion. The kiss became urgent, filled with hunger.

Lifting her onto his lap, their mouths fused together. What had been a gentle searching became demanding, tendrils of desire rushing through them. Tongues colliding, they explored each other, moaning their pleasure as the passion increased.

One strong, broad hand moved to her hip, caressing as he shifted her closer. Raising his head, he nibbled at her earlobe before searing a path down her neck to the hollow at the base of her throat. Stroking his hair, she whimpered when his hand moved up, settling over the fabric below the curve of her breast. A moment later, his lips recaptured hers, their hunger growing.

In the distance, the sound of a door slamming and footsteps crunching on fallen leaves had Dom easing away on a regretful groan. Settling her next to him, he swiped errant strands of hair from her face as their breathing began to calm.

"Dom? Josie?" Nick's voice rang over the sounds of the rippling water.

"Here, Nick," Dom called, flashing her a grin before looking over his shoulder. Seeing the worried expression on the older man's face, he stood.

"What is it?"

"Bernie brought this telegram for you. Apologies, but I already read it. Didn't want to bother the two of you unless it seemed urgent."

Which meant it was. Taking it from Nick's hand, he read through it, color draining from his face. "My father was injured during the drive. Cruz took him to the clinic in Big Pine." Lowering the telegram, his brows furrowed. Turning, he held out a hand for

Josie, whose glassy brown eyes searched his. "I need to go."

Josie gave a slow nod. "Of course you do." Seeing the hesitation, she tightened her fingers on his. "I'm fine, Dom. Go to your father."

"Nick, would you send a rider to let Bull know where I am and the news on the herd?"

"I will, but you should take someone with you. If the Crow are active again, the trail between here and Big Pine could be trouble."

Running a hand down his face, his mouth twisted. "There's no one to ask."

"Rafe."

Eyes widening, the men looked at Josie.

"He's an excellent rider," she said. "And he has nothing urgent pressing, except to bother me about returning to New Orleans."

"It's not a bad idea," Nick added. "Let him see how life is out here. I'll wager he's never seen a cattle drive. And it will give Josie time to adjust to the news about their parents without Rafe hovering."

Grimacing, Dom removed his hat, threading fingers through his hair. "Do you think he knows how to shoot?"

"I know he does." Josie shot him a satisfied grin. "He's won competitions with both his pistol and rifle."

"Doesn't mean he'd shoot a man," Dom countered.

"If he's in danger, Rafe will shoot to survive," Nick answered. "Take him along. It'll give you two time to settle your disagreements."

"Or kill each other," he muttered under his breath.

After a good deal of persuading by Nick, Suzanne, Dom, and Josie, Rafe agreed. He had to admit his curiosity about cattle drives was the deciding factor. It certainly wasn't to spend several days with a man determined to have Josie stay in Splendor.

Packing saddlebags, Rafe took a few minutes to speak with Josie alone before joining Dom at the livery. Noah already had his horse saddled.

"Do you have plenty of ammunition?" Dom asked from atop Blue.

Thanking Noah and taking the reins, Rafe slid his rifle into the scabbard and mounted. "Enough."

"I need to send a reply to my brother before we ride out."

Sitting atop Ajax outside the telegraph office, Rafe took time to look around. Although not as large as Big Pine, Splendor had a good number of shops, two saloons, one hotel, and the boardinghouse. He'd been surprised to learn how many businesses Nick and Suzanne owned or had partnered with others.

The vehemence from Josie about not leaving had been unexpected. Rafe had a hard time understanding why an educated, refined young woman would choose a small frontier town over the constant activity of New Orleans. Mostly, he couldn't reconcile how she'd come to build such a fondness for a man who made little money doing a dangerous job.

Dom didn't seem a bad sort. He just wasn't the man for Josie. Rafe believed any number of his friends back home would be much more suitable, if they could handle her independent ways.

So lost in thoughts of his sister, Rafe hadn't noticed Dom reining Blue next to him. "Are you ready?"

"Let's go," Rafe answered, following him out of town.

Almost an hour passed in silence, both watching the territory around them. Dom had mentioned what happened at his ranch, but no one seemed too concerned about the Crow attacking riders on the trail to Big Pine. Even if food was scarce, they'd be more likely to raid ranchers with stores of supplies rather than men with little in their saddlebags. Still, the knowledge of what could happen stayed with Rafe, making him more cautious than usual.

"What are your intentions toward Josie?"

Dom didn't take his gaze from the nearby hills as he responded. "Honorable."

"Do you truly believe you can support my sister on the wages of a marshal? She's used to much better."

How well Dom knew it. "It doesn't seem to bother Josie."

"She's a woman ruled by emotions. Of course the money, or lack of it, doesn't matter. Not now anyway. In a year or two, it could matter a great deal."

Dom snorted a chuckle. "Are we talking about the same woman? From what I've seen, she has a solid grasp of life and a good mind. She'd shrivel up if forced to become one of those women expected to have a fulfilling life by hosting teas and soirées." Feeling his temper beginning to rise, he bit back what else he wanted to say.

"You saw her today. She broke down."

Blowing out a curse, Dom shot Rafe a withering look. Before he could reply, Blue and Ajax began to dance around. Glancing over his shoulder, Dom stiffened.

"Hope you're as good on a horse and with your weapons as Josie says."

"Why?" Rafe turned at shouts from behind them.

"Because there's a band of Crow after us. Ride!"

# Chapter Nineteen

Chandler took the trail Nick said would lead to Dom's ranch. With nothing better to do, he hadn't hesitated to ride out and let the man in charge know about Dom's father. It took little time to reach the property.

The barn came into view first, followed by the bunkhouse. From this far away, both appeared completed, which explained why all the men he could see were working to frame what he guessed to be the main house.

Riding closer, he stiffened, letting his right hand move to the handle of his gun. A tall man with broad shoulders and authoritative air walked toward him, a rifle in his hand. Seeing him lift it, Chandler reined up about ten yards from the house.

Deciding it better to show deference than provoke the man, he raised his hands. "I'm looking for Bull Mason."

"You've found him. State your business."

"Nick asked me to ride out." He dropped his hands to rest on his thighs.

Gaze narrowing, Bull lowered the rifle. "And?"

"Dom received news his father was injured. His older brother took him to the clinic in Big Pine. Dom and Rafe rode there today."

Brow lifting, Bull stepped closer. "Who's Rafe? And who are you?"

"Mind if I get down?"

"Suit yourself."

Dismounting, he held a hand out to Bull, who clasped it. "Chan Evans. I'm Gabe's youngest brother." He almost laughed at the stunned look on Bull's face. "Rafe is Josie Dubois's brother." His features sobered. "He came to Splendor to let her know their parents died on their return trip from Europe."

"Dammit," Bull muttered, rubbing the back of his neck. "Sorry to hear that. Josie's a real fine lady." Glancing over his shoulder, he shifted back to Chan. "Gabe's brother. You must be the one who took off, the same as him."

"That's true." He nodded at the workers. "How's it coming along?"

"Slow. We need a few more men. I'm guessing the herd is closer to Splendor than we thought."

"Twenty miles south of Big Pine. How long would it take to get the herd here?" Chandler asked.

"Four days, maybe five, depending on weather. We're ready for them, but not Dom's father and brother. At the rate it's going, it'll take at least another two weeks to get the house ready."

"Where can I put my horse?"

Lifting a brow, Bull nodded toward the barn. "You staying?"

"You need help, and I have nothing else to do. Just tell me what you need."

Following Dom's lead, Rafe drew his gun, bending low in the saddle. Their horses tore up the ground, as anxious to put distance between them and the Crow as were their riders. When bullets whizzed past, Rafe turned and fired.

"How'd they get rifles?" He fired another couple shots, hitting one of their attackers.

"White traders or off dead soldiers and settlers." Dom fired twice, downing another brave.

"How much farther?"

"Too far. We'll go for those boulders up ahead and hope we can pick them off before they kill us." Dom reined left, kicking Blue twice more as they raced for cover.

Jumping from their horses, they grabbed rifles and their saddlebags, crouching behind the rocks as the shouts got closer. Aiming the rifle, Dom fired, feeling instant satisfaction as one of the Crow fell to the ground. Firing again, he clipped another, who managed to remain on his horse.

Beside him, Rafe fired three shots, missing each time. The fourth bullet hit its mark, as did the fifth. When he aimed once more, Dom placed a hand on the stock, stopping him.

"Hold up. They're either regrouping to make another attack or riding out." Digging into his saddlebag, Dom removed a box of ammunition. "Reload in case they try again. If they do, their intent will be to surround."

Glancing around, Rafe snorted. "Won't be hard to do."

Several minutes passed before four Crow riders appeared to gather those wounded or killed. Waiting with their rifles in place, Rafe and Dom watched as they quickly lifted their comrades, mounted, and rode off.

Shifting around, Rafe slumped against the boulder, slipping to the ground. Setting the rifle between his legs, he bent over, his breath irregular, thoughts jumbled.

"Never been in a fight like this?"

Shaking his head, Rafe didn't look up from his spot on the ground.

Dom clasped him on the shoulder. "You did well, for a big town boy." Straightening, he whistled.

It didn't take long for Blue to appear. Thankfully, Rafe's chestnut gelding trotted behind him. Retrieving their canteens, he offered Rafe's to him. Taking a couple small sips, Dom capped his, waiting until Rafe stood and took a swallow.

"You ready to ride out?"

Giving a terse nod, Rafe put the canteen away and mounted.

Riding alongside, Dom kept a watchful gaze both around them and on Rafe. It didn't take much to recognize the symptoms of a man who'd never been involved in an Indian attack. Or any gunfight where men were killed.

It took another hour to reach Big Pine. Riding straight to the clinic, Rafe took care of the horses while Dom hurried inside. By the time he finished at the livery, the sun had set, traffic on the main street beginning to thin. Stopping at one of the saloons, Rafe took his time sipping a whiskey while watching the goings on inside.

The piano player belted out a tinny tune, causing most of the barmaids to swing their hips to the rhythm. Rafe grinned, watching one of the ladies deliver a drink before running her hand up and down the man's arm. An instant later, she laughed when he tugged her onto his lap.

The scene made him think of the woman he'd been seeing in New Orleans since before his parents left for Europe. The thought reminded him of how he'd never see his mother or father again. Might never see the woman again, either.

When she'd asked to travel with him to Splendor, Rafe had refused. Being with her a couple nights each week filled his need for the woman. The realization of how little he cared to be around her surprised him. There'd been times he considered bringing her home, introducing her to his parents and sister. As the months passed, he understood the idiocy of the idea.

Taking another sip, he thought of Josie, the reason he'd traveled thousands of miles. Watching the ladies move between the men at various tables, he wondered if assuming his sister would be anxious to return home had been another idiotic idea.

"Assuming we can keep away infection, your father is going to be all right. He'll almost certainly have a limp for the rest of his life, but he'll be alive." The doctor looked back into the room where Antonio Lucero lay unconscious. "I'd expect him to be ornery for quite some time."

"No change there." Cruz, Dom's older brother, let out a relieved breath.

Dom offered a slight grin. "Our father can be difficult."

"Well, he'd better behave in my clinic or I'll let the sheriff take care of him."

Chuckling, Dom nodded. "Two of a kind."

"You know Sterling?"

"I'm a U.S. Marshal," Dom answered.

The doctor grinned. "Say no more. You're welcome to stay, but you can't go into the room until he's awake and I've explained his injury to him. It'll be at least two days before he can leave. Longer if he gives me any trouble."

Dom gave him a sympathetic look. "Then it could be a long stay, Doc."

*Denver, Colorado*

Hex Boudreaux stared down at the blonde terror who glared right back. He hadn't known what to expect when receiving the summons from Alice's mother. Certainly not an ill-behaved little girl who stared at him as if he were the devil.

"I'm sorry Alice never tried to find you, Mr. Boudreaux."

"Hex, Mrs. Moore," he reminded her for the second time.

Forcing a painful grin, she nodded. "Hex." Shaky hands reached for a glass on a nearby table.

"Let me help you." Hex grabbed it, holding it to the older woman's lips. When she finished, he sat down.

"I tried several times to convince her you'd want to know. After all, Alice talked about you all the time, wishing she hadn't been such a fool to let you go."

Hex ignored the sharp pain piercing his chest. "Why did you want her to contact me, Mrs. Moore?"

Before she could answer, her body spasmed with wracking coughs. Grabbing the water, he held it to her lips again.

"Sorry, but the cancer gets worse each day."

He'd already figured out an illness clawed at her, slowly taking her life.

The older woman met the gaze of the little girl, wishing their lives could be different. "Lucy is four years old. Spirited, but sweet. She's real smart and isn't any trouble. Sometimes makes meals for both of us. Cleans up after."

Confusion clouded his mind, wondering what the woman was trying to tell him.

"Lucy, why don't you get Hex a cup of coffee. We do have some, don't we?"

A combination of fear and bewilderment flashed across the young girl's face before she nodded. "Yes, Gramma." Lucy left the room, her gaze never leaving Hex's until she disappeared into the kitchen.

"She's a beautiful little girl."

Mrs. Moore's eyes lit for the briefest of moments before becoming glassy. "Yes, she is. She won't be any trouble. People tell me she acts much older than four."

Leaning forward, he rested his arms on his knees, trying to form his words so as not to sound unkind. "Mrs. Moore, I rode hundreds of miles at your request. You mentioned Alice dying, but I don't understand what that has to do with me."

Her breath caught before she coughed again, waving him away when he started to stand. Relaxing back in her chair, a regretful expression met his.

"Alice died a year after Lucy's birth."

Although she'd mentioned it in her telegram, hearing it aloud shook him. "I'm sorry, Mrs. Moore."

"I should've tried to locate you right away, before the cancer started. But my husband died several years ago and money was scarce. Certainly not enough to hire a private investigator."

Something about the look in her eyes made him squirm. Ignoring the sense of foreboding, he remained silent.

"All her belongings are packed, but I haven't told Lucy yet. I thought it best to do it with you present."

"Here's your coffee, mister." Lucy held the large cup in her small hand, extending her arms toward him. "We don't have any milk or sugar."

Taking the cup, he took a moment to study her face, seeing Alice in her blonde hair and wide, blue eyes. He saw something else in the olive tone of her skin. The same color as his and Zeke's.

"Black is fine. Thank you, Lucy."

She refused to look away as she moved next to her grandmother.

"Would you mind getting my shawl, sweetheart? I believe it's on my bed."

The look on the little girl's face showed she didn't want to leave again. Without a word, she turned and ran up the stairs.

Taking several sips of the weak coffee, he set down his cup. "I'm sorry about Alice, Mrs. Moore. She was a wonderful girl. I cared a great deal about her."

"She felt the same about you, Mr. Boudreaux."

This time, he ignored the use of his last time and her comment about Alice. "How serious is your illness?"

"I'm dying. The doctor says I have a month, maybe two. That's why I sent word to you."

Hex's stomach dropped.

"Lucy is your daughter."

*Big Pine*

"I'm not staying here another minute." Antonio Lucero tried to toss off his blanket, cursing when Dom stalled his movements.

"You're not going anywhere until the doctor gives his approval. Now, lie back down."

"Why are you here? You should be getting the ranch ready for us," Antonio growled.

"Cruz sent for me, and the ranch is coming along fine."

"How's he doing?" Cruz walked in, followed by the doctor.

Dom shook his head. "How do you think?"

Stepping next to the bed, Cruz glared down at his father. "Don't give the doctor any trouble. He saved your leg, maybe your life. We're going to do what he says."

In that moment, Dom recalled how much his older brother and father were alike. Their similarity was a major reason he'd left the family ranch. He'd found more than his sister in Splendor. The small town became the future he hoped to find.

Antonio glared at his oldest son. "You're going to do what I say, the same as always." Again, he tried to sit up.

"Not this time, Father." Dom moved to the opposite side of the bed from Cruz, both shoving their father's shoulders back down. "If I have to tie you down, I will."

They ignored the red blaze on Antonio's face.

"Dom is right. We'll both tie you to this bed, Father. The men are driving the herd and will meet us west of Big Pine in a few days. Assuming the doctor says you're ready to travel. If not, Dom and I will catch up with them before riding back for you."

"You damn sure aren't leaving here without me."

Cruz leaned down close, poking his chest. "Then you'd better get well, Father, because we don't have time for you to stall our progress."

"Never thought I'd see the day my sons would turn against me," Antonio muttered.

Dom joined Cruz in staring down at him. "We aren't turning against you, Father. We're trying to keep you alive."

# Chapter Twenty

*Splendor*

Zeke Boudreaux walked along the boardwalk, unfolding the telegram Bernie gave him. Lifting his head at a greeting, he nodded in return, then began to read, stumbling on the first sentence.

*On my way home with my daughter.*

Murmuring a curse, Zeke sat down on a nearby bench and continued reading.

*Ask Noah if he can add a bedroom to our place. Will contact you from Big Pine.*

Lowering the message to his lap, he looked up, trying to make sense of what he'd read. Hex had traveled to Denver at the request of Alice's mother. He'd tried to talk his brother into ignoring it. After all, Hex hadn't seen the woman he once loved for five years. And she had been the one to walk away.

Raising the telegram again, he read through the brief message twice more, giving himself time to adjust to the changes in their circumstances. He and Hex lived in a two bedroom house Noah owned not far from the jail. They ate most meals at the boardinghouse or McCall's, sometimes subsisting on beans, canned fruit, hardtack, and jerky from the pantry at home.

With the addition of a little girl, their life would be forever changed. Zeke figured she had to be close to four, not old enough to send to school, which meant they'd need to find someone to watch her while he and Hex worked. It also meant his brother would no longer be able to perform his deputy duties at night.

Folding the telegram and stuffing it into a pocket, he scrubbed both hands over his face.

"You doing all right, Zeke?"

Recognizing Caleb's voice, he stood, pulling the paper from his pocket. "Read this."

Scanning it, his fellow deputy blew out a slow breath. "Hex has a daughter?"

"You know as much as me." Taking back the telegram, he slid it away. "I need to speak with Noah, get some more supplies in the house, and find someone to take care of the girl when we work."

"His message doesn't say how old she is."

"Gotta be about four." Zeke explained about Hex's history with Alice and how she'd walked out.

Caleb listened, understanding Hex's difficult predicament. He'd gone through a similar quandary a few short months ago.

"I might be able to help. Isabella, Travis Dixon's wife, loves children. She takes care of Isaac while May and I work. I'm certain she'd be glad to help with the little girl. If you want, I'll talk to her." Caleb rubbed his brow. "You know Noah will do whatever he can about another bedroom. 'Course, someone can always sleep on the floor for a while."

"True." Zeke suspected that person would be him. "I would appreciate you talking with Isabella. The telegram came from Denver."

"They taking the stage?" Caleb asked.

"Hex rode his horse. I don't know his plans for getting her back to Splendor. Guess I'd better go speak with Noah. Maybe I'll adjust from the shock by then."

*I'm an uncle,* Zeke thought as he headed toward the livery, a goofy smile forming on his face. "And I'm going to be a darn good one," he mumbled to himself.

Rafe choked on the dust, adjusting the bandana over his face. He, Dom, Cruz, and Antonio rejoined the herd a few days after arriving in Big Pine. By then, Antonio's men had driven the animals a few miles west of the territorial capital.

Antonio's injuries had healed enough the doctor allowed him to leave, but only if he traveled by wagon, not on the back of his horse. The news set off a whole new round of robust arguments between the father and his sons. He had relented only after Dom and Cruz had threatened to ride out without him and take his horse.

The elder Lucero rode in a covered wagon not far from Rafe's location on the herd's right flank, one of the ranch hands holding the lines. They'd brought it from Texas, Dom's mother filling it with furniture from his bedroom, plus additional items she felt certain he'd need.

Traveling in this fashion hadn't been what the elder Lucero expected. Even through the noise of the bawling animals, Rafe could hear Antonio's shouts, as if he still led the drive.

"How are you doing?" Dom reined next to Rafe, drawing his handkerchief over his face.

"I'm fine. Your father doesn't seem to be doing too well, though."

Glancing behind him, Dom chuckled. "The man doesn't know how else to act. If he can't grumble about something, he might as well stay silent."

"Can you arrange that?"

"Getting my father to stay silent? Afraid not."

The two rode in silence for quite a while, Dom pulling a few yards ahead every few minutes to keep the herd in line before returning to Rafe.

"I'm going to do all I can to keep Josie in Splendor."

Dom's comment didn't surprise Rafe. He expected as much since seeing the two together. His sister didn't hide her great affection for the lawman. Rafe's initial assessment had changed little since meeting him.

Hardheaded, the same as Josie, he came from a successful Texas ranching family interested in expanding their holdings by crossbreeding long and shorthorns. The knowledge still didn't make him Josie's equal.

She'd attended the best schools in New Orleans, been introduced to the finest families, and her name was connected with some of the most eligible prospects. Although their father hadn't felt any worthy of his daughter. Consequently, she had little experience with men, other than Dom.

"She deserves better than a life with a struggling rancher and lawman with low pay."

Dom understood Rafe's concerns. He'd feel the same if he had a daughter.

"I won't argue with you on that, Rafe. Josie deserves more than any man I know can offer."

Rafe glanced at him, his thick, dark brows narrowing. "Then let her go."

Dom choked out a mocking laugh. "We tried that. It didn't work out for either of us."

He could hear Rafe's curse over the sounds of the herd. "She ran away from our parents because of our father's insufferable control. With our parents gone, there's no reason for her to stay in Splendor."

"Except for her friends, the shop, and me." Dom kicked Blue forward, rounding up some stray cattle before moving back close to Rafe.

"She'll forget about all of you once I get her back home. Did you know she has a substantial trust from our parents' estate? Josie can live anywhere, travel the world. She deserves a man of her status, educated, sophisticated. One who'll give her everything."

*Except love*, Dom thought.

But for the first time since meeting Josie, doubts began to surface. His reservations before had to do with time away as a marshal, the ranch, which needed more time than he had to give, and a family who wanted to insert themselves into his new life in Montana. The misgivings were about what he might have to give up to have Josie, not what she'd be giving up if they fell in love.

Rafe continued to prod Dom. "I understand she has a responsibility to Olivia and their shop. They've worked hard and deserve to give it a chance. Still, there's no reason she can't get the store ready to open before leaving. They can hire someone to work with Olivia." Choking again, he untied the bandana, shaking it out before retying it. "It could work to their advantage. Josie could be their buyer in the east. After all, she'll have the means to try new products personally, deciding which are worth offering."

Doing all he could to ignore Rafe's words, Dom found himself wavering.

"Do you know how many men Father allowed to court her?"

Shaking his head, Dom tightened his grip on the reins. "No."

"None. She has no experience with men. Do you ever wonder if she has feelings for you because Father never allowed her to get to know anyone else?"

Stomach twisting around a hard rock of unease, he stared ahead, focusing on anything but the uncertainties rippling through him. Until Rafe's arrival, he'd been certain approaching Josie to rekindle their interest had been right.

"Dom!"

Cruz's shout drew the attention of both men. His wave had Dom kicking Blue to join his brother riding point, giving him time to think.

Reaching the front of the herd, it took a couple seconds to see his brother's concern. A large band of Crow sat atop a hill several hundred yards away. At least twenty mounted riders holding rifles stared back at them.

Pulling out his six-shooter, Dom checked the cylinder. "They want food."

"How do you know?" Cruz followed Dom's lead, checking his own gun.

"I don't know if they're the same ones, but a group of Crow raided my ranch. They didn't kill anyone, but stole all the provisions. They must be a renegade band. Most Crow get along pretty well with whites. From what I heard, a group splintered off from the main village several years ago. They've been marauding ever since. The Pelletiers believe they're the same group who took some children hostage a while back. They escaped and were found living in a cave near Redemption's Edge. The Pelletiers took them all in."

Cruz massaged the back of his neck. "They can't take the entire herd."

"We have a choice. Cut out one steer for them to take, or fight. I'd rather lose a steer than one of the cows or heifers." Dom glanced at his brother. With their father recuperating, Cruz was the trail boss.

"We don't have enough men to protect the herd and fend off the attackers. Cut out a steer, Dom."

"I'll ride it out as far as I think safe, then let the animal go."

"Not alone," Cruz said. "I'll go with you."

"No. You're needed here. Pick someone to ride along." Reining around, it took little time to cut out one of the steers and join the man Cruz selected.

Dom continued to shoot quick looks at the ridge, glad the Crow numbers hadn't grown. Rigging a simple white flag, he nodded to the ranch hand before checking the hill again.

They were gone. Disappeared in a few short seconds. Dom's chest squeezed, his gaze whipping around, praying he'd see something to give a clue as to where they'd gone. No sounds, no dust. Nothing.

Their disappearance brought an additional danger. He didn't know where they'd gone or their intentions. Were they curious, or planning an attack farther down the trail?

Either way, the journey became much more dangerous.

*Splendor*

"You have to eat, Josie." Olivia slid a bowl of stew toward her, pursing her lips when the food went untouched. "I'm sure they're both fine. We would've heard something if either Rafe or Dom were hurt."

They sat at the table in the kitchen, Josie staring at the unappetizing stew. She knew it would be delicious and did need to eat. Suzanne had brought a small pot of it, a basket of biscuits, and part of an apple pie home from the boardinghouse the night before, well after everyone else had eaten supper. Everyone except Josie.

"We've heard nothing for over a week, Livvy."

"They rode to Big Pine to see about Dom's father and help bring the herd to the ranch. It's just taking longer is all. I'm sure you'll hear something from one of them soon." She tapped the edge of Josie's bowl. "Eat so we can go back to the shop. There's still a good amount of work for us. The sign and the lettering on the front window are going up this afternoon. We're so close to opening, Josie."

She had to chuckle, bringing a forkful of stew to her mouth and chewing. Most days, Josie's enthusiasm lifted any doubts Olivia had about their venture. Today, her friend took on the job, which should've made her feel better. It didn't.

Josie had a strange sense of foreboding. It began a couple days after Dom and Rafe left for Big Pine, a slow burn in her stomach, which increased each day until a roaring blaze seared her insides. She'd never experienced anything similar. No matter what she did to take her mind off Dom, her discomfort increased.

If only she hadn't suggested Rafe leave with him. She'd been overwhelmed with grief over her parents' deaths, angry because her brother assumed she'd leave her life in Splendor and return to New Orleans.

It hadn't occurred to him to ask what she wanted or if she was happy. The brother she'd been close to her entire life acted more like their father. The change confused Josie. The result had been her encouraging Dom to take him along, using the excuse he'd never been on a cattle drive.

It would've been much better to keep Rafe close, show him how well she fit into the growing frontier town. Introducing him to her many friends, accepting invitations to supper, might have impressed him enough to reconsider the reason he came to Splendor.

He'd always had a knack for business, helping their father with his different investments and ventures. Offering advice on the store would've been a better way to spend his time than on the trail with Dom.

Who knew what her brother had told him about their lives in New Orleans. She prayed he hadn't mentioned the trust her parents left for each of them. Combined with the money her great-grandfather provided upon his death, most would consider her not only comfortable, but wealthy. Josie shuddered, wondering how Dom would take the news.

Taking a few more bites of stew, she shoved the bowl aside. "I can't eat another bite."

Grabbing the dishes, Olivia washed them, wiping her hands on a towel. "Are you going to tell me what's bothering you so much?"

Lips thinning into a taut line, Josie gave a short shake of her head.

"I'm your closest friend, and your business partner. Maybe I can help."

"It's just a feeling. I can't stop believing something awful is going to happen when Dom returns to Splendor."

"What do you mean?"

"I'm not exactly sure, but I know it won't be good."

"If he were hurt, we'd have gotten a telegram from Big Pine or Rafe would've gotten him back here."

Pursing her lips, slender brows furrowing, Josie shook her head again. "I don't believe it will have anything to do with an accident. Of course, it might." Groaning, she clasped her hands together. "I'm probably worrying about nothing." Straightening her spine, Josie forced a small smile. "Whatever it is, I'll figure a way to live through it, the same as the deaths of my parents."

Slipping an arm through Josie's, Olivia guided them to the front and out the door. "You worry too much. Dom will return to court you the same as Clay is courting me."

Josie wished she felt as confident as her friend. Fighting the warning tremors in her stomach, and the uncomfortable tightening of her heart, she feared Dom's return wouldn't be the joyful reunion Olivia predicted.

# Chapter Twenty-One

"Keep them moving. There's a narrow canyon up ahead. A perfect place for an attack." Dom waited until Cruz's nod before riding ahead.

The band of Crow they'd seen earlier had appeared and disappeared two more times over the last few hours. They hadn't gotten closer than a couple hundred yards either time. Their presence unnerved the men and the cattle.

Which was the reason for Dom riding out now. Someone needed to act as scout, locating the band and trying to judge their intentions. Although he had no doubt they meant to swoop down, steal one or two head of cattle, then ride off. The Luceros would fight them taking the animals, but they wouldn't allow their men to be picked off one at a time.

Most of the Lucero ranch hands were experienced with the Comanche and Apache tribes in Texas, but knew little of the Crow. Dom figured this particular group were renegades, living on their own, apart from the main village. The distinction was important. Most of the Crow people found a way to get along with the white settlers.

The renegades were dangerous, raiding and marauding at will. They had no use for the whites, other than to steal their cattle and kidnap women and children. From what he'd learned from Bull and the Pelletiers, the attacks were swift, without warning, often leaving people injured or dead.

If they didn't need all the ranch hands to guard the herd, Dom would continue to the ranch and warn Bull. Knowing the Pelletier foreman, he'd have men on watch.

Taking a trail up a steep hill, he dragged his rifle from the scabbard and slipped to the ground. Dropping down, he belly crawled to the crest, peeking through low sagebrush to the valley below. What he saw made his breath hitch.

Instead of the number of riders who'd shown themselves earlier, he stared down the slope to see at least fifty people. Some on horseback, most milling about in an area of less than an acre. Several Crow lodges covered in hides were scattered about, women and children staying close to them.

Dom guessed at least thirty of the men were warriors. They were proficient with bows and arrows, rifles, and knives. And could be merciless when their people needed food.

Their location and size gave Dom two choices. Continue on their current path, traveling within a mile of the village, or turn the herd around. The alternate route would move the herd through thick brush and over treacherous terrain with few places to rest for the night. It would also take them miles away from the Crow village. He didn't see any real choice.

Moving back to Blue, he grabbed the reins, leading his horse several yards down the trail before mounting. Holding the rifle in one hand, he continued to glance behind him as he hurried away.

The herd hadn't moved far from where he'd left them. Regardless, they still had to turn the cattle around and backtrack a good mile.

"What'd you find?" Cruz joined him at the front of the herd.

Dom explained what he saw, as well as the choice of trails. His brother agreed about taking the longer, tougher route.

A couple hours later, they'd made the change, ambling along at a slower pace. The drovers spent more time keeping the herd together. The thick brush on either side of the trail made it easy for strays to disappear if the men weren't alert.

As they ambled along, Dom pondered Rafe's words.

Chandler set the last window into place, securing it before stepping away. They'd made incredible progress over the last week. The day before, a good-sized breeder herd of shorthorns and Herefords arrived from Kansas. Two weeks earlier than planned.

Bull and the men had taken it in stride, directing the trail boss where to take the cattle. They'd cull the herd once Dom arrived with the longhorns, a breed Chandler understood better than those delivered yesterday.

Bull bounded up the porch steps, removing his hat to drag an arm over his forehead. "The downstairs is finished. Shouldn't take long to do the same upstairs when Dom's ready. Don't know what's taking them so long. They should've arrived before now."

"It's not the weather. What about rustlers?" Chandler stepped to the edge of the porch, taking a look around.

Bull joined him at the rail. "Wouldn't be smart with the number of Lucero ranch hands. The renegade band of Crow might've slowed them down." Bull's head whipped toward the south. "Did you hear that, Chan?" He didn't wait for an answer before dashing down the steps. A moment later, he pointed toward a plume of dust. "Here they come."

"I'll let the men know." Adjusting his gunbelt, Chandler swung atop his horse. Shouting at a couple men near the corral, he continued toward the pasture where the other men worked.

Crossing his arms, Bull couldn't hide his smile at seeing the herd of Texas longhorns approaching with Dom at point. Grabbing the reins to Abe, he mounted, shouting as he closed the distance to the herd.

"You're a sight for sore eyes. Did you have trouble?"

Drawing the bandana down his face, Dom nodded. "We were followed by a band of Crow most of the way."

"They didn't attack?"

"No, but wouldn't surprise me if they showed up here."

Glancing over his shoulder, Bull's gaze lit on the covered wagon, an older man sitting next to the driver. The Lucero chuckwagon brought up the rear.

"Let's get the longhorns where you want them, then we'll talk about placing men to watch the herd." Dom's jaw clenched when he thought of what else he had to do. "Tomorrow, I'll be riding to town. Get me a list of supplies, Bull. I'll bring them back with me."

In truth, his mind wasn't focused on provisions. His thoughts were on a beautiful blonde with wide brown eyes and a trusting soul.

*Splendor*

"Move the mirror to your right a little bit, Josie." Olivia stood several feet away.

"You just said to move it left." She struggled with the weight of the heavy, gilded frame.

The bell over the door stopped Olivia's response, giving Josie a moment to lower the frame. When she looked up, her heart skipped more than a few beats. Dom stood inside.

"Dom." She couldn't stop her feet from moving toward him, her smile growing with each step. Reaching him, Josie raised a hand to touch his arm, drawing it back at the sober expression. Her stomach clenched when he failed to hold her gaze. Not at all what she expected after almost two weeks of him being away.

"Good morning, Josie, Olivia."

Glancing behind him and onto the street, she forced a smile. "Did Rafe ride to town with you?"

"No. He decided to stay at the ranch another day or two." Dom wouldn't tell her Rafe didn't want to leave the place short of men if the Crow attempted another raid.

Stepping around her, he studied the vast number of items displayed on the shelves and atop counters. The doors of a wardrobe on one wall were open, offering a view of the clothes hanging inside. Two Tiffany lamps brought color to a desk in the front. On the top sat stunning inkwells, as well as several ornate fountain pens. The ladies had created a beautiful environment of upscale, difficult to find accessories and trimmings not sold anywhere else in Splendor.

"You've been busy." Dom directed the comment to both women, unable to meet Josie's puzzled gaze.

Before Rafe arrived, sharing the details of Josie's wealth, he'd have had a different reaction to seeing her. The response his heart urged him to express. Instead, he held back, her brother's pleas to consider her future foremost in his mind.

For over a week, he'd considered Rafe's reasons for her to return to an opulent life in New Orleans. Lifetime friendships, teas, soirées, travel, fine dresses, rides along the waterfront, parties in the parks, and men considered her equal in social status.

Dom could come up with three reasons for her to stay. Olivia, the shop, and him. Not one offered her the opportunities available back home. Advantages she might long for after a few years living in Splendor.

With her substantial wealth, she *could* travel between New Orleans and Splendor. Dom knew the trips would grow old after a while, ending with her spending more time at home than in Montana. More time away from him.

After several sleepless nights, Dom came to the only conclusion possible. He'd let her go, forcing Josie to make a decision not based on her feelings for him. Emotions had no place in the choice she had to make.

If Dom didn't step aside, he knew Josie would choose him with little thought as to what she'd be giving up. With him out of her life, she'd be free to make a decision with a clear head and no emotional entanglements.

He needed to do this for her. *Wanted* to do this for her, even if it would shatter his heart.

"Do you have time for a walk, Josie?"

Resting a hand on her stomach, she shot an anguished look at Olivia, reminding them both of her premonitions about Dom's return. So far, nothing about it had been expected. Except perhaps a quiet walk.

Mind swirling, throat tightening, she tried to draw a breath. Words failed as she fought to contain her unease.

"It is a good time to take a break, Josie," Olivia said, seeing the agitation on her friend's face.

Forcing a smile, she met his gaze. "A walk would be nice, Dom."

Without reaching for her hand, he opened the door for her to step onto the boardwalk. Her heart sank lower when he kept several inches between them, not taking her hand to slip it through his arm. The silence stretched until Josie couldn't take it any longer.

"Is your father all right?"

Continuing to stare ahead, he nodded. "He's still recuperating, although he's doing all he can to fight it."

She gripped her hands in front of her. "It must have been a difficult trip for him."

"Father is a demanding, difficult man. No trip is easy for him."

Spotting the church, Dom placed his hand on the small of her back long enough to guide her to the new structure. The fire which destroyed the church before Christmas had been a brief casualty for the town. Within a couple weeks, ranchers and townsfolk had erected a new building. Christmas Eve service had been held as planned, followed by Caleb and May's wedding. What Dom planned wouldn't have such a joyous ending.

"Are we going into the church?" Hope flared for an instant. Josie couldn't imagine him delivering bad news inside a building offering such optimism.

"If you don't mind."

Walking up the steps, he tried the door, not surprised when it opened. Motioning her inside, he guided her toward a pew in the back. Sitting down, she waited for him to join her. Instead, he leaned against the back of the pew in front of them, his arms loose at his sides.

"Rafe convinced you to break the courtship, didn't he?"

The question stunned him, as did the moisture building in her eyes. The calm he'd worked so hard to achieve drained away under her searing scrutiny. Clearing his throat, Dom shoved aside his doubts.

"He told me enough to realize what you'd be giving up if you stayed in Splendor."

"There's nothing at home for me, Dom. Everything I want is here, not hundreds of miles away." She couldn't hide the anxiety in her voice.

"You're a young, wealthy woman, Josie. A woman with no experience with men."

"Except for you," she blurted out, unease turning to anger.

Jaw tensing, he gave a curt nod. "Except for me. You deserve a chance to meet someone who's—"

"More suitable?" Josie interrupted.

"Yes." Straightening, he paced a few feet away. "You're a beautiful, educated woman who's used to fine things. I'm a marshal and rancher. Although my family has a certain amount of wealth, it's nothing compared to you. Other than money from my grandparents, I have little. You deserve so much more than what I could ever provide."

Chest heaving, she stood, hands clenched in the fabric of her dress. "I don't care how much money you have, Dom. I never have."

"You may not now, but in time, you will."

Stepping into the aisle, she closed the distance between them. "Fine. If I need to get away, I'll take

Olivia and travel to San Francisco. It's what Caro and Isabella did before they married Beau and Travis. You *do* know they are both wealthy, yet their husbands don't care."

He did know about both couples. "It's different for them," Dom almost bellowed before taking a breath to calm his rising irritation. "Caro and Isabella were widows, and older than you when they came to Splendor. Both had more experience with life before making the decision to come west."

"What about Abby Brandt? She's the wealthiest woman in Splendor, and possibly Big Pine. She was about my age with no experience when Noah proposed. A wealthy woman and a blacksmith, yet they're one of the happiest couples I've ever known."

"They're happy because they're in love, Josie." The instant the words were out, Dom wanted to pull them back.

A gasp of pain escaped her, lips quivering. Swiping at an errant tear, she glared up at him. "I love you, Dom. Are you saying you don't feel the same?"

Closing his eyes, he gave a quick shake of his head. "No, Josie, I don't." The lie caused a sharp stab of pain to slice through his chest.

The answer had her staggering backward. When he reached out to steady her, she slapped his hand away. "Don't."

The anguish on her face almost buckled his knees. He fought the knot of regret in his stomach threatening to double him over. "I'm sorry, Josie."

Squaring her shoulders, she raised her chin, studying his face. Sucking in a strangled breath, she raised her hand, shoving a finger at his chest. "You're nothing but a coward, Dom Lucero."

Nostrils flaring, his eyes flashed in surprise. "You don't know what you're talking about."

Poking again, she let the fury on her face show. "You're in love with me but are afraid to admit it. Afraid to take the chance on us, on a life together. Instead of facing the truth, you latch onto Rafe's reasons for wanting me to return to New Orleans. They aren't *my* reasons, Dom, but *his*. And you're willing to tuck tail and skulk away."

The deep red color on his face a moment earlier began changing to a flushed purple, his eyes sparking with indignation.

"No one has asked what *I* want."

"Rafe wants what's best for you," he ground out, not trusting himself to say more.

"My brother is a wonderful man, but he's also selfish and controlling, the same as our father. Well, I won't allow him to force me into a future not of my choosing." Stomping a few feet away, she whirled back to him. "If you truly don't love me, fine. I'll learn to live with your rejection."

His heart twisted at her phrasing.

"No matter what Rafe wants, I *will* stay in Splendor. I *will* open the shop. And, over time, I *will* fall in love with someone else and marry. Forgetting you won't be easy, Dom, but it *will* happen." Taking one last look at him, she turned around, walking the short distance to the door.

"Josie, wait."

Refusing to look back, she quietly closed the door behind her.

# Chapter Twenty-Two

Josie brushed tears from her face as she almost stumbled down the steps of the church. Making her way to the door behind the shop, she took several moments to compose herself before entering.

The sound of Clay's voice caught her attention. Peeking into the front of the shop, she slapped a hand over her mouth to stifle a gasp.

Clay knelt in front of Olivia, his hands holding hers. It took little effort for Josie to realize what the display meant. Olivia's eyes were wide in surprise as a deep sob tore from her lips.

The scene scorched through Josie, a reminder of what she'd never have with Dom. The raw pain of his words clung to her. He didn't love her. Rafe had planted enough doubt in his mind that he refused to accept what Josie already knew. Dom *did* love her, but he wasn't willing to stand up to her brother. Josie had no such reservations.

Anger swelling, she hurried back outside, picking up her skirts as she ran toward the livery.

"Good morning, Josie." Noah straightened from where he worked pounding a new tool into shape near the forge. Setting aside the hammer, he pulled an already soiled rag from a back pocket, doing what he could to clean his hands. "Is Dom with you?"

Spine stiffening, she answered with a quick shake of her head. The entire town would eventually know of his decision to stop seeing her. For now, she chose to ignore the ache and humiliation at his rejection.

"Would you have a horse available to ride?"

Lips twitching, Noah nodded. "How about the mare you usually ride?"

A wave of relief washed over her. "She would be perfect."

"Give me a few minutes and I'll get her ready."

Glancing behind her and into the street, she followed him to the back door. She absolutely didn't want anyone to spot her and ask questions.

"Do you mind if I come with you?"

"Of course not." Swinging the door open, he motioned for her to go first. Slipping a bridle over a shoulder, he picked up a blanket and saddle before going to the mare's stall. Brushing her down, he made quick work of getting the horse ready to ride.

"Where are you headed this morning?"

"I thought I'd ride out to Gabe and Lena's house."

Gaze narrowing, he clutched the reins, walking the mare to the gate. "You do know they're both in town this morning."

No, she didn't, but it made no difference in her plans. "Oh, yes. I thought to ride along the creek behind their house before returning to town."

Accepting Noah's help to mount, she took the offered reins. "Olivia and I have been putting in long hours getting the store ready."

"A ride will do you good, Josie. Still, you shouldn't be riding alone. Is anyone going with you?"

Brushing aside his concern, she tightened her hold on the reins. "Not today. I'll only be gone a short while, Noah. Not long at all, really." She saw her response as just a small lie compared to the one she'd heard from Dom.

Rubbing a finger over his thick, dark brow, he didn't try to hide his concern. "I saw Dom ride in. Maybe he could take time to go with you."

"He came by the shop this morning. Since he's just returned from the cattle drive, I wouldn't think of asking him to accompany me. Dom's much too busy for something this frivolous." She felt a slight measure of satisfaction at her ability to stay calm when her heart felt as if it had been crushed. "Thank you so much. May I settle my account when I return?"

Sensing something wasn't quite right, he stroked the mare's neck. "That would be fine. Just, well...be careful."

"Always." The smile she offered felt forced, which it was.

Taking the trail to Gabe and Lena's, she drew in a deep breath. Josie didn't like lying to anyone. The fact Noah's concern was justified made her feel even worse. If it hadn't been for Rafe, and Dom supporting her brother's desire to see her return to New Orleans, there'd be no need for this ride. Or what would transpire once she reached her destination.

She'd loved her parents, still mourned their passing. Would for a long time. Her grief, however, didn't excuse the way her father did everything in his power to control every aspect of her life. And it didn't justify Rafe trying to take over the task after their father's death.

Josie would always love her brother. But she refused to accept his meddling in her life.

Reaching a fork in the trail, she stopped, sucking in a frustrated breath. Feeling the searing pain of earlier slow to a tolerable ache, she stared ahead. Staying to the right would lead her to the Evans's home. Turning left would take her north, past Baron Klaussner's almost completed mansion.

Not much farther and she'd cross the boundary onto Dom's ranch. The showdown with Rafe couldn't be put off any longer.

"She rode off alone?" Dom's incredulous tone ripped through Noah. "And you let her go?"

He sat atop Blue, knowing it wasn't fair to blame his friend. Josie had a mind of her own. No one could stop her once she decided on a course of action. Plus, he'd hurt her. His intentions were honorable, and for her own good. Reflecting on what he'd said and how she'd responded, he realized how ridiculous the reasons sounded. The fact she now saw him as a coward, a man not willing to fight for what he wanted, galled him.

All Dom intended was to give her the freedom to make the right choice. In hindsight, he realized she'd already made her decision. She'd chosen him. Now Josie wanted nothing to do with him.

What he refused to do was give her time to ponder new choices. He darn well wouldn't step aside to let other men near her. She was his, no one else's. Too bad he didn't realize how much he loved her until expressing his reservations aloud. Now she'd ridden off alone. Probably without protection.

"I tried to stop her, but you know Josie. The same as Abby, the woman has a strong will."

Massaging the back of his neck, Dom nodded. "Yeah, she does. Which way did she ride?"

"She planned to ride to Gabe's place, then along the creek for a while before coming back. I'd appreciate it if you'd let me ride along, help you find her. It'll just take a couple minutes to saddle my horse."

A part of Dom wanted Noah to join him, but the man always had a backlog of work. "Thanks, but I won't ask you to take time away. Josie's probably doing exactly what she told you. It shouldn't be hard to find her."

Lifting a hand to shield his eyes from the late morning sun, Noah stepped away. "If you don't find her, hurry back and we'll grab a couple other men to help locate her."

Dom hoped he wouldn't need to take Noah up on his offer. "I'll do that."

Taking the same trail Josie had an hour before, he kept his gaze moving, hoping to spot her. Reaching Gabe's house, he rode around back to the creek. He saw no sign of her or recent hoofprints.

Backtracking, he headed to the fork in the trail, spotting fresh prints going north. Keeping his attention on the tracks, he continued, coming to a stop near Klaussner's house. Several minutes passed as he sorted out the various prints, finally locking on those he believed to be Josie's horse. It wasn't hard to guess where she headed. Straight to his ranch and a probable confrontation with Rafe.

Dom should've figured out her destination sooner. She'd see her brother as triggering what transpired in the church. If anyone was to blame, it was him, not a brother seeking the best for his sister.

Dom could've ignored Rafe's concerns. Wished he had. Now he had a great deal to make up for, and hoped she'd give him the chance.

It didn't take long to reach the boundary of his ranch. Riding closer, he spotted Josie and Rafe outside the barn, her arms flailing as she spoke. Grimacing, he ignored the churning in his gut at what he'd be riding into.

Focusing all his attention on the dueling couple, his back stiffened at the sound of loud cries. Glancing to the side, his blood chilled. A band of close to twenty Crow riders yelled and whooped, approaching at a fast pace. An instant later, bullets whizzed past.

"Get inside!" Dom shouted the command more than once before reaching them. Sliding to the ground, he grabbed his rifle as Rafe ushered Josie through the barn entry. Shoving her to the back, he returned to join Dom. He might not have his rifle, but at least Rafe was armed with a six-shooter.

Firing at the approaching raiders, Dom and Rafe lost sight of Josie, their concentration fixed on the threat. The sound of shots coming from the bunkhouse indicated his men saw the danger. He hoped the men guarding the herd could hear them, as well.

"They're after the cattle," Dom shouted, hoping his men heard before he retreated into the protection of the barn. The cover didn't last long.

Hearing a strained curse, Dom saw Rafe slump to the ground, blood pouring from a wound to his head. Taking several shots, he rushed to him, grabbing his collar to drag him away from the door. Before he had time to raise his rifle, a bullet pierced his left arm, another grazing his thigh.

Shouting his own string of curses, he tried in vain to lift the rifle. Feeling it slip from his grasp, his frantic gaze landed on Josie. Instead of the fear he expected, her features were locked in anger and determination. Before she could move from her hiding spot, his shouted order stopped her.

"Stay there, Josie." It was all he remembered before another bullet grazed his forehead and he lost the battle to remain conscious.

Dom didn't know how long he'd been out. When he came to, the shouts and gunshots had stopped. Trying to sit up, he slumped back to the ground, his head fuzzy and throbbing. Behind him, Rafe lay still, blood still oozing from the shot to his head.

Blinking several times, he tried again to sit up. This time, determination won over the dizziness. Dom knew his wounds weren't life-threatening. He didn't know about Rafe's.

Ignoring the pain in his leg and arm, he shoved himself up, limping to Rafe's side. A relieved breath burst from him as he inspected the head wound. The shot grazed his temple, knocking him out but not a lethal shot. Pulling the bandana from his pocket, Dom used it to stop the bleeding, ignoring his own wounds.

Edging awake, Rafe raised a hand to his head, groaning in pain. "What the..." His voice trailed off on a rush of light-headedness.

"You were shot." Opening his own shirt, Dom shrugged out of it to inspect the damage to his left arm. Wadding the material into a ball, he pressed it against the wound.

As Rafe became more coherent, his eyes widened as he took in Dom's injuries. "Appears you were shot three times."

"Yeah. All of them grazes, but they still hurt like hell." Glancing up, his gaze roamed the barn, chest constricting. "Josie!" The shout went unanswered.

Forcing himself to stand, Rafe held the bandana to his head. "Josie! Where are you?"

No response. Blowing out a stream of obscenities, Dom limped toward the stall where she'd been hiding, fear wrapping around him.

"She's not here."

"Maybe she's helping the other men." Rafe's comment held no hint of conviction. Both men knew if they needed help, she'd start with them.

"Are you two all right?" Bull stormed into the barn, resting his rifle against the wall when he saw their injuries. Turning, he shouted for help before checking their wounds.

"We're fine. You need to find Josie."

Bull knelt beside him, checking his wounds, brows lifting at Dom's command. "Josie is here?"

"*Was* here. She took cover in a stall. Now she's gone." Another flash of pain shot through Dom. "It's my fault she was at the ranch in the first place."

Shaking his head, Rafe groaned in agony. "It's not your fault she rode out. I should've spoken to her myself."

"I'll get word to the men to search for her as soon as we get your wounds cleaned."

"Not soon enough, Bull. You need to start looking now," Dom gritted out when Bull pressed a handkerchief to the wound on his thigh.

"Hold on." Standing, Bull rushed out of the barn, yelling orders before returning. "Cruz and Antonio just rode in from where the herd is grazing. They're going to start a search. I'll join them once we get you two inside the house."

"Dammit. I don't need coddling. I need to find Josie."

"No, you don't," Bull shot back. "What you need is to have these wounds cleaned before they become infected. Help me get him into the house, boys, then one of you ride to town and bring back one of the doctors."

It took three men to get him up the steps and into the house, Bull barking orders for someone to gather blankets and form a pallet on the floor. Another ranch hand supported Rafe, lowering him to a bench they'd dragged into the house.

"Cruz and my father will need help if it looks like the Crow took Josie."

Bull slipped Dom's pants down, exposing the wound on his thigh. "That's why I sent a couple Pelletier men with them. They're good and will figure out real quick if she's somewhere on the ranch or if the Crow took her."

The words felt raw in Bull's throat, remembering how his wife, Lydia, and the other orphan children had fared at the hands of the same band of Crow. It had been over two years, yet no one had forgotten how they had suffered.

"And if they believe she was kidnapped?" Rafe asked.

Bull shrugged, as if the answer were obvious. "We gather as many men as possible and go after her."

# Chapter Twenty-Three

"Let me go." Josie squirmed and kicked, unable to get her arms free to swing at him. He had her slung in front of him, swatting her each time she kicked the sides of his horse.

They rode fast, keeping pace with the other riders who'd attacked the ranch. The group herded a single longhorn steer with them, no doubt the reason for the raid. But why take her?

Anger seethed through her, eyes burning at the memory of both Rafe and Dom lying on the ground, bleeding. She didn't know if either lived. When she'd emerged from the stall, meaning to examine their injuries, the brave scooped Josie up, tossing her in front of him. No amount of screaming, kicking, or hitting had loosened his grip.

Her ankles and hands weren't bound. Even so, Josie's continued attempts to free herself did nothing except cause him to strike her on the rump. A sharp, cracking sound which angered her even more.

Calming, she tried to think. Her view was limited, as were her choices. When he wasn't swatting her, the brave's hand pressed down on her neck, forcing her gaze forward. Reaching a steep hill, his hold released long enough for her to shift, giving her a view behind them.

No riders followed. At least she couldn't see any from her new position. What Josie did see had a small grin playing across her face. The rider had a knife strapped to his thigh with a thick length of leather. Her unbound hands hung loose above her head, swinging as they continued up the steep grade.

The pressure on her neck decreased, the man either not noticing or caring that she'd shifted to stare behind them. He also seemed unconcerned about the knife, which appeared within easy reach. If she could just shift a little more toward the back. Which meant inching her hips, stomach, and chest closer to the man's thighs. It wasn't a pleasant thought, but neither was ending up in the Crow camp.

Josie had been in Splendor long enough to hear Lydia's stories of her life as a Crow captive. Bull's wife spoke of the warrior who'd kept her near him, claiming her for all to see. It was the reason she, her brother, and younger sister ran before his threats of taking her turned to action. Two other young captives learned of their plan to escape and insisted on going along.

The five had traveled long miles on foot with little food and no cover. Some settlers provided meager provisions, but no one offered shelter. Not even blankets during the cold nights. She understood their fear of the Crow tracking the runaways. Still, the five had never forgotten the ordeal, or their rescue by Bull and a group of Pelletier men.

Josie had no intention of experiencing the same fate. Staying as still as possible, she waited until the brave's grip loosened further. Keeping her gaze locked on the knife, she carefully reached out, missing the handle by a couple short inches.

Steadying her racing heart, she let out a long breath before trying a second time. Again, the knife lay just beyond her grasp. Frustrated, she tried to shift her body closer, coming to an abrupt stop when the rider slapped her twice on the rump.

The jolt of pain fired her blood, determination to free herself driving her next actions. The instant his hand lifted from her, Josie arched her body to the side, gripping the bone handle of the knife.

A roar of excitement ripped from her lungs. Bucking, she felt herself falling, slipping from the horse to land on the hard ground. By some miracle, her tight grip on the weapon hadn't loosened. By another, she hadn't landed on the blade.

The steep terrain helped Josie, propelling her down the hill in a fast roll. Rocks dug into her, tearing at her clothing, but she refused to let go of the knife. Closing her eyes, she allowed herself to roll as far as the ground would allow, coming to rest against a thick shrub.

Hearing the pounding of hooves and whoops of her captor, she struggled to stand, holding the knife in front of her. She frantically looked around, seeing no place to hide. Behind the raider who'd captured her, two other riders rushed down the hill, their shouts adding to his.

Her skin stung from dirt and pebbles, back and ribs aching from being flung over the horse. She refused to be taken again. Not without a fight. Glancing at the knife, her courage rose, then fell when the three riders charged toward her.

Screaming, she rushed to the other side of the brush, knowing it provided little protection.

"Stay away from me!" Her scream echoed over the open ground. Looking behind her, she spotted a stand of trees yards away. Too far for her to run, yet she couldn't stay put or they'd surround her. Refusing to give up, she picked up her skirts, legs pumping toward escape.

Yelling after her, the three Crow plunged down the hill. The initial amusement on their faces turned to irritation as she continued to search for escape. Slipping between three large tree trunks, Josie turned in the circle of their protection, praying someone would appear.

Knowing it ridiculous, she shouted. "Help!"

Repeating it twice more, she winced at the angry stares of her pursuers. They slid from their horses, all three holding long strips of leather, their intent clear.

"No," she muttered to herself as they drew closer. She sent up one last prayer of rescue.

The sounds of approaching horses and gunfire caught their attention. Screaming at the top of her lungs, she whipped the knife around.

"Help me!" She continued screaming until her throat grew raw. Tears of relief pooled at the sight of several riders dressed as ranch hands.

Seeing the same, the three braves swung onto their horses. Shooting venomous glares her way, they kicked their mounts, shouting as they rushed back up the hill.

Bending over, Josie sucked in gulps of air. The knife fell from her grasp, her body sagging as the men rode up. She briefly recognized a familiar voice before her eyes rolled back and she slumped to the hard ground.

Rafe held Josie against his chest, the same as he'd done all the way back to the ranch. She'd been pale, shaking, and unable to stop her wracking sobs. Cruz had offered to hold her, citing Rafe's head wound. He'd waved him off, unwilling to allow anyone else to take care of his sister. It was his fault she'd been at the ranch when the Crow attacked, and it was his duty to make certain Josie recovered, body and soul, from the ordeal.

Rafe's tense body relaxed at the sight of the ranch house. "We're almost there, Josie." She nodded against his chest. The tears had long ago dried, but he could still feel her tremble.

His heart had almost stopped at the sight of her gripping the knife, eyes glazed with fear, surrounded by three menacing Crow braves. Once she'd been secured on his lap, he'd sworn to never allow her to face danger again. A ridiculous thought, but one he vowed to do his best to achieve.

Her bravery still stunned him. He'd never expected Josie to fight against her captors. Before riding out, Rafe had recovered the knife she'd taken from the brave, keeping it as a sign of her courage.

During their explosive quarrel before the Crow attacked, Rafe had realized the gravity of his mistake. Josie's raw anger and the disgust in her voice forced him to accept the depth of Josie's love for Dom. He'd been about to tell her as much when the first bullets whizzed past them.

Then she'd been taken.

Dom had insisted on riding with the men searching for her. Three men had to hold him down, Bull threatening to bind his wrists and ankles if he gave them any trouble.

Thank goodness Rafe's head injury hadn't been as severe. Bull had argued with him, but after a couple minutes, he'd relented. Josie needed at least one familiar face if the search party caught up with the Crow. Since Dom couldn't be there, Rafe was the best choice.

Reining to a stop in front of the house, Rafe handed Josie to a waiting Bull before dismounting.

"Thank God," he blew out, taking the steps to the house. "I never thought you'd find her so soon. The Crow are usually good at disappearing into the numerous valleys and hidden caves."

"How's Dom?"

Entering the house, Bull snorted a laugh. "As you'd expect. Right now, he's out. Clay left a while ago. I can get one of the men to fetch him back to examine Josie."

"She has a number of scrapes and bruises. We'll need to remove several small pebbles and dirt imbedded in her skin."

Placing her on a pallet close to Dom, Bull grabbed a leather pouch. "We'll find what we need in here. We'll need whiskey to disinfect the wounds. We used what was here on Dom."

"I have a bottle in my saddlebags." Rafe glanced at Dom's prone form a few feet away. "I'll get it."

Dom's eyes cracked open at the rustle of blankets, the stomping of boots on the wood floor. His head swam, gaze blurry as he tried to focus on the activity around him. Touching the wound on his head, he winced, then did the same with his arm and leg.

Ignoring the injuries, he tried to sit up, searing pain shooting through his entire body. He hadn't thought the wounds too serious. Clay McCord hadn't agreed, ordering Dom to stay down and the men to keep watch on him. It couldn't have been more than a few hours since the attack, yet it felt as if he'd been laid up for days.

Groaning in disgust, he turned enough to see Bull kneeling beside the nearby pallet. Then his gaze moved to the person he tended.

"Josie." His whispered words accompanied another attempt to sit up.

"Stay down, Dom." Bull didn't lift his gaze when he gave the terse command, causing Josie to stir.

Opening her eyes, she shifted enough to see him. "Rafe told me you'd survived the attack." Her words held no hint of warmth or concern.

Grimacing at her cool tone, he lifted his body enough to support himself on an arm. Watching Bull clean her wounds, he studied her injuries. Seeing her flinch when Bull used tweezers to remove tiny pebbles and dirt from her skin, he had the intense urge to hold her. The cold look in her eyes chilled the thought.

Josie hadn't recovered from what she perceived as his rejection. He hadn't meant to hurt her.

Watching the play of emotions on her face, a knot of regret flashed through him.

Recalling the tears in her eyes, pale skin, and agonized features, he knew he'd failed in his attempt to offer her the freedom to leave with Rafe. What he hadn't seen was the depth of her love. She'd offered him everything he ever wanted. Instead of grasping it and responding favorably to her admission of love, he'd dashed her hopes with three cruel words.

*"I'm sorry, Josie."*

If he could go back to earlier in the day, their conversation would begin and end in a much different way. It had taken his ride to the ranch to realize they'd *discussed* nothing.

Instead, he'd told her what Rafe wanted, saying he agreed. Other than admitting her feelings and lashing back at him, she'd had no say in what transpired in the church. Josie had been told what would happen. As foolish as it now seemed, he'd expected her to understand.

Dom hadn't anticipated her fiery reaction.

"Did they hurt you, Josie?"

She knew he meant the Crow. "Besides being thrown over a horse and swatted each time I squirmed, no."

His lips twitched, but his features remained impassive. "How did you get those injuries?"

Wincing as Bull removed more dirt, she exhaled. "I stole a knife, bucked myself off the horse, and rolled down a hill. A rather steep hill, I might add."

"You should've seen her, Dom." Rafe strolled into the room, handing the whiskey bottle to Bull. "She attempted to shield herself between the trees, swinging the blade toward the three Crow braves. It was a sight I won't soon forget." His features sobered on the last.

"It should never have happened." The words were out before Dom could stop them.

Josie's eyes widened in disbelief. "You couldn't have stopped the attack."

"I mean *you* shouldn't have been at the ranch. Taking you away from your work at the store was a mistake, as was our conversation at the church."

Bull shot a look at Rafe, but neither commented.

Remembering the hurt of his rejection, Josie's jaw clenched. "You were honest."

Nostrils flaring, he snorted a derisive laugh. "And were *you* honest, Josie?"

Staring straight into his intense deep brown eyes, she gave a curt nod. "To my regret, yes."

Not interested in revealing more to the two men listening, Dom settled back onto the pallet, closing his eyes. Grimacing at the stab of pain in his left arm, he rested it over his chest.

A long minute passed before Rafe cleared his throat. "This house isn't yet ready for injured people to recuperate. As soon as Bull is finished, we'll settle both of you into a wagon and return to town."

Dom didn't open his eyes. "I'm fine here, Rafe."

"He's right, Dom." Bull poured whiskey over Josie's wounds, hearing her sharp intake of breath. "Sorry, but the scrapes need to be disinfected." Setting the bottle aside, he stood. "You and Josie should be close to the clinic so the docs can watch for infection. We have plenty of men here for what needs to be done."

Dom opened his mouth to argue, then stopped. Bull and Rafe were right. He'd yet to purchase mattresses, bedding, and most of the items required for the kitchen. The men were content eating hardtack, beans, and meat cooked over an open fire. Josie needed more than the minimal provisions on hand.

"It's dark outside, Rafe. What if the Crow see us?" The fear in Josie's voice had all three turning to look at her.

Bull's mouth twisted. "We can't spare any men to ride with the wagon, Rafe. After the attack, we need all of them here."

"All right. We'll wait until first light tomorrow." Rafe walked toward the kitchen, returning a few minutes later with hard biscuits and jerky. Dividing it between the four of them, he lowered himself to the floor.

"You really do need to get furniture, Dom." Breaking off a chunk of hardtack, Rafe leaned back. "Take Josie with you to Big Pine. She's excellent at selecting what's needed for a home."

Choking on a piece of jerky, Josie shook her head. "I'm too busy with the store. Perhaps one of the other single women in Splendor would be willing to accompany him."

Hiding the knot of frustration in his stomach, Dom shrugged. "Are you certain you don't want to go, Josie?"

She hesitated a moment before giving a reluctant nod. "Yes. I'm certain you'd have a much better time with someone else." Josie glanced away, the words a bitter reminder of the way he'd scorned her love.

"Sleep on it, Josie. Perhaps when you're rested, you'll change your mind." Swallowing the last bite of jerky, he cursed himself again for his rash behavior in the church.

He had a great deal of work ahead of him to get Josie back. After facing his own mortality and almost losing her to Crow raiders, Dom's determination hardened.

Josie belonged to him, and he'd do anything to win her back.

# Chapter Twenty-Four

Hex Boudreaux rode alongside the stagecoach, glancing inside every few minutes to check on his daughter. *My daughter.* He still had trouble accepting the change in his life.

After Alice left him, he'd shoved the idea of a family from his mind. Wanderlust became his ambition in life. Traveling across country with Zeke, taking jobs when they needed money, suited them both.

Their days had been consumed with playing cards, eating fine food, drinking copious amounts of whiskey, and bedding any woman they chose. They never stayed more than a few months in one town. Usually much less.

Jobs as deputies almost always came with room and board, making it the perfect profession for two men who refused to settle down. And they were good at it. Affable, with a core of steel, wearing a badge came easily to both.

Although neither had voiced any interest in leaving Splendor, they knew the option always existed. The frontier town had grown on them, as did the people. Unlike most places they'd lived, the townsfolk and ranchers took care of each other.

"Hex?"

His name shouted from the window of the coach by his precocious four-year-old daughter tipped his mouth into a smile. When Lucy spoke of her mother, it was Mama. Her grandmother was Gramma. Hex remained Hex.

She'd shown little interest in seeing him as her father, even after a long talk with her grandmother. Without blaming Alice, the older woman had taken a great deal of time explaining to Lucy why Hex hadn't been a part of her life.

It had been a hard, albeit necessary, discussion. Lucy listened, asked a few questions, then kissed her grandmother and ran outside to tend the chickens.

Hex had offered to bring Mrs. Moore back to Splendor with them. She'd refused. The older woman had no desire for Lucy to witness her demise to cancer. Honoring her wishes, he'd purchased passage on the stage.

Some days he rode inside with her. Most times, he rode alongside, keeping watch on Lucy while serving as an additional guard.

"What do you need, Luce?" He'd begun using the nickname his daughter preferred.

"Millie is sick."

When they'd boarded the stage in Denver, three sisters had joined them. Nineteen-year-old twins, Chrissy and Millie McKenna, and their eight-year-old sister, Cici. They'd shown an immediate fondness for Lucy, taking her in as if she were another sister.

Reining his horse toward the coach, he looked inside. Millie was bent over, moaning louder with each bump in the trail.

"Chrissy, do you need the stage to stop?"

Glancing up from leaning down next to her sister, she nodded. "It would be best, Mr. Boudreaux." Hearing Millie wretch, her eyes shimmered with concern. "Now would be good."

"Hold up," Hex yelled to the driver. It had been the second time during the trip they'd had to make an unscheduled stop. Not bad, considering Millie seemed to have a weak constitution.

Sliding off his horse, Hex drew the door open, helping Millie and Chrissy out. "Luce, Cici, stay in the coach unless you have business to attend to."

They'd stopped not two hours before in Big Pine. By sunset, the stage would pull into Splendor. Home, and Hex couldn't wait to get there.

Chrissy knelt beside her twin, rubbing her back in a circular motion as Millie lost the food she'd eaten for lunch. The same meal consumed by everyone else.

"She feels hot." Chrissy shot a worried look at Hex.

Grabbing the canteen from his horse, he soaked a bandana, handing it to Chrissy. After a minute, she held it out, waiting until he'd soaked it again.

"We need to move on, Boudreaux."

The driver's order had Chrissy biting her lower lip, worry etching the corner of her eyes and mouth. "She's worse than I first thought."

Dropping down beside Millie, he touched her forehead. "We need to get her to a doctor." Scooping her into his arms, Hex placed her back inside the coach. "There's a blanket under the seat. If she starts shaking, wrap it around her."

"Is there someone in Splendor who can examine her?" Chrissy's voice broke on the last.

"There are two real fine doctors in Splendor. The clinic is new, and we have two nurses who help when needed." Hex glanced at Lucy. She watched Millie, her eyes wide. "Are you all right, sweetheart?"

Lips parted, she nodded, not taking her gaze off Millie. "Will she be all right?"

"We just need to get her to Splendor."

"We gotta go, Boudreaux."

Lifting a hand to the driver, he closed the door before swinging into the saddle. "Let's go."

The stage took off with a jolt, the driver slapping the lines to get the horses racing forward. It would take them at least four hours to reach Splendor. Assuming they didn't encounter any highwaymen or Crow raiders.

Hex hoped Millie made it that long.

Josie swept the wood floor of their shop, heart heavy. She should've been delighted, and not just because of the opening on Saturday.

Olivia and Clay were betrothed. In a few days, they'd make the announcement at the celebration planned for the new Splendor Emporium, and Josie couldn't be more excited for them.

Setting the broom aside, she slumped against a counter. It had been a week since returning to town after the ordeal at the ranch. Doc Worthington had checked her wounds, then sent her home. He'd been more concerned with Dom's injuries.

Clay had told her they'd made Dom stay at the clinic two days, wanting to make certain no infection took hold. Cruz had ridden into town with Dom's horse, both men leaving the minute Doc Worthington gave his approval.

Josie didn't know what she'd expected from him. Maybe to seek her out, admit he'd been wrong about his feelings, possibly confess he'd changed his mind about the difference in their situations. An issue which seemed to mean a great deal to Dom, but nothing to her.

If only Rafe had stayed in New Orleans.

If only he'd kept his concerns to himself.

There were days she hated her brother for pushing her and Dom apart. If he'd had concerns about her staying in Splendor, he should've brought them to her. Josie could've told him no matter what happened between her and Dom, she'd be staying.

She'd built her own life, would be opening a business in a few days. Neither would've been possible in New Orleans, where strict social barriers, wealth, and gender dictated what was and wasn't possible. None of those mattered in Splendor. Not a single one.

"May I escort you to lunch?"

Startling, Josie shoved away from the counter, her dark gaze landing on Rafe. "I'm too busy to eat."

After he'd delivered her and Dom to the clinic, Rafe had stayed long enough to make certain they were all right before riding back to the ranch. It had been for the best. Josie wanted time away from him and his meddling. Time to sort out her thoughts, come to terms with no longer having Dom in her life. Time to grieve all she'd lost.

"You can't go all day without eating, Josie. A few minutes away won't hurt." Rafe walked toward her, hands shoved in his pockets. It was the first time she'd seen him in a week.

"Another time." Picking up the broom, she began to sweep.

"If I could take back what I said to Dom, you must know I would."

His words surprised her, but not enough for Josie to set down the broom. "Well, you can't." Her swipes at the floor became erratic as hurt rose within her.

"If you keep that up, you're going to destroy the broom."

Shrugging, her movements didn't slow. "Will you be at Nick and Suzanne's for supper tonight?"

"I'll be going back to the ranch once the supplies are loaded."

Dropping the broom, Josie took a step toward him. "So this is a way for you to spend a little time while you're helping Dom." Crossing her arms, she glared at him. "At least one of us is still on good terms with him."

Rubbing the back of his neck, Rafe took another step closer. "I don't know what else to say, other than I'm sorry."

Snorting a disbelieving laugh, she cocked her head. "Do you remember what Father used to tell us about being sorry?"

Grimacing, Rafe nodded.

"I'll repeat it anyway. *'Sorry is for those who couldn't do their job right the first time. It means nothing and fixes nothing'.*" Reaching down, she grabbed the broom. "It doesn't matter about Dom anyway. He doesn't love me or want me."

"How do you know?"

"Dom said as much, right after he called off our courtship. He also said I was now free to claim the life I deserve." Swallowing the bile in her throat, she continued. "The problem is, I already have the life I want, Rafe. It's right here in Splendor. You see, shoving Dom out of my life won't change what I want for myself."

Scrubbing both hands down his face, Rafe shook his head. "So you aren't ever returning to New Orleans?"

"I don't know. Perhaps I'll go back for a visit one day, but I have no plans to ever live there again."

Crossing his arms, he leaned a hip against the counter. "I see."

"How long will you be staying?"

"I don't know. A few more weeks maybe. Surprisingly, I'm enjoying my time at the ranch. There are some extremely interesting people living in this part of the country."

"Yes, there are." Letting out a slow breath, she glanced around the store. "We will be having an opening celebration on Saturday. You're welcome to come. Suzanne and Lena are bringing refreshments. Oh, and Clay has asked Olivia to marry him. They plan to announce it during the shindig."

"I'll let Dom and the men know."

"That's fine, but with all the work at the ranch, I doubt he'll come."

The defeated tone of her voice and lack of spark in her eyes, made him feel worse than if she'd slapped him. Rafe knew she'd get over what happened, excuse his meddling, and move on. She'd always been quick to anger. She'd also never held onto it long, forgiving sooner than most. Still, it hurt to see what his interference had done.

"I'll see you on Saturday, Josie."

She didn't bother to respond.

"It'll take a while, but I do believe crossbreeding shorthorns and longhorns is going to be a success." Antonio Lucero clasped Dom on the shoulder. "It was worth all the effort to get the herd up here."

They watched as a bull danced around a skittish heifer, finally bending her to his will.

Dom rested his arms on the top of the corral fence. "It could take a couple seasons before we have enough to sell at market."

Cruz stepped onto the bottom rail. "We planned that long before we made the decision to bring some of the longhorns north. We've already made a deal with the Pelletiers to buy cows and heifers to take back with us."

"Dax mentioned it when we had supper at their place." Dom remembered little of the conversation between the cattlemen, unable to keep his thoughts off Josie. Soon, he'd have to ride into town and try to get her to talk with him. "You two are planning to head into town with Rafe and me on Saturday, aren't you?"

His father nodded. "Wouldn't miss a chance to meet your lady friend, Dom."

Shrugging, he headed toward the barn, his father and Cruz walking next to him. "She isn't my gal. At least not right now."

"Rafe did mention you two had a little misunderstanding."

He snorted at Cruz's phrasing. "Might be a bit more than a little. I hope to rectify that when I see her Saturday."

Looking up at the sound of an approaching wagon, Dom changed direction, waving at Rafe. "You get everything on the list?"

Stopping, Rafe jumped to the ground. "All but the extra rope you wanted. Noah will have it ready on Saturday." Removing his hat, he swiped an arm across his forehead. "One of the deputies, Zeke Boudreaux, asked me to let you know his brother, Hex, rode back in today. Brought a daughter with him."

Dom's jaw dropped. "I didn't know he had a daughter."

The news brought another complication to his plans. Dom had asked Hex to consider taking over his U.S. Marshal job once the ranch was operational. He doubted a single father would be interested in all the travel. Dom would have to start looking for someone else.

Chuckling, Rafe shook his head. "Neither did he. Found out about her when he rode to Denver. Someone said she's four and a handful. The stage also carried three sisters. One of them is pretty sick. They took her right over to the clinic."

The men reached into the back of the wagon, removing sacks of beans, flour, and sugar, plus crates loaded with canned goods, an iron pot, and other supplies. Walking up the steps, Rafe felt Dom's gaze on him.

"I saw Josie at the shop. She and Olivia are having an opening celebration on Saturday."

Dom's jaw tightened. "Already heard about it."

"I'm going to ride in. What about you?"

"Father, Cruz, and I plan to. They want to meet your sister." Setting down one of the crates in the kitchen, Dom brushed his hands down his pants. "She say anything?"

Rafe waited until Antonio and Cruz had set down their loads and headed back outside. "Did you tell Josie you don't want her?"

"Dammit. She told you that?"

"And more. No matter what happens between the two of you, Josie still plans to stay in Splendor."

"I figured as much."

"Look, Dom, you might consider setting her straight on a few things when you see her on Saturday."

Hooking a thumb under his belt, he lifted a brow. "Such as?"

"How you feel about her. The truth this time."

Rubbing his chin, Dom muttered a curse. "Suppose I should. So she forgave you for interfering?"

"Hell no. I'm hoping you'll have better luck."

Pinching the bridge of his nose, Dom nodded. "Yeah. So do I."

# Chapter Twenty-Five

"We're as ready as we're going to be, Livvy." Josie settled her hands on her hips, taking one more look around the shop.

Signs were up, merchandise displayed, and hot coffee sat atop the stove in the front corner. On a table next to it, Lena and Suzanne had set a bowl of punch and a plate filled with gingerbread cakes and molasses squares.

"Is it time?" Olivia's eyes twinkled, excitement rolling off her.

Clasping her hands together, Josie released a tension-filled breath and nodded. "Yes."

Hand hovering over the sign on the door, Olivia flipped it to *Open* and unlocked the door. Several minutes ticked by without anyone entering, their anxious anticipation building. Fifteen, then twenty minutes passed before the bell chimed. Pasting on smiles, trying to hide their apprehension, Josie and Olivia turned toward the door.

A man of average height dressed as a ranch hand, a six-shooter strapped around his waist, stood in the entry. Removing his hat, he took a few tentative steps forward.

"Good morning. Can we help you?" Josie felt a surge of self-satisfaction at the calm tone of her voice. A calm she didn't feel.

Ignoring her question, he strolled toward the stove, pouring a cup of coffee. Taking a sip, he turned back toward them.

"Good coffee." Taking another sip, along with another look around, his features softened. "Heard you ladies were opening your shop today. Thought I'd take a look at what you had." His gaze lit on a locked counter containing gold rings, pendants, and watches. "Quite a selection."

"Thank you. I'm Miss Josephine Dubois and this is Miss Olivia Barnett. And you are?"

"Everyone calls me Tater."

"Do you work around here, Mr. Tater?"

"Just Tater, and no, I don't."

Cocking her head at Olivia, Josie lifted a brow. "Passing through?"

"Most likely." Swallowing the last of his coffee, he set the cup down and picked up a gingerbread cake. Taking a bite, the hint of a smile touched his lips. "This is good. One of you make 'em?"

"My stepmother, Suzanne Barnett, made them," Olivia answered.

"Well, you let Mrs. Barnett know they're real fine." Brushing his hands together, he took a slow tour of the shop, asking a few questions, not requesting to see any of their merchandise. "I'd best be going, but I'll be back with a couple friends of mine." Touching the brim of his hat, Tater walked out.

Staring at the door a few seconds, they turned toward each other.

"He certainly was, well...interesting," Olivia said.

Before Josie could reply, the door opened again. Ruth Paige, followed by a group of church women, stepped inside. Eyes wide, their gazes searched the shop for a few moments before broad smiles spread across each face.

"This is lovely." Ruth moved through the front half of the store, fingers grazing over silk and wool scarves while the other ladies sent admiring glances at Olivia and Josie. "You both are so talented."

"And brave," another woman answered.

"Few women would have the courage to take on such a big task," a short, stout woman of indeterminable years added.

Josie and Olivia spent the next thirty minutes describing the different merchandise and providing prices. Several ladies, including Ruth, purchased at least one item before indulging in coffee or punch and sweet cakes.

Several others came in, looked around or made a purchase, enjoying the banter of the group of church women before leaving.

"I should get back home." Ruth set down her empty punch glass, gripping her purchase under her arm. "Reverend Paige will be expecting his midday meal."

287

Josie moved to her, but before she could thank the woman for coming in, the front door burst open. Tater stepped inside, flipping the sign on the door to *Closed*. No bandana hid his face, even though a hand rested on the gun strapped to his side.

A moment later, two more men entered, closed the door, and took positions near the last display case.

Corralling all of her courage, Josie stepped toward Tater. "What do you want?"

Without warning, his hand latched onto her arm, dragging her against him. "You, Miss Dubois." Straight, white teeth sneered at her, eyes glinting in satisfaction. "The rest of you ladies will keep your mouths shut and move toward my companions."

Ruth stormed forward, her package slipping to the floor in her rush to help Josie. "Absolutely not. I demand you let go of her at once and leave."

A deep, belly laugh burst through Tater's lips. "Whoever you are, you've got spunk."

"I'm Mrs. Paige, Reverend Paige's wife. If you want money, take it, but leave us alone."

Again, he laughed. "The minister's wife, huh?" His gaze lifted to his two men. "Seems we got ourselves a passel of real ladies." Amused, hoarse chuckles followed before the room quieted. "I don't care if you're the Queen of England. You and your friends need to get in the corner before someone gets hurt."

Ruth gasped her indignation. "Certainly you don't mean to hurt any of these women."

Eyes flaring in irritation, Tater tightened his hold on Josie. "Lady, I don't care who gets hurt as long as we get who we came for." Thrusting Josie forward, he motioned with his gun for the women to do as he asked. Tater sent a pointed look at Josie. "You and I are going to have a nice chat in the back."

Whirling toward him, she crossed her arms. "I've nothing to say to you."

"Well now, you might be real surprised at what you do have to say, Miss Dubois."

Grabbing her shoulder in a painful grasp, he shoved her ahead of him, and through the opening to the back room.

Tater pointed to the lone chair. "Sit down."

"I'd prefer to stand."

His hand connecting with her cheek caught Josie unaware, the sound reverberating through the small room and into the front. Before she could stop herself, Josie fisted her hand and reared back, landing a well-aimed punch against his nose. The shock on his face, blood spurting, provided a moment's satisfaction.

Grabbing the chair, she used it as a barrier to the man cursing a few feet away. "Don't ever slap me again."

Hand clasped over his nose, Tater's venomous gaze locked on her a moment before he pointed the barrel of his gun at her heart. "Don't think I won't shoot you. I've done worse in my life than killing an innocent woman."

His words, and the intent behind them, sent a chill through her. Breath coming in short gasps, heart stuttering, she gripped the back of the chair, hoping for a chance to use it. Then she recalled something important.

*The knife.*

Rafe had recovered the weapon stolen from the Crow brave. She'd scoffed when he'd told her it was a sign of her courage. Maybe it was, maybe not. The important part was its location. Strapped to her thigh.

Dom tightened Blue's cinch, still struggling with riding into Splendor for the emporium's opening. It wasn't that he didn't want to see Josie. He did, but assumed there'd be enough of a crowd to make it almost impossible to have a private conversation.

"Are you going to keep wasting time or finish up and ride in with us?" Cruz stood next to him, a hand on Dom's shoulder. "Even if you can't have much of a discussion, at least you can let her know you want one."

Dom glowered at him, frustrated at his brother's continued ability to read his thoughts. It galled him how often Cruz was right. Releasing the stirrup from the saddle's pommel, he let it drop to the horse's side.

"Might as well get this over with," he grumbled, slipping his boot into the stirrup.

Squeezing Dom's shoulder, Cruz chuckled. "Damn right. Besides, I'm eager to try some real food instead of what we've got here."

"You haven't been complaining about the food." Dom hated to butcher one of the steers, but the men needed meat.

"I'm doing that now," Cruz shot back, mounting his horse, reining it to join Antonio and Rafe.

The group didn't push it, taking the trail to town at a leisurely pace. Antonio, Cruz, and Dom had met Sylvia and her husband, Mack, for supper at the Eagle's Nest earlier in the week. At first, the meeting between his sister and her family had been strained. Once her father and oldest brother accepted Mack, the tension had eased and they'd enjoyed a couple hours of lively conversation. He'd been tempted to go to Nick's after supper, requesting to see Josie. By the time supper was over, he'd decided to leave their meeting until the store opened.

Today, they planned to arrive in plenty of time to get lunch at one of the restaurants, then visit the shop. Dom's chest pinched at the thought of seeing Josie for the first time since the attack. Their last conversation hadn't gone well. Both had been injured by the Crow raiders and forced to talk in front of Bull and Rafe. At least that was how Dom remembered it. He also recalled the flash of pain on her face, the way she fisted her hands at her sides. She'd wanted to remain civil, something Dom cared nothing about when it came to what needed to be said.

"How long have you known this gal?" Antonio rode a couple feet away, his injuries a distant memory.

"A few months. She arrived before Christmas to visit a friend."

His father's brow lifted. "And decided to stay?"

"Seems so." Dom ignored the sting of regret, recalling what he'd said in the church.

He'd been a fool to expect her to leave with Rafe. She loved him. Dom could see it each time their eyes met, yet he'd ignored the signs. He'd wanted to give her an easy out, and she'd taken it. Walking right out of his life.

"Are you planning to marry her?"

"First, I have to convince her to speak to me again, Father. She's one of the most stubborn women I've ever met."

"Except for your sister," Antonio said.

Dom choked out a chuckle. "Sylvia and Josie are a lot alike. Both headstrong. Mack is a good man. They're lucky to have found each other."

Remorse passed over Antonio's face before he could conceal it. "I suppose. Your mother and I miss her, though. The same as we miss you. I never expected two of my children to up and leave the ranch."

"Mack's talked about heading to Texas, maybe becoming a Ranger."

Antonio's face lit up, then dimmed. "I wouldn't put much stock in it. Sylvia mentioned them buying a small spread close to town and buying some stock from you."

Dom recalled the short conversation at supper between his sister and father. "If they're serious, I'll supply whatever they need."

"Cruz and I figured you would. That's why we plan to drive another herd of longhorns up here in a few months."

Dom glanced behind him at his brother, seeing him give a swift nod. "Mother is going to like it."

"If she's willing to come, I'll bring her with me. I don't like not having her close by for such a long period."

His father's words brought back a flood of memories about his mother. She was an excellent rider, had worked alongside her husband to build the ranch while taking care of three children. Never complained and never ran out of energy. Sylvia was the same. So was Josie.

"You know she'll come if you ask her."

A slow smile curved his father's mouth. "I'm hoping she will."

The next bend in the trail signaled Splendor was less than a hundred yards away. Dom's throat constricted, an unexpected wave of dread moving through him. As they rode closer, the odd churning in his gut increased. He'd always been one to heed his instincts, especially in his role as a marshal. Today, they warned him something wasn't right.

"You go on to the boardinghouse. I'm going to stop at the shop before meeting you."

"You got some reason for going there first?" His father could always tell when something disturbed Dom.

"My gut isn't doing too well."

Antonio glanced over his shoulder at Cruz and Rafe. "We'll go to the shop first, then get a bite to eat."

Although each raised their brows, neither argued. As they approached the shop, Dom's concern increased. It was almost noon, yet the sign showed the store as closed.

"Cruz, Rafe, something's wrong. You come in the front. Father and I will enter from the back. Watch your backs."

Rafe's sharp gaze showed his confusion. "What's going on, Dom?"

"I don't know, but I'm going to find out."

# Chapter Twenty-Six

"I don't know what you want from me." Josie's chest heaved, heart racing, brain muddled with dread.

She'd finally done as Tater had asked and sat down. Thankfully, the man threatening her hadn't tied her hands or ankles. A mistake she hoped he'd regret.

Reaching the knife concealed under her skirt couldn't be accomplished with him in the room. Even with her hands free, she'd never be able to release and slide it out without Tater seeing. Next time, she'd sheath it at her ankle. Josie stifled a groan at what most would consider a ridiculous thought.

But twice in as many weeks, she'd been threatened, used as bait. For a brief moment, she thought of Rafe's plea for her to return to New Orleans. After today, she might have to give it serious consideration. Stubborn determination might not win against continual threats to her life.

"Did you hear me, Tater?"

Leaning a shoulder against the wall, he shrugged with the other. "You want to know what I want from you."

Trying to appear unconcerned, she nodded. "It's a fair question."

Setting his gun on the counter, he stalked to her, crouching down to look into her eyes. "I don't intend to tell you since I'm certain the man we want will be walking through the door real soon."

Eyes narrowing in confusion, she shook her head. "That makes no sense."

Trailing a finger down her arm, he straightened. "Not to you maybe." Returning to his spot against the wall, he picked up the six-shooter, checking the chambers for what had to be the hundredth time. "I hear you're a fine lady from New Orleans."

Again, her brows furrowed. Instead of answering, Josie clamped her mouth shut.

"I also hear you've taken up with a lawman from Texas."

Her body stilled. How had he learned about her and Dom? Or maybe he was just taunting her. "I've no idea who you're talking about."

The denial made Tater chuckle. "No? You aren't poking around with a U.S. Marshal?"

Feeling her face flush, anger rising, she forced herself to stay seated. "I'm not *poking around* with anyone."

"Word around Splendor is you two are real cozy. I figure if it's true, he'll be coming by your shop today. What do you think?"

Crossing her arms, she leaned back in the chair. "I believe you're delusional. If you know all about me, then you'd know there is no man in my life.

None. Zero. Whoever you got your information from is wrong."

"You're bluffing."

"On the contrary. I believe you're the one who's bluffing, Tater. If any such man does come in here today, it will be a coincidence. Not because he has any attachment to me."

A flash of doubt crossed his features before a bland smile edged up the corners of his mouth. "You're lying."

Returning a small grin, she gave a quick shake of her head. "No, Tater, I'm not."

Removing his hat, he shoved a hand through his damp, dirty hair before turning toward the front. Biting her lower lip, her hand gripped the hem of her skirt, lifting it enough to feel the knife. Keeping her gaze on Tater, Josie wrapped her fingers around the handle, pulling slowly, quietly, hoping he wouldn't turn around.

Her hand grew damp as she tugged on the weapon now caught on a fold of her skirt. Praying for time, she held her breath, refusing to look away from the outlaw. She'd almost freed it when her grip slipped, the knife hitting the floor with a thud.

Whipping her hand from under her skirt, she closed her eyes and sent up a quick prayer.

Tater abruptly shifted, his dark eyes boring into hers. "What was that?"

Opening her eyes, she cocked her head to the side. "I don't know what you're talking about."

Shoving his hat back down on his head, he closed the distance between them. "Something dropped to the floor." Dropping down, Tater lifted her skirt.

A scream tore from her lips. Outraged, she brought both hands down on the top of his head. Before Tater could recover, the back door flew open. Dom stood in the open doorway, his gun aimed at the man holding up Josie's skirt.

Releasing the skirt while drawing his six-shooter, Tater got a quick shot off at Dom before wrapping an arm around Josie's neck. Tugging her in front of him, he fired again, forcing Dom to take cover outside.

Backing toward the opening to the front of the shop, Tater dragged a squirming Josie with him, her screams making his ears ring.

"Shut up," he growled into her ear, tightening his hold. "I'm going to kill him. You can live to see it or die along with him."

Refusing to cower, she stomped on his boot with the heel of her shoe. Tater gave no indication he felt the blow. It didn't matter. Pounding on the front door and shouts halted his progress, giving Josie a momentary advantage.

Stomping down hard on his boot once more, she thrust her head backward, landing a blow to his chin. His hold loosened for an instant, long enough for her to drop to the floor. Seeing Dom in the doorway, she stayed low, allowing two shots to pass over her. Both missed, the bullets plunging into the wall behind Tater.

"What's going on?"

Rafe stepped away from the front door, turning toward Gabe, while Cruz put his face to the window to peer inside. "The sign says the shop is closed."

"There's two men holding guns on a group of women inside." Cruz shoved away from the window. "I don't recognize either of them." He'd met the sheriff when they'd journeyed to town earlier in the week. Cruz would now have the chance to observe the competence of the lawman.

Gabe looked through the window in the front door, assessing the situation. Cursing, he stepped away. "Whoever those men are, they're holding the reverend's wife and a group of church women hostage. Rafe, go to the jail. Let Mack and Caleb know I need their help. If there are any other deputies there, bring them, too."

Crossing the street, Rafe rushed toward the jail. Gabe grabbed Cruz's arm, dragging him out of the way an instant before a bullet from inside broke the glass. Another stream of expletives burst from his lips at the screams from the women.

"Dom and my father are in the back." Cruz drew his gun, preparing to go inside.

"Not yet. We can't risk hitting the women. We'll wait for my deputies." Unholstering his gun, Gabe opened and checked the cylinder, already knowing each chamber held a bullet.

"What can we do?" Mack stopped next to Gabe, Caleb and Rafe soon following.

"Stay here and don't let the outlaws get past you. I'm going around back to join Dom and his father."

Drawing their guns, Mack took a position next to Cruz, Caleb beside Rafe. Gabe hurried to the back, rounding the corner at the same time Dom leaned into the building, firing twice. Joining him at the doorway, Gabe tensed at the panicked scream. Glancing inside, he saw another man, gun still aimed at the back door as his hand snaked out to grab Josie's ankle.

"No!" She clawed at the wood floor, grasped at the chair leg, the bottom of a work counter, anything to enable her escape.

"Let her go," Dom ground out, the muzzle pointed at Tater's chest.

The answer came quickly as another bullet whizzed past Dom, missing him by an inch. Gabe motioned Antonio to take cover before raising above Dom and firing, only to have it go wide when Tater swung away. Recovering, the outlaw again stretched out an arm, gripping Josie's calf before she could crawl away.

"Let me go."

Her terrified words punched into Dom's chest.

When he leaned into the room this time and fired, his bullet struck Tater in his leg. An enraged howl preceded wild pops of gunfire, each shot splintering the doorframe close to Dom and Gabe.

A scuffling noise had them both glancing inside, Dom's heart stopping at what he saw.

Josie struggled out of Tater's grasp, her hand searching for something on the floor. The knife Rafe had recovered and given to her. Screaming again when Tater's fingers dug into her leg, she thrust her hand toward the knife once more, grasping the handle.

With a guttural sound of fury, she pushed herself to a kneeling position and raised the blade.

"Josie!" Dom yelled, entering the room an instant before she thrust the knife into Tater's arm.

Tearing it out, she lunged again, plunging the blade into his chest. Wracking sobs tore from her as she raised the knife again, not realizing Tater's body had gone slack.

"Josie, stop." Voice calm, Dom wrapped his hands around her wrists, stopping the downward stab.

Screaming in fear, hate, and anger, she whirled on him, shattering the air with another body-wracking shout of despair.

"Josie, sweetheart, it's Dom. You need to let go of the knife." His grip held tight around her wrists, controlling any additional motions.

At the same time, one of Tater's men rushed to the back, Gabe dropping him with a pop of his gun. Moving past Dom and Josie, he hurried forward, stopping the third outlaw with a shot to his chest. Whirling around, his gun still held in front of him, Gabe stayed in fighting mode.

Seeing no more threats, he gave a cursory glance to the women huddled on the floor on his way toward the front door.

"Help the women. I need to check on Josie and Dom." Shooting a grim look at Ruth Paige and the others, he hurried to the back, halting in relief.

Dom's arms wrapped protectively around Josie, whose hands dug into his arms, deep sobs shaking her body. The outlaws were dead, all the hostages safe. Gabe's work was done.

Dom refused to leave the clinic until Doctor McCord allowed him to take Josie home. Indeed, he refused to move from her side. The wounds to her body weren't serious. The injuries to her soul were of greater concern.

She'd fallen into an exhausted sleep on the clinic bed, waking to her own screams of terror. Drawing her into his arms, Dom rubbed his hand along her back, whispering soft endearments until she calmed. With tears streaming down her face, Josie buried her face into his shirt.

After long minutes, she pulled away. Swiping away moisture, her red-rimmed eyes met his. "I want to thank you for coming to my rescue, Dom."

"There's no need to thank me."

"Yes, there is. I would've expected Rafe, Gabe, and his deputies. I was surprised to see you put yourself in danger for me."

A slow build of confusion mixed with anger crawled up his spine. "Why wouldn't I do whatever I could to help you?"

Sliding away from him, she worked to calm the wretched ache in her heart, wrapping her arms around her waist. "You were quite clear you have no feelings for me, Dom."

"Josie..."

Shaking her head, she forced herself to continue. "I've come to accept your decision and want, no, need you to know how grateful I am you chose to come to my rescue."

Leaning forward, he cupped her face in his hands. "You are so wrong, Josie."

Brows furrowing, she had no chance to respond before he brushed his lips across hers. On her gasp, he lifted his head enough to stare into her eyes.

She wrapped her hands around his wrists. "What am I wrong about?"

Dropping his hands from her face, he inched them down her arms. "I was an idiot."

"About what?"

Threading his fingers through hers, he glanced down at their joined hands. "About almost everything." His slight, self-deprecating chuckle felt bitter on his lips. "The first error was not fighting for you when you broke off our courtship in Big Pine. I knew it was a mistake, as was staying away from you for weeks afterward."

"It was my fault, Dom. I never wanted to end the courtship. I just, well..." She drew in a breath. "I was afraid you still had feelings for Miss Lawson." She touched a hand to her temple, feeling her face heat. "I couldn't bear the thought of you choosing her when I'd become so fond of you."

"Ah, Josie. I have no feelings for Mattie other than friendship. It's why I came to my senses and called on you again, determined to change your mind about us."

A small smile tilted her mouth upward. "You did." Sucking in a shaky breath, she let it out on a slow whoosh. "Then you changed your mind."

"I didn't change my mind. That's what I need you to understand." Stroking fingers down her face, he caught her gaze. "Rafe made a great deal of sense when he spoke of all you'd be losing by staying in Splendor. The mistake I made was believing you'd be better off without me."

"I'm not better off, Dom. I've been miserable since our conversation in the church."

A slow grin appeared on his face. "So you don't mean to forget me and switch your affections to another man?"

Glancing down at her hands now clasped in her lap, she shook her head. "I'm afraid I may be hopeless where you're concerned. Of course, it doesn't matter. You made it clear you don't love me."

"I lied."

"Whaaat?" She drew the word out, trying to grasp his meaning.

Unable to stop himself, Dom cupped her face again. "I love you, Josie. I'm sorry for what I said, the pain I caused. Can you forgive me?"

Ignoring his question, she stared at him. "You love me?"

Pressing a kiss to her lips, he pulled back. "I have since the first day I saw you in Splendor."

Brow lifting, she allowed a hopeful smile. "Since I arrived?"

"I couldn't get you off my mind. Every time I was called away to attend a trial or escort a prisoner to Deer Lodge, I feared you'd meet someone else."

"You did?" She still could quite accept what he was telling her.

"Yes. The question is...do you still love me, Josie?"

Fear clutched her chest. She could admit the truth, or lie to shield herself from more pain if he changed his mind. Looking into his deep brown eyes, she had to tell him the truth.

"Yes, Dom. I love you."

"Then marry me, Josie."

Her doubts slid away at his words and the intense gleam in his eyes. Feeling tears well, she choked out a laugh. "Are you certain?"

"I've never been more certain of anything. Say yes, Josie."

Leaning up, she brushed a kiss across his lips. "Yes."

# Epilogue

*One week later…*

"Explain to me again why the rush to marry Dom."
Abby Brandt flashed a smile at Josie, taking a sip of
punch.

Josie's gaze followed her husband as he moved
from one group to the next, thanking them for
attending the wedding on such short notice. She
found it hard to believe she was Mrs. Dominic
Lucero. Two weeks ago, they weren't speaking.
Today…

A bright smile, filled with love, appeared on her
face. "Cruz and Antonio must leave for Texas, but
they refused to go until Dom and I married. His
father said if his wife couldn't attend, it would be up
to him to describe the ceremony."

"He didn't try to talk Dom out of it?" Abby
asked.

"After Sylvia married Mack, I believe Antonio
had no intention of alienating another of his
children. He already plans to drive a second herd of
longhorns north, and hopes Dom's mother will
accompany him."

"Oh, that would be lovely. I know Sylvia misses
her mother." Abby's attention fixed on Hex

Boudreaux and the little girl beside him. "I wonder how he's doing."

Josie's features softened. "Dom says he and Zeke are doing everything possible to make a good home."

"Noah is adding another bedroom to one of our houses. As soon as it's finished, they'll move out of their existing house. The three sisters who arrived on the stage with Lucy Boudreaux will move into it."

"The twins?"

"And their younger sister," Abby said. "Betts Jones says the twins' father remarried when their mother died. They had a daughter before their father and stepmother were killed in a flash flood near Kansas City. The twins became the recipients of their trust, with the provision they become Cici's guardians."

Josie's gaze moved to the three sisters, one of the twins gaunt and pale, the light all but gone from her eyes. "Why would they travel all the way to Splendor?"

Shrugging, Abby shook her head. "I've been wondering the same. Once you and Dom have a few days alone, we should invite them to join us for lunch."

"That would be wonderful."

Josie sought out and found Dom, now standing next to Chandler. They were deep in conversation, their faces animated. Wondering what they were discussing, she excused herself, moving toward them. Before she crossed the room, the two men shook hands, both smiling.

"Josie!"

Stopping, she shifted toward the familiar voice. "Suzanne."

Lena stood beside her, news of their pregnancies no longer a secret. The two hard-working women had never looked more beautiful or more serene. Reaching them, she kissed both on the cheek.

"Thank you both for all your help in arranging the ceremony and reception so quickly."

Suzanne's face brightened. "We loved every minute. It also gave us a chance to focus on something other than our increasing stomachs."

"You ladies look happy." Dom joined them, wrapping an arm around Josie's waist to draw her close. "I have two bits of good news," he announced to the three.

Josie looked up at his handsome face. "Do you plan to tell us, or are you going to play the tease?"

Chuckling, he nodded. "First, I spoke with Dax and Luke about hiring Mal Jolly."

Her face brightened in excitement. "And?"

"They approved. I've already spoken to Mal and he accepted. He'll be moving over in the next week."

Lena touched his arm. "That's wonderful news, Dom. I've heard Mal is quite capable."

"I'm fortunate he accepted. It saves a great deal of time looking for the right foreman."

"And the second piece of good news?" Josie leaned into him, trying to quell her desire to rest a hand on his chest. Although the night ahead frightened her, being with Dom always brought waves of excitement.

"Chan Evans agreed to take over my job as U.S. Marshal."

Before Josie could express her joy, an agonized scream from across the room caught their attention. Chrissy McKenna dropped to the floor, wrapping her arms around her twin.

"Millie...no...please, no...." Brushing hair from her sister's face, Chrissy stared into blank eyes. Her frantic gaze shot across the room, spotting Clay McCord hurrying toward them.

Kneeling, the doctor checked Millie's pulse, listened for a heartbeat, then cupped her face, looking into unseeing eyes. "I'm sorry, Miss McKenna. She's gone."

"Gone?" Beside her, Cici began to cry, her small body trembling.

Sensing movement beside her, Chrissy took hold of Cici's hand, a broken sob escaping as a strong arm wrapped around her shoulders.

"How can I help, Clay?" Hex's voice barely registered as Chrissy turned her face into his chest.

"If you would carry Millie to the clinic, Doc Worthington and I will take care of her."

Nodding, Hex bent down to whisper into Chrissy's ear. "We must take her to the clinic."

Looking up, confusion spread across her face. "The clinic?"

"The doctors will take care of her until arrangements are made." Feeling her stiffen, he tugged her closer.

Clearing his throat, Hex glanced up to see Lucy staring at him, her four-year-old eyes filled with tears. "Luce, please stay with Cici."

For once, his daughter didn't argue. Reaching out, she slipped her hand into Cici's.

Helping Chrissy stand, he sent a look at Zeke, silently asking for his help. When his brother stepped beside her, taking her hand to slip it through his arm, Hex bent down.

Scooping Millie's limp body into his arms, he straightened, taking a quick look at the shocked faces around them. Expression dark, Hex turned away, stalking out of the crowded room.

Thank you for taking the time to read Restless Wind. If you enjoyed it, please consider telling your friends or posting a short review. Word of mouth is an author's best friend and much appreciated.

Watch for the next book in the Redemption Mountain series, Storm Summit.

Please join my reader's group to be notified of my New Releases at:
https://www.shirleendavies.com/contact-me.html

I care about quality, so if you find something in error, please contact me via email at
shirleen@shirleendavies.com

# About the Author

**Shirleen Davies** writes romance. She is the best-selling author of books in the romantic suspense, military romance, historical western romance, and contemporary western romance genres. Shirleen grew up in Southern California, attended Oregon State University, and has degrees from San Diego State University and the University of Maryland. Her passion is writing emotionally charged stories of flawed people who find redemption through love and acceptance. She lives with her husband in a beautiful town in northern Arizona.

I love to hear from my readers!

Send me an email: shirleen@shirleendavies.com
Visit my Website: www.shirleendavies.com
Sign up to be notified of New Releases:
www.shirleendavies.com
Check out all of my Books:
www.shirleendavies.com/books.html
Comment on my Blog:
www.shirleendavies.com/blog.html
Follow me on Amazon:
http://www.amazon.com/author/shirleendavies
Follow my on BookBub:
https://www.bookbub.com/authors/shirleen-davies

Other ways to connect with me:

Facebook Author Page:
http://www.facebook.com/shirleendaviesauthor
Twitter: www.twitter.com/shirleendavies
Pinterest: http://pinterest.com/shirleendavies
Instagram:
https://www.instagram.com/shirleendavies_autho
r/

# Books by Shirleen Davies

## *Historical Western Romance Series*
### MacLarens of Fire Mountain

Tougher than the Rest, Book One
Faster than the Rest, Book Two
Harder than the Rest, Book Three
Stronger than the Rest, Book Four
Deadlier than the Rest, Book Five
Wilder than the Rest, Book Six

### Redemption Mountain

Redemption's Edge, Book One
Wildfire Creek, Book Two
Sunrise Ridge, Book Three
Dixie Moon, Book Four
Survivor Pass, Book Five
Promise Trail, Book Six
Deep River, Book Seven
Courage Canyon, Book Eight
Forsaken Falls, Book Nine
Solitude Gorge, Book Ten
Rogue Rapids, Book Eleven
Angel Peak, Book Twelve
Restless Wind, Book Thirteen
Storm Summit, Book Fourteen, Coming next in the
series!

# MacLarens of Boundary Mountain

Colin's Quest, Book One,
Brodie's Gamble, Book Two
Quinn's Honor, Book Three
Sam's Legacy, Book Four
Heather's Choice, Book Five
Nate's Destiny, Book Six
Blaine's Wager, Book Seven
Fletcher's Pride, Book Eight
Bay's Desire, Book Nine
Cam's Hope, Book Ten, Coming next in the series!

# *Romantic Suspense*

## Eternal Brethren, Military Romantic Suspense

Steadfast, Book One
Shattered, Book Two
Haunted, Book Three, Coming Next in the Series!
Untamed, Book Four, Coming Soon!

## Peregrine Bay, Romantic Suspense

Reclaiming Love, Book One
Our Kind of Love, Book Two
Edge of Love, Coming Next in the Series!

# *Contemporary Romance Series*

## MacLarens of Fire Mountain

Second Summer, Book One
Hard Landing, Book Two
One More Day, Book Three
All Your Nights, Book Four
Always Love You, Book Five
Hearts Don't Lie, Book Six
No Getting Over You, Book Seven
'Til the Sun Comes Up, Book Eight
Foolish Heart, Book Nine

## Burnt River

Thorn's Journey
Del's Choice
Boone's Surrender

**The best way to stay in touch is to subscribe to my newsletter.** Go to www.shirleendavies.com and subscribe in the box at the top of the right column that asks for your email. You'll be notified of new books before they are released, have chances to win great prizes, and receive other subscriber-only specials.

Made in the USA
Monee, IL
09 April 2023

31591738R00184